DEAD
DRIFT

Center Point
Large Print

Also by Dani Pettrey and available from
Center Point Large Print:

Sabotaged
Still Life
Blind Spot

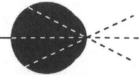

CHESAPEAKE VALOR
—— BOOK FOUR ——

DEAD DRIFT

DANI PETTREY

CENTER POINT LARGE PRINT
THORNDIKE, MAINE

ISBN: 978-1-68324-884-2

Library of Congress Cataloging-in-Publication Data

Names: Pettrey, Dani, author.
Title: Dead drift / Dani Pettrey.
Description: Center Point Large Print edition. | Thorndike, Maine :
    Center Point Large Print, 2018. | Series: Chesapeake valor ; book 4
Identifiers: LCCN 2018020473 | ISBN 9781683248842 (hardcover)
Subjects: LCSH: Murder—Investigation—Fiction. | Large type books. |
    GSAFD: Suspense fiction. | LCGFT: Thrillers (Fiction)
Classification: LCC PS3616.E89 D43 2018 | DDC 813/.6—dc23
LC record available at https://lccn.loc.gov/2018020473

To Dave Long

For signing an unknown author and believing in me. For all the input, feedback, and fun brainstorming chats over octopus and, even occasionally, in sub-zero temperatures. You've had such an impact on me as an author, and I'm deeply grateful. Thank you!

This one is for you.

PROLOGUE

CHESAPEAKE HARBOR, MARYLAND
EIGHT YEARS AGO

Excitement bubbled through Jenna McCray, gooseflesh rippling along her skin in the cool night air as she hurried to meet Parker. Her Parker. It was almost too amazing to be real.

He was bright, tender, manly, and hers. How it had happened, she didn't know. She'd spent years daydreaming about marrying him, but now her dream was coming true. They were talking marriage.

She looked both ways before crossing the neighborhood street, though at midnight in her tiny town there was really no need. Yet, to her surprise, two headlights appeared in the distance.

Crossing the street with a skip in her step, she hopped up on the opposite sidewalk and shoved her hands into her pockets, praying whichever neighbor was out driving at this hour didn't rat her out. She'd be an adult in a few weeks, and then it wouldn't matter, but tonight it still did. If Griff found out . . .

She winced, hating to think what her big brother would do. Parker would have no problem holding his own, but she wanted to avoid that battle until she turned eighteen—and then Griffin couldn't say anything at all. Well, he could and probably would, but it wouldn't matter. She and Parker would be engaged soon.

The headlights lit her from behind, casting her shadow on the sidewalk in front of her. *Great.* She was going to get busted.

She turned and lifted her hand to shield her face, the glare of the headlights blinding her momentarily. Trepidation shot through her as the van stopped. A shiver raced up her spine. She was being silly. She was in Chesapeake Harbor, for goodness' sake. Nothing bad ever happened in Chesapeake Harbor.

A man stepped out of the van, and instinct bade her to run, her internal warning flaring red hot.

The man moved toward her, and despite the shelter of her hometown, she heeded her instincts, turning to run. Whoever he was, she could face them with Parker at her side. She was only a half mile from the park.

Heavy footfalls echoed after her. He was chasing her.

Panic flashed. Something was wrong. *Very* wrong.

As the man closed in on her, she hollered, "Parker!" praying maybe, just maybe, Parker hadn't made it to the park yet and would hear her.

The man called her a name that made her ears burn. Who was he? Certainly no one she knew.

Tears beaded in her eyes as she ran as fast as her slender legs would carry her. Racing for Parker and safety.

A thick hand clamped down on her shoulder, another wrapping around her throat. She kicked and screamed, but the man only tightened his grip. A nasty odor enveloped her face, a cloth smothering her nose and mouth. She blinked, and everything went black.

1

Luke extricated himself from the vehicle to find shattered convoy debris littering the ground.

Ebeid had blown up the convoy. It didn't make any sense.

He covered his face with his shirt as smoke billowed into the air, sirens wailing dimly over the ringing in his ears.

The ringing grew louder. His phone. Coughing, he pulled it from his jeans pocket and answered. "Yes?"

"I'm assuming you survived what I just learned was a convoy explosion."

"Yes, but I don't understand. Why would Ebeid blow up his own scientist?"

He realized the reason before Malcolm answered.

"It appears they found a replacement with Bedan."

"Any idea where he is?" Luke asked.

"No, but that's not the worst of it."

"What happened?" What had they missed?

"Fort Detrick was transporting a supply of anthrax to the CDC, and it was just hijacked. The guards are dead, and the truck carrying somewhere in the neighborhood of six ounces of anthrax is gone."

"Why didn't we know about that transfer?"

"We did, but we didn't consider it a target."

He was so sick of being given only bits of intel when there was a far bigger game at play. His frustration with Malcolm soared. "And you can't find the truck?" Surely helicopters were searching, but why hadn't he been notified about the anthrax transport? If only he'd known. . . . Of course Ebeid would go for the anthrax. Dr. Kemel's transport was just another diversion. Ebeid had been feeding them false intel. Righteous anger flared hotter than the flames dancing a hundred yards from him as fire trucks converged on what remained of the convoy.

He covered his free ear, trying to hear as Malcolm continued. "We believe they must have switched vehicles somewhere undercover, but we're still looking."

His chest compressed. Both the bridge and Kemel's transfer were diversions. Ebeid and his team had just outmaneuvered them. But how did he know to play them? Did he have a man on the inside, or had Ebeid discovered *their* man on the inside and fed him false intel?

Either way, Ebeid and his crew now had six ounces of anthrax along with Dr. Bedan. Luke fought the urge to stagger backward. Instead, he leaned against his car, which was still warm from the blaze that had engulfed it only moments ago. It was mind-numbing to think the convoy

12

explosion and the bombing attempt on the Bay Bridge were nothing compared to what anthrax could do. A few grams were deadly, and Ebeid now had six *ounces* in his control.

Luke swallowed. He couldn't even begin to fathom the level of destruction Ebeid could cause or what deployment method he was planning. This case had just shifted gears—and the ramifications were terrifying. "We need to bring in the FBI. I'm sure they've already been alerted to the hijacked anthrax."

"Yes. I'll make sure the case is directed to Declan Grey, as he's already somewhat looped in. Looks like you'll be reunited with your old friends after all. Guess we're going to see how well trained you actually are in not letting attachments come into play."

Elation and unease churned inside Luke. The idea of working side by side with Katie and the guys thrilled him, yet it also terrified him. He wasn't the same man they'd once known, and he was nervous that they wouldn't like who he'd become. He didn't like who he'd become half the time, and yet he knew he was doing what the job required.

"I need you to come in. We need to talk."

Luke gazed back at the remnants of a war zone—shattered debris littering the scorched ground, gray smoke plumes funneling into the hazy air, flames dancing in the carcass of the transport van.

He swallowed at the sight of the charred remains, regretting the action as pain shot down his parched throat, the smoke sucking the oxygen from the air. "I'll be there in an hour."

Dr. Isaiah Bedan entered the lab Ebeid built for him—designed, it appeared, to his exact specifications. A combination of trepidation and searing joy surged through his limbs. *This is it.* This one act would be regarded as the zenith of his life's work. He was creating something others had only dreamt about. Yes, it would cause destruction, but that's what they deserved—destruction and decimation.

Bedan appraised the finest in lab equipment and, much to his pleasure, adequate space and light. Everything he needed to make his mark on history. To *be* history.

"Your living quarters are this way," Cyrus said, gesturing to the back of the lab.

The living space consisted of a small galley kitchen, a desk, sofa, and armchair, and a bedroom with a twin bed and full bath.

"It will suffice?" Cyrus asked.

Bedan nodded. Not the luxury accommodations he'd expect from a man like Ebeid, but it was sufficient.

"If you require anything we have not provided"—he handed Bedan his business card—"call me and I will see you get it. The kitchen is fully stocked," he said, opening the refrigerator door to reveal shelves stuffed with food. "The pantry is equally full."

Bedan nodded his thanks.

"How soon can we expect results?"

"If everything goes smoothly, the finished product will be ready in a matter of days."

"Meaning?"

"In time for the anniversary." He'd had a working prototype before Ebeid moved him to the States. Now he had a privately funded lab and the opportunity to fully concentrate on putting the finishing touches on his design. He narrowed his eyes at Cyrus's displeased look. "Has something changed in the timeline?"

"No. The date stands, but we don't want to wait until the last minute to make certain it works. We need time for testing."

"Of course." Bedan set down his bag and rolled up his shirtsleeves. "I'll get started right away." A day or two of concentrated time, and he'd be finished. "You may tell Ebeid he *will* have his retribution."

Luke strode across the leaf-covered grounds of his alma mater. Seven and a half years since he'd been a student here. His mentor, Malcolm Warner, had recruited him into the Agency just prior to graduation. He'd still gotten his degree—Malcolm saw to that—but he'd never walked across the stage or seen Katie do so.

He blinked, his mind flashing back to a simpler time, when the dreams he and Kate Maxwell had were the same. Join the Bureau, get married, fight injustice, and make a life together. But all that had changed during a conversation with Malcolm. Instead of embarking on a life with Katie, he'd gone through advanced training at the Farm and had been sent into the field in a black ops unit under the leadership of Lauren Graham. Talk about someone who was not quite right. . . .

Passing a couple clearly in love jolted his mind and heart back to Katie. But she was his past. Ebeid was his present. And the future . . . ? That was up to him to define—not Malcolm.

Seeing Katie a couple nights ago—seeing the life he'd once been a part of, a life that could maybe still be his—had convinced him he was done with the Agency as soon as Ebeid was behind bars or dead. Whether that meant he returned to his old life remained to be seen, but he doubted he could just waltz back in. Not after the hurt he'd caused or the man he'd become.

Reaching Malcolm's door, he knocked, and the man he both loved and loathed answered. Over seven years had passed since he'd set foot in Malcolm's office, and now he was here for the second time in less than a week.

Malcolm gestured him in, shutting the door behind him.

Luke took two steps in and froze as a blonde on

16

the couch stood and turned to face him. *Lauren Graham.*

He swallowed, unsure if he wanted to politely greet her or strangle her.

He glared at Malcolm. "What is *she* doing here?" This was *his* op. His man. Ebeid was no longer hers. Not since she'd nearly gotten their entire unit killed in Afghanistan.

"Nice to see you too." She linked her arms across her chest.

Wearing a red turtleneck sweater, gray pencil skirt, and black heeled boots, she had the same allure. Long blond hair hanging straight to the middle of her back, deep blue eyes—cold as ice—five feet seven, one thirty, max. She was a killing machine in a pretty package. A package he wanted absolutely nothing to do with.

"Please sit down," Malcolm said.

Lauren took instruction. He did not. He remained standing, leaning against the far wall, still perfectly able to hear whatever possible explanation Malcolm had for bringing one of the Agency's top wet work assets, or assassins, back into his life.

Malcolm sighed but ignored Luke's positioning and continued all the same. "I brought in Lauren in case we need help with Ebeid."

"It's not necessary," Luke said, knowing that was not the true reason for her presence. He could easily read Malcolm's lies.

Malcolm looked at him as if he'd anticipated the response. "It may not be, but she's our contingency asset."

"Meaning?" If he failed? He hadn't failed at a single mission yet. Lauren, on the other hand . . .

"Meaning you're walking back into your past. I want to make sure you don't get distracted."

Luke pushed off the wall, anger and frustration flaring through him. "So she's here to babysit me?" He knew that was the real reason she was here. To run interference. To make sure he didn't get any ideas about returning to his old life.

"No." Malcolm shook his head in that flustered way of his, dabbing his brow with his handkerchief. "She's here to keep another set of eyes on Ebeid. He's too close to home, and he needs to be stopped."

"Which is why *I'm* here." But there was still a question burning in his mind. Why had Ebeid chosen Baltimore? Because it was a port city and easy to get what he needed transported in? Because the cultural office he worked out of needed a new leader? Or was there a deeper significance to it all? One they didn't yet understand?

"It's why I'm here too," Lauren said, her slender legs crossed and angled slightly off to the side. Such poise for a ruthless killer.

Ebeid wasn't the reason for her presence. She was here to ensure he didn't leave the Agency, that his old life didn't pull him back in. He understood the former, but the latter was none of her business. If she went anywhere near Kate, she'd regret it.

2

Luke stood in front of Charm City Investigations in the chilly October night air, watching them— the woman he loved and the men who had once been his best friends. So much time had passed, so much had happened, so much compromise on his part to protect the country he loved, to protect those he loved. He'd felt it was worth it, but Kate's stinging slap the other night said she certainly didn't view it that way, and he couldn't blame her. He'd gone in with the belief it would only be for a short while, just until they'd caught Ebeid, but the months had quickly grown into years and the years to nearly eight. And now he was back.

Inhaling a steadying breath, he grabbed the door handle. He'd faced down armies, suicide bombers, and spies, but walking back into what had once been his world was far more terrifying.

He strolled inside and through the foyer, the sound of laughter and cheering in the air.

"Thanks, guys, but it wasn't just me. It was a lot of folks working together," Declan said as Luke stepped through the doorway.

"You did a great job," Luke said. All eyes swung toward him, and he stuffed his hands into his pockets, feeling the sting of uncertainty.

"But we've got a far more lethal threat on our doorstep."

Kate stood, her gaze wary. "Luke?"

He surveyed the room, especially taking note of the additions to the group. His friend Mack, stationed behind a desk in the Baltimore office because of a permanent on-assignment injury, kept tabs on Luke's loved ones. If Malcolm knew, he'd be furious, but Mack was gracious enough to keep updates strictly between him and Luke. They had come up with a coded system so Luke's loved ones stayed safe, and so none of them, or his attachment to them, could be used against him or them. He didn't check in as often as he wanted to, but in his weak moments . . .

That was how he knew Griffin had married and that Kate never had—which gave him hope. But he was a fool to think she'd ever forgive him or that he could ever again be the man she deserved. He was tainted by his job, by actions taken and choices made. Yes, they'd been in service to his country, but he was finding the assignments harder and harder to swallow.

Declan's cell rang.

"You're going to want to take that," Luke said.

Declan lifted his phone and strode out of the room. "Grey," he answered. "Yes . . ." His voice trailed off as a door opened and shut down the hall.

Luke shifted his hands in his pockets.

"What happened to you?" Kate asked. "Looks like you got into a battle with a curling wand."

Luke lifted his hand to his face. He hadn't even realized he'd been burned. "There was an explosion."

"I've got some salve," Kate said, striding to the room on his left.

Everyone stared at him.

"I'm going to . . ." He indicated he was going to join Kate and pushed through the swinging door.

In the kitchen, Kate opened and shut drawer after drawer, her cheeks flushing. "I know it's here somewhere," she said, looking up at him and then straight back down.

He moved behind her and reached his arms around her waist, placing his hands on hers, hoping to steady her shaking. It was the wrong move. He should maintain his distance, but once in her presence . . . he couldn't seem to keep away. This was Katie. After more than seven long years, she was right in front of him, in his embrace.

Her skin was soft and warm, and she smelled of cassis. His brief assignment in France, where the flower bloomed, flashed through his mind, but he quickly shifted his focus back to her. He was indulging in a moment of his old life, even if it was the wrong thing to do.

Kate's shoulders shrugged at his touch. He

leaned in, lowering his face flush with hers, cheek nestled against soft cheek. She needed to know the pain he felt. "I'm sorry, Katie," he said, his words hoarse and throaty, nearly a whisper, though he hadn't intended them to be. She felt *so* good, so right in his arms. All he wanted to do was . . .

She stiffened in his embrace. "For what?" Anger and hurt mingled in her cracking voice. "Leaving in the first place or showing back up?"

Ouch. He'd endured bullet wounds that stung less.

"For everything." He swallowed, his throat still burning from the effects of the explosion. Why had he been foolish enough to hope for anything other than her anger? He shouldn't have come. He was only causing her pain. "I'm sorry I ever left. I thought it would be a short, grand adventure. I never imagined we'd be standing here seven years later. I know none of this can be easy for you, but we've got a crisis and I need Declan's help."

She turned in his hold, facing him, her chin tilted up, her gaze a mix of wariness and defiance. "Why?"

He bit back the urge to kiss her, to feel her soft lips against his, and he quickly reined in his thoughts. "Because there's an imminent threat on U.S. soil, and I don't have jurisdiction here."

The kitchen door burst open.

"How on earth did Ebeid get ahold of six ounces of anthrax?" Declan roared.

Luke lowered his head and exhaled. The brief reprieve from the demons he battled was over. He straightened. "He must have someone on the inside."

"At which end? CDC or Fort Detrick?"

"I don't know, but I could use your help determining which one."

"This is the Bureau's jurisdiction." Declan raked a hand through his brown, spiky hair. "But I'd be a fool not to take advantage of your knowledge and intel. You clearly know Ebeid."

"Yes, I do—far more than I'd like to. So . . . it appears we're in this together." The word *together* sounded foreign on Luke's lips. He'd worked alone for so long, his contact with anyone other than targets severely limited. How would he function in a dependent dynamic?

"Excuse me," Kate said, shifting under Luke's arms, which were still wrapped around her. She slipped out of his hold as easily as he'd let her go the first time. He'd left her and his friends behind for a purpose—to stop this terrorist threat to America. There still was a purpose, but it was one he was ready to be done with, ready to face down once and for all.

He looked to Declan as the door swung shut behind Katie.

"She's never going to forgive me, is she?"

"Would you?" Declan asked.

No. He wouldn't, and he couldn't expect Katie to either. He couldn't be the man she wanted, not anymore.

"Let's head back into the front room and get started," Declan said, moving for the door. "You have a lot to catch us up on."

Luke nodded and followed Declan out to the curved sofa that the gang was seated around. There was an open spot beside Katie, but he leaned against a wooden post instead, Declan beside him. Everyone was present except Avery, who Parker said would be right back. She'd just run to grab something from their office down the hall.

Luke exhaled. "Where do you want me to start?"

Declan rubbed his hands together. "Let's start with the anthrax."

"I know—" Parker paused and smiled at Avery as she entered the room and passed between him and Luke.

A shot pierced the glass. Shock paled Avery's face, and Luke lunged forward, knocking her to the ground. "Everyone down!"

Another round of shots cracked the windows along the back wall above the sofa, shards of glass cascading around them.

Parker army crawled to Avery, horror on his face. "Avery?"

25

Her breathing was labored, and blood seeped from her shoulder.

"She'll be okay," Luke said, having made a rapid but sure assessment. "Someone call 9-1-1. We need an ambulance." That was a luxury he often couldn't afford when undercover in the field. He'd self-bandaged more wounds than he could count and removed two bullets from his own flesh.

The shots stopped.

"No one get up. Not yet," Luke instructed. The sniper could just be waiting, though it couldn't have been a professional sniper taking those shots. Luke was almost positive he had been the gunman's intended target.

"I called 9-1-1," Griffin said. "Two minutes out."

Luke slid off his jacket, bunched it up, and pressed it to Avery's wound. "Apply pressure," he instructed Parker. "She'll be okay. No organs hit and straight through."

"It's okay, baby," Parker said, kissing her brow.

Luke surveyed his friends, his loved ones crouched low on the ground, glass shards in their hair, anger and concern marring their brows. It was surely his fault. He'd brought this on them. If Avery hadn't walked in front of him at just that moment, he'd be dead. Ebeid not only knew he was in town but knew where he was and, far more frightening, knew *who* he was with.

3

Sirens wailed in the distance, growing closer in sync with the pounding of Luke's heart.

How had Ebeid found him so quickly? Or . . .

Maybe the shots were in retaliation for Declan stopping the Bay Bridge attack.

Declan *had* been standing right next to him. What if that shot had been intended for Declan?

Either way, Ebeid had just knocked on their front door, and from this point on they had to ramp up security.

Parker held Avery in his arms, keeping pressure on her wound, whispering words of love to her as she grew paler, all color leaching from her cheeks.

She was going to be okay, but he was sure that didn't make this hurt any less for her or Parker.

Sirens howled out front, and soon the stomping of boots filled the room as SWAT swarmed in, their own snipers no doubt already in place.

The team moved quickly, medics taking Avery to the waiting ambulance, Parker going with her. He glared at Luke as he followed the medics out.

Kate stood, glass shards still clinging to her hair, shock blanketing her face, though she moved with purpose and spoke with the agents questioning her with a steadfastness few possessed in such crisis situations.

Declan strode over to him as he stood back and watched Declan's FBI cohorts handle the situation valiantly.

Declan cleared his throat. "You think that was intended for you or me?"

Luke swallowed. "I was just wondering the same thing."

"Either way, Ebeid just declared war on us."

Luke nodded. That was one way to put it.

"We'll give our statements and then head to the hospital for Avery," Declan said.

Luke had forgotten what it was like to have a group of friends be there for him. Of course they'd go to the hospital and he'd go with them. Whether the bullets were intended for him or Declan, he was not letting Kate out of his sight.

Luke drove alone to the hospital, keeping a close eye on Kate's car. He hadn't been to the University of Maryland Medical Center since his sophomore year in college, when he'd broken his leg playing rugby, but entering the sterile-smelling building brought a rush of memories flooding back.

A nurse directed them to a small peach room off the larger waiting area, and they found Parker pacing. The furniture was covered in a green-and-peach tropical print, the palms and winding vines reminding him of the jungles of Thailand. He blinked back the awful memory of that place, of his mission there. Dark eyes haunting him.

A bullet wound to his thigh, nearly hitting his femoral artery . . .

"Any word?" Tanner asked, a frantic look in her deep brown eyes.

Parker raked a hand through his hair. "Not yet. She's in surgery." He turned to Luke, his eyes bloodshot and his countenance fierce. "*You* had to bring whatever world you've been living in to our doorstep."

"Hey." Declan quickly stepped between them. "I know you're upset. We all are, but that assault could have just as easily been aimed at me for my role in stopping Ebeid's Bay Bridge attack." He swallowed, the stark reality of that possibility washing over his face.

Parker looked at Luke and then Declan, and then took a step back. "If anything happens to her . . ."

"I know." Declan clamped his hand on Parker's shoulder. "Let's pray."

They all circled up, and Tanner pulled Luke into the group.

"Father, we lift Avery up to you. Please bring her through surgery with no lasting harm. She's a fighter. Help her to be strong, and be with Parker too. Let Ebeid pay for what he's done and guide us to finally stop him," Declan said.

A chorus of "amen" rounded the room.

Luke swallowed. How often had he taken time to pray—*really* pray—for guidance? He'd called out in anger and frustration, begged God to spare his life, but true, heartfelt, intentional prayer outside of a crisis? It'd been far too long.

An hour and a half passed before the surgeon finally appeared at the door, a nurse at his side. "Mr. Mitchell?"

Parker lurched to his feet. "Yes?"

"Miss Tate did beautifully."

Relief washed over Parker, the tension in his jaw and shoulders loosening with his exhale. "She's okay?"

"She'll need some recuperation time and possibly some physical therapy to regain her range of motion, but that just depends on how she heals. But yes, she'll be fine."

"Can I see her?"

"She's still out from the anesthesia, but as soon as she's awake and they've had a chance to check her over, they'll call you back."

"Thank you." Parker shook the surgeon's hand.

"You're welcome. I'd tell you to get some rest, but I have a feeling you're not that type of man."

"No, sir."

"I didn't think so." The surgeon smiled as he and the nurse left the room.

"I hate to leave," Griffin said. "But now that we know Avery is okay, Finley and I better get some sleep. We have to be up for our flight to Texas in a few hours."

Griffin is a husband. A guy he'd known since they were four. It was surreal.

30

"Arriving two hours before the flight is the stated suggestion for BWI," Finley said, rolling her eyes as Griffin shifted her toward the door. "For a flight at six, that means *four in the morning*. It's not natural."

Griffin wrapped his arm around her. "I know you hate mornings, but you can sleep on the plane."

She looked less than pleased but followed him to the door.

Parker stepped toward Griffin. "If you come across anything you need my help on, just call. I'm happy to help you . . . to help Jenna . . . in any way I can."

Griffin clapped him on the shoulder. "I know and I appreciate it. I'll call if I need your input. You take good care of that lady."

Parker nodded, clearly torn between the desire to find his first love's killer and to be at his current love's side. He'd made the right choice by staying, at least in Luke's mind, but what did he know about relationships anymore?

After Griffin and Finley departed, Parker said, "It's late. I appreciate you all being here, but it's not necessary. Take Tanner home, Declan."

Declan looked to Tanner and nodded. "Kate, how about you take my second guest bedroom? Tanner and I haven't been comfortable with you staying alone since the shootout on the boat, and after tonight—"

"Shootout?" Luke could feel his eyes widening, his brows hiking. What were they talking about?

"It's a long story," Kate said.

"One I'm very interested in hearing," he replied.

"One that can wait until morning," Declan said.

"I'm fine," Kate said. "I'll stay on my boat."

"Katie," Luke said.

She gave him an are-you-kidding-me look of exasperation. "I can take care of myself."

"I'm sure, but . . . why don't you stay with me?" Luke countered.

"What?" she and Declan said at the same time.

"I would feel best if we stick together. I have a motel room. You can take the bed. I'll take the floor."

Declan looked at Kate.

She swallowed. "I'll stay on my boat."

Stubborn woman. "Fine, then I'm staying with you," Luke said.

"No, you're not."

"Yes. I am."

"And we're exiting this throwback to a decade ago," Declan said, taking Tanner's hand and turning to Luke. "See you at the office at nine. We have a lot of work ahead of us." He left with Tanner, closing the door behind them.

"Shall we?" Luke said.

Kate looked at Parker.

"I'm going to get a cup of really bad coffee," Parker said, leaving them to duke it out as they always had. There'd always been a strong love between them, but strong wills to match. It was addictive, really, the fire that existed between them, fueling the other until they ended up in a passionate embrace. They'd been a mess but a magnificent one. And he'd let it all go.

She linked her arms across her chest and stared at him.

"I'm coming with you whether you invite me or not," he said.

"So you leave for over seven years, then suddenly I'm your responsibility?"

"You just got shot at." He was trying to protect her. Didn't she get that?

"It wasn't the first time. Doubt it will be the last."

"What?" What kind of PI jobs was she working? And what was the shootout at the boat?

"It comes with the territory." She shrugged.

"Then even more reason for me to stay."

She glared at him, but he held his ground. After a long stalemate, she finally relented. "Fine. You can have the couch," she said as Parker entered with a Styrofoam cup of coffee sloshing in his hand.

"Just like old times, I see." A shadow of a smile crossed his scruffy face. The kid who'd tried for years to grow facial hair now had a five-o'clock shadow. Times had changed.

According to Katie, they had *really* changed. Had he expected time to stand still?

4

Luke followed in his rental car as Kate drove to her houseboat, *Barefoot*. He hated that she'd insisted on driving alone to the hospital, but he'd followed her every inch of the way and would continue to stay with her until Ebeid and whomever he'd hired to shoot at them was in prison or dead.

Though given the poor job the shooter had done, Luke bet he was either already dead at Ebeid's hands or ready to take another strike before admitting his error to the unforgiving Ebeid. Either way, he or Declan was still in danger—more than likely, both of them. And that meant they were all in danger.

"I appreciate your offering to stay," Kate said as they exited their cars and headed for her houseboat, "but—"

"It's not an offer," he said, pulling his sparsely filled duffel from the trunk and hitching it over his right shoulder. "I'm insisting."

Kate cocked her head. "You really think that's the best way to get me to respond positively?"

"No." He inched the duffel strap higher up on his shoulder. "I know you hate it when people attempt to order you around." He took a step closer. "It brings fire to your eyes." Her beautiful, captivating eyes.

"So why go there?"

"Because you also know I don't take no for an answer." Never had.

"Fine." She exhaled. "But *just* for tonight. We reassess in the morning."

"Sure." He shrugged, knowing full well there'd be no reassessing, but if that was what it took for her to let him stay the night, so be it.

Kate led the way and, after unlocking the sliding glass door, allowed him passage inside.

"You really ought to get a security system," he said, stepping on board the small houseboat he'd first entered a few nights ago when following and then killing Ebeid's right-hand man, Xavier Benjali.

Kate shook her head. "You sound like Declan." Flipping a switch on the wall, she turned on the recessed lighting all along the pine-paneled ceiling. The galley-style living room decorated in creams, rustic oranges, and bright yellows showed her love of Tuscan-style interiors hadn't decreased.

He was so incredibly thankful the guys had looked out for Kate while he'd been gone. They had been good friends to her, and it appeared—at least with Declan and Griffin—they were still his friends, too, despite the years they'd spent apart. Parker would come around eventually, after he got over the shock of his girlfriend being shot. Luke felt horrible about that.

35

"I have a guest room," Kate said, moving through the living space to the galley kitchen.

He glanced at the couch. "I'm fine here. It lets me keep an eye on the door. I don't sleep much." He tried to, but in his profession sleeping soundly was rarely an option. He spent most nights reading, analyzing his ops, or exercising. He'd bother her less in the living room.

She shrugged. "Suit yourself. I'll grab you some bedding."

"Thanks." He dropped his duffel on the floor and took more time to look around, since his last visit had been pretty intense.

The space was clean and uncluttered, though he expected no less from Kate. She'd always been a minimalist when it came to stuff and wasn't the sentimental type. It had never been her nature to linger over things. He moved to the kitchen to find two photos in colorful magnetic frames stuck to the stainless-steel Kenmore. One was an image of her and the gang hiking at Bandelier. So they'd taken a trip to New Mexico. He wondered if it had been on business or for pleasure. He bet a combo of the two.

Sandia Labs, Los Alamos, and Kirkland Air Force base were located in New Mexico. According to Mack, Kate had been offered jobs all over the world, but she stuck to in-country. He wondered why, especially when it'd always been her dream to travel. So many questions he wanted to ask, so much he wanted to know about the woman she'd become.

Was she still devoted to Christ? It appeared so, from small actions he'd witnessed and the fact that her dog-eared Bible sat with a highlighting kit on the side table by the chaise longue.

Based on the Bandelier and cliff-jumping pictures on the fridge, she still loved the outdoors and adventure. Leaning in, he studied the cliff-jumping one but couldn't place the location.

"Hawaii," she said.

He turned, shoving his hands in his pockets at her nearness. He felt strangely out of place where he used to feel so at home in Kate's presence.

How could he have been so stupid as to leave her? To leave such a blessed life behind?

He cleared his throat and switched his attention back to the photographs. "Which island?" he asked.

"The big one."

He leaned in closer to examine the photo. "Cool shot."

"Thanks. Tanner took it when we all traveled there a couple months ago after Griffin and Finley's wedding. We kind of crashed their honeymoon," she said sheepishly but with a hint of the smart-aleck smirk he loved.

"Seriously?" He laughed. "I'm sure they appreciated that."

"Their travel agent made it sound so awesome,

and we stayed on different islands—hopping opposite them, so when they were on Maui, we were on the Big Island, when they were on the Big Island, we were on Kauai."

"Sounds like a great trip." He'd never been. Measures of national security never seemed to occur in paradise, at least not since Pearl Harbor.

"It was. We hiked up volcanoes, went swimming with sea turtles, and snorkeled with dolphins."

"And went cliff-jumping," he said, gesturing to the picture.

"Yeah, that too." She smiled.

She had remained the adventurous, wanderlust-filled girl he loved. "What's been your favorite place to visit?"

"Oooh." She grabbed a flavored sparkling water from the fridge and offered him one. He passed. They tasted like bubbly nothingness to him, though everyone else seemed to be crazy about them.

She held up a Mighty Mango Naked juice.

"Great," he said.

She tossed the cold bottle to him and he caught it. "Thanks."

She nodded, took a seat on a barstool facing him, and tracked back to his question. "My favorite place to visit. Hmm. That's a tough choice, but I'd have to say the Big Island."

He leaned against the counter, loving the way her face looked as she mentioned it. "Why?"

"Because it's breathtaking, full of adventure, and low on people."

"Sounds like your perfect spot." He untwisted the bottle cap and took a swig of the fruity drink.

"How about you?" she asked, managing to sit cross-legged on the barstool.

He'd seen a lot of beautiful places, but hardly ever under pleasant circumstances. "I'd have to say Barcelona."

She leaned forward. "Why?"

"Because it's gorgeous, has beautiful beaches, and, of course, is home to the best *futbol* team."

"Barca fan?" she asked, tapping her water bottle decorated with bright pink berries.

"Yeah." He narrowed his eyes. "You know Barca?" She'd been a hockey fan in college.

"It's hard to not know who Lionel Messi is."

"True."

"So, Barcelona . . . ?" she pressed.

"Oh, it's a city that doesn't feel like a city." He moved to lean over the counter. His hands mere inches from her, his head dipped under the cabinet overhanging the galley bar where she sat on the opposite side. "It's got quirky but fantastic architecture, all thanks to Gaudi."

"I've seen pictures of his work. I can't decide which is my favorite, the fish house or the cool park."

"Casa Batlló is cool and totally does look like a fish, but Park Güell is amazing." He'd spent a lot of time relaxing there on his leaves, rare as they had been.

She stared at him the way she used to when they'd chatted like this before he'd abandoned her. He leaned closer, his fingers caressing hers. She leaned in, then quickly yanked her hand away. "I better get to bed."

"Right," he said, straightening and clearing his throat. "Night."

"Night." She looked back one last time before shutting her bedroom door at the end of the short hall.

Cyrus entered Ebeid's study, surprised to find him still awake at this late hour. "I followed Agent Grey like you asked, and you'll never believe who showed up," Cyrus said, leaving out the fact that he'd acted on his own and tried to kill the man, and failed. If he 'fessed up now, he'd be the dead one. Besides, he was about to rectify that situation posthaste and get on Ebeid's good side with the intel he had to share. By the time Ebeid learned of the botched hit at CCI, it wouldn't matter because Garrett Beck and Kate Maxwell would be dead.

"I'm hardly a fan of guessing games. Get to it, Cyrus."

"Garrett Beck." The CIA black ops agent known most often as Garrett Beck had been a chigger under Ebeid's skin for almost eight years.

Ebeid lurched forward. "*Here* in Baltimore?"

"Yes, and you're never going to believe where I followed him to."

"What did I just say about guessing games?"

"The boat the Shaw woman was staying on with Kate Maxwell."

Ebeid straightened, stiffened. "What?" His dark eyes narrowed. "Are you certain?"

"Positive."

"So she has ties not only to Grey's investigation and to Tanner Shaw, but also to Garrett Beck?"

Cyrus nodded, pleased at his boss's half smile.

"You know what to do."

Kate rolled over, unable to sleep. The time with Luke at the counter had stirred intense feelings. The stark reality was that she was falling in love with the man he'd become, and not just the boy she'd known. *Disconcerting* didn't come close. Shaking her head, she sat up. She'd bolted so quickly before anything deeper could begin that she'd neglected to get ready for bed—hadn't even washed her face or brushed her teeth.

It would only take a couple of minutes and would make her feel far more comfortable.

Cold from the hardwood floor seeped through her fuzzy socks as she opened her bedroom door. Getting a glimpse of Luke, she forgot to breathe.

He hung in the doorframe of her bathroom, doing chin-ups, his fingertips braced on the edge of the frame. His back contracted, his muscles flexing, his sinewy arms rippling with each pull and release.

He glanced over his shoulder at her, perspiration slipping down the center of his back as a heated ripple cascaded through her limbs.

"Sorry," he said, hopping down and planting his bare feet on the floor. "Did I wake you?"

"Nuh-uh." *Nuh-uh?* What was she, some star-struck teenager who'd just met Tyson Ritter? She smoothed her tousled hair. "I forgot to brush my teeth."

"Oh." He grabbed a hand towel to wipe his face.

She swallowed, his sculpted abs even more impressive than his back. "You couldn't sleep?" she said, barely managing a coherent sentence.

"Nah, like I said, I don't need much sleep."

"That must get exhausting." She stepped around him in the tight quarters, trying not to stare. *Focus on his eyes. No, don't do that. His eyes always melted you.*

"Comes with the job, I'm afraid." He shrugged, his muscles again flexing with the motion.

Her lanky college boyfriend was now a beautifully sculpted man who could rival Michelangelo's *David*.

Swallowing, she scooted into the bathroom and, with one last glance, shut the door. Her eyes widened, and the desire to call Tanner and share what had just happened raced through her, but she refrained and instead splashed her face with cold water.

Katie?

Luke bolted upright and scanned the room. It took a moment to acclimate himself. Katie's boat, and he'd crashed out?

Rubbing the sleep from his eyes, he glanced at the clock. Just after midnight. Normally he didn't crash this early and then was up at dawn. His job didn't allow for a long or sound night's sleep, but his body and mind had adjusted, allowing him to perform at his best on four hours of sleep a night without issue or incident. It was amazing what a body and mind could endure with rigorous training, the strength and fortitude one gained.

He glanced back at Katie's door. All was silent.

He was so thankful she'd finally let him stay. Why did the girl have to fight him on *everything?* Even more frustrating, why did he enjoy the verbal jousting so much?

Because she was unlike any other woman he'd ever met. Smart, witty, quick on her feet, and more than able to hold her own while still possessing—although she rarely showed it to anyone—a tender side. He'd spent seven-plus years away, and not a day had gone by during which she hadn't danced through his mind.

He raked a hand through his hair, back to his natural shade of dark brown for the first time in a while.

It was amazing the love he still held for Katie. He'd always known he loved her, but even he hadn't realized how deeply or all consumingly until he was back in her presence. But what did he do with it? So much had happened, so much time had passed.

He dropped to his knees in prayer at the side of the sofa bed.

Father, I know it's been too long.

Oh, he'd said prayers, offered up quick ones as he needed help and as they fit in his schedule, but he couldn't recall the last time he literally dropped to his knees with a bared-open heart before his Savior. Though he feared after all he'd done . . . after all his sins . . . he might be beyond the point of redemption.

I'm sorry, Lord, for choices I've made and some of the orders I've followed. They were contrary to my soul, and I did them regardless. I'm wrestling with demons. They're always haunting me, trying to keep me in darkness.

Being back, all I want is to return home to You, to Katie, to the guys, and to my family, but I don't know if that's even possible.

Help me, Father. Guide my steps and keep the gang safe. Don't let evil touch them because of me. Help me to keep my focus when it's being pulled in two vastly different directions—Katie and Ebeid.

He lay back on the couch, fully expecting to remain awake, but an hour later he was roused from a deep slumber. This time something was wrong. Once again he sat up, pulling his .45 Sig from under the pillow.

He moved to check on Katie, cracked her door, and found her sound asleep. He moved back through the boat and then heard it—a click by the sliding glass door.

Was someone trying to enter?

With a deep swallow, he inched back the privacy curtain.

A man in black, a shadow in the dimness of the dock lights, stood less than a foot away on the opposite side of the glass. Wires were on the door. On the handle. A black box fixed to the glass. It was a bomb. Its red countdown numbers reflected backward on the sliding door of the ship opposite. *Two minutes.*

He raced for Katie.

Please, Father. Don't let anything happen to Katie!

Kate awoke to a large thump on top of her legs, a heavy weight pinning them in place.

Fear ricocheted through her.

She grabbed her gun from under her pillow.

"It's me," Luke said, shifting off her legs. "Don't shoot."

Cold October air swirled in through the open hatch above. "Luke? What are you doing? Why is my hatch open?"

"Your sliding door is rigged to blow in under two minutes. We've got to get out of here *now*."

"What?"

"No time to explain." He kneeled on her bed beneath the hatch. "Climb up me and out the hatch. Hurry!"

She stared at him. Was she dreaming?

"Now, Katie!"

She shook off her slumber and did as instructed. Once through the hatch, she dropped to the deck and lay flat on her stomach for better stability. She offered her outstretched hand to Luke. "Thanks," he said, climbing up like a spider scaling a wall, "but I've got it."

Reaching the top, he grabbed her hand and they slid down the rear boat ladder to the main deck. They leapt to the pier and raced for the parking lot, seconds ticking away along with the rapid thumping of her heart.

An explosion shuddered the earth below as her home shattered into a thousand pieces. Luke yanked her to the gravel-strewn pavement behind his rental car, shielding her body with his as the ground quaked in rippling waves.

Once the charred pieces of her home ceased raining down, Luke slowly released his hold on her and stood, assessing the damage.

Mr. and Mrs. Braverman stumbled onto their deck, gaping at the destruction. "Oh, Kate!" Mrs. Braverman wailed.

"I'm ok—"

Luke covered her mouth and tugged her hard against him. "Shh. Better to let them think they succeeded—that you went down with your ship."

"But I don't want folks to worry."

"Better they worry than to have whoever did this try again."

Excellent point. How did she argue with that?

He helped her into his rental car and handed her the keys. "Just don't start it until I give you the okay."

She nodded.

He opened the glove box and pulled out a flashlight.

Dropping to the ground, he slid under the vehicle. Then a moment later he stood, walked to the edge of the harbor, dumped something in, and ran back and climbed in the car.

"What was that?"

"A second incendiary device, in case the first didn't do the job."

"And you just threw it in the harbor?" she asked as he started the car and pulled out of the lot.

"I disabled it first."

He shifted gears and tore down the road, checking the rearview mirror.

She looked back, anticipating a follow, and sure enough, one came.

Luke exhaled, shifted gears, and tore down an alleyway. Several minutes and impressive maneuvers later, he lost the tail but continued to check the rearview and side mirrors.

"Where are we going?"

"My hotel."

She swallowed, both a thrill and shot of trepidation bolting through her. After a minute, she found her voice. "Was that Ebeid back there?"

"One of his men. A dead one for failing."

"What happens now?"

He shifted gears and banked a hard right down another alleyway, checking the rearview mirror yet again. "You don't leave my side."

5

"When we were at the hospital, Declan said there'd been a shootout at your boat." It'd been nagging at Luke.

"Ebeid's men were after Tanner and Declan," she said.

"On *your* boat?"

"Tanner had been staying with me. Declan was walking her home and Ebeid's men opened fire."

"Obviously, they survived."

"Do you think they blew up my boat assuming Tanner was still staying with me?" Kate asked. "In retribution for Declan stopping the Bay Bridge attack?"

"It's possible, but my gut says they were there for you—and possibly me." And the man in black would have succeeded if he hadn't been there, as Kate had been sound asleep. The thought hit him hard. He'd already lost Katie once by walking away. Now that he was back . . . the thought of her gone for good was suffocating.

"Why for me?" she asked, her hands fidgeting in her lap.

He tapped the wheel with his thumb. How real was he willing to get? "Either because of your connection to Declan's investigation or . . . because they've figured out what you mean to me."

49

"How could they possibly know what I mean to you when *I* have zero clue?"

After the kiss they'd shared the other night and his apology, he'd hoped she at least knew he still loved her. Not that he could necessarily do anything about it, but he wanted her to know he'd carried her with him all these years. "I guess I hoped . . ."

"Hoped what?" She shifted to face him, and the unease reflecting in her eyes tugged at his soul. "You took off without a word and have been gone for over seven years. How on earth could I assume—let alone know—that I mean *anything* to you?"

The breath left his lungs in a whoosh. She really *didn't* know. But how could he blame her? If the roles had been reversed, what would he be thinking? He swallowed hard, the stinging reality of the depths of pain he'd caused hitting home. "I'm sorry, Gracie."

She stiffened, tears glistening in her eyes as an oncoming car's headlight beams bounced off her beautiful face.

Apparently the use of her nickname hit a raw nerve.

She stayed silent the remainder of the ride, and he left it there. He'd said little but already caused her pain. The last thing he wanted to do was cause her more. She deserved nothing but the best, and he most certainly wasn't it.

● ● ●

The sound of *Gracie* on Luke's lips—the nickname he'd whispered during their most tender, most in-love moments—echoed through her soul. She swallowed, hugging her knees to her chest as they drove to Luke's hotel, but where that was, she had no clue.

Luke had apologized for leaving, the words sincere and pained, and he'd kissed her—a kiss that tickled her soul. But what did that all mean after so much time? And why should it even matter?

But it did. It mattered immensely, and that realization heated the frustration pulsing through her veins. How could her feelings betray her so easily? All it took was an apology and a kiss, and love pounded in her for a man who'd wounded her beyond measure.

Speaking of wounding . . . She blinked as her mind shifted to the realization that she'd just lost her home and most of her belongings. Everything was a blur, a distant dream, as if she were sleepwalking. She was in a combination of shock and survival mode, but as soon as the adrenaline wore off, the real pain would come. She braced herself for it, praying Luke didn't know she was fighting off tears, but surely he'd seen . . .

Luke pulled into the rear lot of what could aptly be described as a down-on-its-luck motel.

Not that she was a hotel snob like her mom—far

from it. She'd done her fair share of backpacking across states, camping on beaches, staying in three-star hotels, but this looked like something out of *Deliverance*.

He rolled to a stop, cut the engine and the lights.

She unbuckled. "Please tell me this is a pit stop on the way to the *real* hotel."

He chuckled. "This is it, at least for the night."

She stepped from the car as he did. "This from the college guy who refused to stay at any hotel chain under four stars." He and her mom had gotten along great.

"Let's just say my time in the field gave me a fresh appreciation for any place with a solid roof over my head, running water, and electricity."

"Never thought I'd hear those words come out of your mouth." She wondered more about his time away, where and how it was spent, but she imagined there was little he could share.

He unlocked his door with an extra jiggle of the key and held it open for her. She stepped inside, and as he flipped on the light switch she felt she'd stepped back in time.

Retro nineties was the style. Either that, or the room had been the same for nigh on three decades. Sadly, she was betting the latter. The walls were a deep charcoal gray with a handful of colors painted in zigzag patterns on the far wall. The chairs around the round chrome-and-glass dining table to her right were padded in black pleather. To the left was a double bed with a black, purple, and aqua-striped comforter, a chrome-and-glass nightstand on either side, topped with chrome gooseneck lamps and a square black clock with green digital numbers, like the one she'd had when she was a kid.

But her focus quickly shifted from the furnishings to the fact that there was *one* bed and—she spun back around to be certain—no sofa. She rubbed her arms. "Um . . . sleeping arrangements?" She gestured to the bed.

He grabbed a pillow off the bed. "No worries. I'll take the floor."

She glanced at the worn gray carpet. "Please don't."

He arched a brow, and she grimaced. "The floor is beyond scary."

"I'll take the extra blanket out of the closet and fashion a makeshift sleeping bag."

"Are you sure?"

"I'll be fine. I don't—"

"Sleep much. I know."

"Go ahead." He gestured to the bed. "Get some sleep. I've got you."

She'd heard that before—mere days before he'd left.

Climbing into bed, she swiped at the tears beginning to fall and shifted her gaze to the phone. "I'd better call Tanner and Declan and let them know I'm okay," she said.

"You think they've already heard about the explosion?"

"I'm sure they heard police dispatched to the marina, and Declan's place isn't far away."

He skimmed a hand across his forehead. "I guess I forgot about keeping others in the loop."

"Yeah, you did."

That wounded him. She could read the pain on his pinched brow. She just kept darting jabs his way.

Why?

Because she wanted him to hurt as she did?

No. She wouldn't ever wish that on another.

Because he deserved it?

Perhaps, but she wanted to believe she was better than that.

It was simply because the hurt inside of her was screaming so loudly, she feared if she didn't lash out in anger, she'd fall right back into his arms. And that *couldn't* happen. She *wouldn't* let it. She was stronger than that, had been for so many years, but something had shifted the moment she saw him standing before her. All of a sudden she was that college girl hopelessly in love with a college boy who'd promised her the world.

"The bedcovers aren't the warmest. Let me get you a sweatshirt, and I'll crank up the heater," he said, after standing awkwardly still while her thoughts ran wild.

He grabbed the sweatshirt, and though the room

wasn't horrible temperature-wise, he insisted on making it as comfortable as he could.

She slipped on his sweatshirt, its scent of Old Spice reminding her of being in his arms so many times. Shaking off the memories clamoring to be remembered, she picked up the phone and called Tanner, assuring both her and Declan that she was fine.

Hanging up, she turned to find Luke standing over a makeshift bed on the floor. She couldn't seriously allow him to sleep on that ratty flooring. "You can't sleep on that."

"I've slept on far worse." He reached for the light switch.

She bit her lip, leery about falling back asleep after waking up the way she had. A man pouncing on her bed—even if it was Luke—a bomb decimating her home, and nearly everything she owned gone in a single blast. She longed for a night of company and old reruns to soothe her soul, just like they'd done back in college, but dare she go there? Dare she let down her guard enough to enjoy a few hours' reprieve with Luke? Could she enjoy simply being in his presence after so many years apart? "Would you leave the lights on for a bit? I'm not quite ready to go to sleep."

He looked poised to argue but apparently thought better of it. "Sure." He gestured to the bathroom. "Would you like to use it before I go in?"

"Nope." She shook her head. "Go ahead."

"Okay. I'll be out in five. I think I have an extra toothbrush for you in my backpack for the morning. I'll leave it and some soap on the sink for you. Anything else you need?"

"I'm good. Thanks." She'd grab a change of clothes at her office before heading to the Bureau. Thankfully, she spent so much time at CCI, she kept a fair number of items and necessities there—so she hadn't lost *everything*.

Luke moved for the bathroom and shut the door behind him. The water trickled in the sink as she clicked on the big, boxy TV set.

Channel surfing, she found *I Love Lucy* reruns. She'd watched less than a minute of the chocolate factory episode when Luke opened the bathroom door. He stood there, his hair combed, face freshly washed, his shirt off and clutched in his hand.

She did her best not to gape, *again*.

"I hoped you'd be asleep. You need your rest."

"Like I said, I'm not ready to sleep yet."

He narrowed his eyes, clearly trying to figure out what he could do to help. "Are you sure I can't get you anything?"

She pulled her knees up to her chest, his sweatshirt soft and comfy. "Any chance this place has a vending machine?"

"Yep. What's your fancy?"

She hadn't heard that question from him since college.

"Doritos and—"

"Ho-Hos?"

It'd been their late-night snack of choice throughout college.

"And Mountain Dew?" he said with a soft smile tickling his lips.

She nodded. He *remembered.*

"Still haven't figured out how that doesn't keep you up all night."

"Just me, I guess." She shrugged, swallowing as he put his shirt back on, slid his gun into the back of his jeans, and headed for the door.

"I'll be back in two shakes," he said. "Lock the door behind me."

She did as he instructed, then glanced out the curtains as he walked down the concrete corridor and out of sight.

Suddenly she felt extremely vulnerable—like the target she was.

Flipping the curtains back into place, she moved away from the window.

"Better to let them think they succeeded."

But the tail following the explosion proved the killer knew he'd failed, that they'd lived.

How long until he figured out where they were?

How long until the next hit?

6

Luke tugged on the knobs of the old-fashioned vending machine, scanning the perimeter while he waited for the bag of Doritos to fall into the bay. Their surroundings were clear. He'd lost the tail, and it appeared no one had figured out where he was staying—at least not yet. They'd switch locations tomorrow night. He prayed Kate wouldn't balk at remaining by his side until this was finally over. He'd no doubt have a battle before him, convincing her of the necessity to remain with him, but it was a battle he'd win—even if it meant he had to sit outside the door of wherever she chose to stay. He would not leave her side until Ebeid was behind bars or dead.

Grabbing the remaining items for Kate, along with a bag of Cheetos and a grape Shasta for himself, he returned to the room. Unlocking the door, he found Kate lying on her stomach, socked feet up in the air, kicking back and forth, her elbows propped an inch from the foot of the bed.

His mind flashed to all the nights they'd spent talking, studying, and watching old reruns throughout college. They'd been the best years of his life.

"Thanks," she said as she shifted to sit cross-legged at the foot of the bed. He handed her the treats, and she wasted no time opening them. She started with the Mountain Dew, which fizzed as she popped it open, and then she took a long, slow sip.

He moved to sit on the floor, his back to the bed, but she shifted to the side and patted the spot next to her. "It's fine."

He looked up at her. "You sure?"

"Don't worry. My hands are occupied." She smirked, dipping her hand back into the Doritos bag. She'd smacked him the night of their reunion, right after they'd shared the most amazing kiss. He'd never gone from a moment of pleasure to one of pain quite so quickly before.

He sat on the bed beside her, not worried about receiving another slap, but rather trying to be conscious of what made her comfortable or, more so, uncomfortable.

He longed for nothing more than to be close to her, to comfort her. She'd just lost her home and all her belongings, and she was taking it in stride. She was one strong lady, but she'd always been so.

It was a huge part of what attracted him to her. Her mix of strength and vulnerability, which stirred his soul like nothing else. It was why he'd believed she could weather his leaving— and Malcolm had promised him it was only to be for a short period of time. One assignment on a team that needed "a man like him." Malcolm had played to his ego and pride, and Luke allowed the persuasion and flattery to work, not to mention Luke's own certainty that he could negate a threat to the country he loved. But time passed rapidly, and the longer he was gone, the harder it seemed to return. After a while, and after *who* the job had turned him into, he thought it might be better for Kate if he didn't come back at all. Besides, until Ebeid was behind bars, no one was safe. He'd stayed in the Agency to protect her and their country, and yet he longed for nothing more than to be back at her side.

He glanced at the TV screen. "*I Love Lucy*," he said, popping his soda open. "Still one of your favorites?"

"Yep, and *Green Acres*, of course."

That show was what she'd fallen asleep to pretty much every night at UMD. She'd crash, and he'd cover her up, kiss her forehead, and head back to his dorm room.

Gratitude welled in his heart for this time together, this moment that felt frozen in time, a gift from God.

The chocolate factory episode ended, and the next began. In it, Lucy headed to the dress store with Ethel in tow. He'd seen this one too. Seen them all. He'd embarrassingly enough bought the entire *I Love Lucy* DVD collection and carried a single season in his laptop DVD drive wherever he went, so he could fall asleep—when he'd actually been able to fall asleep—with thoughts of Kate and better times dancing through his mind.

"I guess I have a good excuse to go shopping now that all my clothes are gone," she said, a hint of laughter forced into her voice, but he saw past the façade—he always had—to her underlying sadness.

"I'm sorry, Katie."

She shrugged. "They were just things."

Kate had never been big on material things, but it'd always been her dream to live on a boat and to sail around the world. She'd accomplished the first part of that dream, and now it was gone. That had to be crushing. Yet one more thing Ebeid had taken away.

Anger flared, and he pumped out his fists to release the adrenaline suddenly surging through him. He'd ask if she had insurance but didn't want to open that can of worms in case she didn't, and even if she did, it wasn't the same. You couldn't just replace a lifetime's worth of belongings, no matter how badly you ached to.

"I guess I'll stay with Tanner and Declan until I can find a new home," she said before popping a Dorito in her mouth, the smell of cheese filling the air.

"You're staying with me until this op is over."

She looked at him with raised brows. "One, I can handle myself. And, two, Declan and Tanner aren't slackers in the protection area either."

"And I respect their skills, but they aren't me."

"Okay, Mr. Cocky. . . ."

"It's not cocky if it's true." His training was on a far higher level than what the Bureau provided. He wasn't trying to be arrogant.

She fluttered her eyes in that way only she could. "You're ridiculous."

"Ridiculous or not, you're at my side until I see this finished."

A knock rapped on Khaled Ebeid's bedroom door, jarring him awake.

He sat up, blinking the bleariness from his eyes, and glanced at the clock. *5:13 a.m.*

He clicked on the bedside lamp. "Yes?" he called, knowing in his gut Cyrus had failed or he'd still be sound asleep.

Cyrus cracked the door open and poked his head in with apprehension. "I apologize, sir, for waking you. . . ."

"But you failed."

"Yes, sir," Cyrus's voice cracked. "Garrett Beck and Kate Maxwell survived the explosion."

Khaled sat up straighter, stiffening. "Explosion?"

"Yes, sir. I succeeded in blowing up Miss Maxwell's boat, where she and Agent Beck were sleeping."

Heat boiled in his veins. "And yet you *still* managed to fail?" Two right-hand men and both had failed him. It was time to bring in a professional assassin, and he knew just the wet asset for the job. One who freelanced to the highest bidder. One they'd never see coming.

"I'm afraid so, sir," Cyrus said.

Khaled pulled the gun with silencer from the nightstand. It was time to get his hands dirty and send a message—he would no longer permit incompetence.

Two squeezes of the trigger and Cyrus crumpled face-first to the floor.

7

Griffin and Finley boarded a plane for Houston, still dragging from only a few hours' sleep, but Griffin was thrilled to be taking his wife out of town after the attack at CCI. Both had requested a period of leave from their jobs to make the Houston trip and to commit a good amount of time to focus on finding his sister's killer.

Griffin balanced the stack of Agent Steven Burke's files on his lap, ready to dig in. On his own time, Burke had been working the case of a friend's daughter, Chelsea Miller, who had been kidnapped and murdered, and her body found washed up on shore. The case quickly turned cold when all leads fizzled out. But Burke refused to give up and kept working Chelsea's case until his own murder two months ago.

Burke's work hadn't been in vain, however. His digging had revealed a similar M.O. in the murders of seven other young women, including Griffin's sister, Jenna, who appeared to have been the first victim. After hers, Burke had found two more murders near Wilmington, North Carolina, and most recently, five in the Houston area—Chelsea's included.

For the first time in almost a decade, Griffin

had real hope Jenna's killer might finally be brought to justice.

Before his death, Agent Burke had surreptitiously marked seven code words in a book—seven words Griffin believed tied to the women's cases. He couldn't be sure that all seven words fit all the murders, but multiple words from Burke's list seemed to fit each case.

Leader. Glock. Handcuffed. Message. Wrists. Barn. Agent.

Seven words. Seven victims. Coincidence? Unfortunately, Griffin believed so. Sadly, in his opinion, the killer wasn't done. And maybe there were others out there Burke hadn't connected to the case.

Every word tugged hard at Griffin, but the one that wrenched most was the last. *Agent.*

Had Burke narrowed the suspect pool down to a profession or, even better, an individual? If so, what type of agent? So many existed—real estate agent, ticket-counter agent for an airline or car rentals, talent agent. Was his profession how he lured his female victims, promising them money or fame?

There was no way Jenna would fall for something like that. She'd had no interest in fame. Her world had wrapped around family, faith, loved ones, the water, and her hometown. She dreamed of being a wife and mom one day—raising her family in Chesapeake Harbor as she and Griffin had been. But that had all been cut short. In the blink of an eye, she was gone.

After nearly a half hour of sitting on the tarmac, their plane *finally* got runway clearance, and within minutes they were soaring up into the bleak, gray October sky.

"Here's hoping we have better weather in Houston," he said, looking over at his beautiful wife. *Wife*.

He still couldn't believe Finley was his, and he hers.

"I checked my weather app, and we're looking at highs in the mid-eighties," she said.

"Nice." That was one bright spot in what would be a very difficult few days. Combing through the poor women's murders would no doubt bring his sister's murder and the gruesome details surrounding it back to the surface—raw and ugly wounds that never fully healed. He'd reached a place of acceptance, but never peace. How could he after what had been done to Jenna?

"What's the name of the agent we're meeting with?"

"Special Agent Lance Thornton, regarding Chelsea Miller's murder—the case Burke latched onto because he was friends with Chelsea's dad. Then we'll let the detectives in charge of the other women's cases know we're in town, and hopefully set up meetings today and tomorrow. I've always found it easier to catch them when you're already local. My hope is to interview them in reverse order—most recent case first, working back to Jenna's."

"Detectives, as in plural?"

"Turns out all the murders were either in different jurisdictions in the Houston metro area or outside of Houston altogether. Same with the two in North Carolina."

"Each murder occurred in a different jurisdiction?"

Griffin nodded grimly. This meant the killer most likely knew something about law enforcement procedure, or at least how to best work around it.

"So how did the FBI get involved with Chelsea Miller's case? I mean, I understand Burke's involvement as a friend of the family and his work on the side, but why Agent Thornton?"

"Because Chelsea was underage and transported across state lines before being murdered. That indicates federal jurisdiction, which Burke no doubt had pushed, being a friend of the victim's family. Though, because he and his partner, Chuck Franco, were counterintelligence—and Chuck still is—the case went to Agent Thornton, who specializes in kidnappings."

"What a rough specialty." She winced.

That was definitely one area of law enforcement Griffin wouldn't want to focus on. The heartache. The fear. Never knowing if the loved one would return.

"Are we speaking with the victims' families?" Finley asked.

He nodded, remembering what it felt like to be one of them. "Yes, all have agreed to talk with us."

"So we're going to have a very busy couple of days."

He clasped her hand, brought it to his mouth, and placed a tender kiss across her fingers. "I'm glad you came with me." It was going to be a very difficult process—however long it took to conduct a thorough investigation—but having his wife at his side filled him with comfort.

"I am too," she said. "Any chance we can look at any of the bodies?" Being a forensic anthropologist, studying human remains for clues was her focus.

"I didn't want to broach that sensitive subject with the families over the phone."

"Of course not."

"But I will ask in person. I know it will be a tough ask, but once we explain how many cases you've solved that way, they might agree. If not, I definitely want you scouring the victims' autopsy files." He reached into his bag and handed her a stack. "Thankfully, Burke had copies or getting these could have been a logistical nightmare."

Finley took a deep breath and closed her eyes in prayer—always praying for guidance, direction, and deep compassion for each victim she studied, and their families. That was yet another reason he loved her. She had a deep devotion to God, coupled with the determination to fight for those who could no longer fight for themselves. She spoke for them. It was a heavy burden to bear. So was his as a homicide detective. But God continued to equip and sustain them both.

He didn't know how people in similar professions who didn't know God dealt with the tragedy and darkness. If they didn't know that one day justice would reign and that hope and healing were possible even through the direst circumstances, it had to be all consuming and overwhelming. It made sense that such professions drove many to drink. Several of his fellow cops tried to drown the sorrow and frustration instead of allowing Jesus to carry the burden. His heart ached for them, and he prayed they would find the peace waiting for them if they'd only ask. He'd recently tried talking with two officers who were really struggling, but they'd just laughed off his "church talk." He continued to pray for an opening, and for God to soften their battle-weary hearts.

After taking Kate by Charm City Investigations and standing guard while she showered, changed clothes, and grabbed some items for the next few days, Luke and Kate entered Declan's FBI office. At nine thirty, according to Declan, they'd be briefing the Bureau chief, Alan King, and then addressing a task force assembled to take down Ebeid. As awkward as it was to be entering an office building and what was essentially a "normal" job, Luke was thankful for the time he'd continue to have with Kate.

If their time together last night had revealed anything, it was that an inexplicable bond still existed between them.

Malcolm had insisted time and time again that the life Luke was now living wasn't one that he, nor any other black ops field agent, could simply walk away from. Even if Luke found a way, how on earth would he function in regular society? For years he'd been living in an entirely different world, with fluctuating rules or complete lack thereof, different objectives, intense focus. . . .

Could he just shut off his brain to the crises surrounding him and be a "normal" citizen? Okay, Declan, Griff, Parker, and Kate weren't exactly "normal" citizens. They still battled darkness and crime, but in a far different manner. Could he adapt to fighting injustice the way they did?

"When does Lexi return?" Kate asked Declan, and Luke's attention shifted back to the conversation.

"Tomorrow," Declan said, looking with longing at Tanner.

"And Lexi is?" Luke asked.

"My partner," Declan said.

Luke's gaze shifted between Declan and Tanner. "But I thought . . . ?"

Declan explained how their boss, Alan, had paired Tanner and himself while his usual partner, Lexi, was on bereavement leave.

"So . . . what happens with Tanner's involvement in the investigation when Lexi returns?" he asked, curious.

Declan smiled at Tanner, clearly madly in love with the woman. "For now, Alan is keeping Tanner on the case and pairing Lexi with another agent." He glanced at his watch. "Time to go to work."

They briefed Alan, and then Luke followed Declan, Tanner, and Kate down the hallway to the briefing room. It'd been years since he'd been in one—most of his briefings since recruitment being clandestine.

The twenty-by-twenty-foot room was full of agents, and he felt every eye on him—the stranger in the room.

Alan strode to the front of the room and cleared his throat. "Good morning. Let's get straight to it."

Alan was tall and broad. Dark hair combed neatly to the side. Brown eyes, an aquiline nose, and a strong jaw. He exuded the strength of his position of leadership. His voice was deep, but he kept it even and on point. "Agent Grey is lead on this investigation and head of the task force, so I want you to give him your full attention. He believes we are facing one of our country's greatest threats, and after yesterday's attempted attack on the Bay Bridge, I have to say I concur."

8

The air was warm and sticky as Finley followed Griffin through the exhaust-filled parking structure to their rental car, her heels clicking along the concrete a few inches behind him, the sound of her presence soothing. A black Chevy Equinox was waiting for them in slot C3 with keys in the ignition.

Griffin glanced at his watch. They had an hour before their arranged meeting with Special Agent Lance Thornton, the federal agent assigned to Chelsea Miller's case. The same agent who'd stopped the investigation within three months of opening it, pronouncing all leads dead.

From Griff's brief conversation with him over the phone, Agent Thornton still sounded unwilling to acknowledge a pattern in the cases. How any law enforcement official worth their salt could deny the obvious connection once the evidence was presented to them was beyond him. To Griff, it sounded like Chelsea Miller's case was fully closed in Thornton's mind and he had zero interest in reopening it. Griffin prayed he was wrong.

After a round of quick calls to the various detectives, and a few return calls, their meetings for the next couple days were set.

Today, after meeting with Thornton, they'd make the hour-and-a-half drive southwest of Houston to Edna, Texas, to speak with Detectives Clint Eason and Joel Hood. Then they'd be on their way to Pasadena, Texas, which was only twenty minutes outside of Houston, where they'd meet with homicide detective Gil Crest. It wasn't the most efficient route drive-wise, but Detective Crest wasn't free until early evening, and it allowed them to work the murders in reverse order. Plus, it would bring them back toward Houston for dinner and their night at their hotel.

Tomorrow's lineup included the final two detectives and speaking with the victims' families. That was the aspect of the investigation Griffin was dreading most, knowing the pain he'd be resurrecting. He wished there was some way to avoid it, but he wouldn't be conducting a thorough investigation without those interviews.

Declan strode to the front of the briefing room, his perfectly shined leather loafers squeaking on the faded white tile floor. Declan had grown from a medium-built youth into a solidly built man—his shoulder breadth and handspan surely intimidating to most people.

Luke had been trained to handle himself in any situation, but Declan's rugged build had given him a moment of pause upon first sight—not out of fear, but out of surprise and a bit of admiration.

And Kate . . . She'd grown into the beautiful, complex, fascinating woman he'd always known she'd become. And he'd missed the joy of seeing her go from a twenty-two-year-old student to a spectacular woman who made his heart thud in a way he hadn't thought still possible. Every nerve ending sparked to life when she entered a room.

"As Alan said"—Declan's deep timbre pulled Luke back into focus—"I fear we are facing one of our greatest terrorist threats yet, comparable to 9/11, and with potential for even more devastating effects."

A murmur trickled through the room, and then a hush fell over the group. Everyone's attention was riveted on Declan, who paced back and forth in front of the LED screen as a photograph—one, strangely enough, Luke had taken in the field—appeared upon it.

"This threat," Declan continued, "has the potential to spread like wildfire." He turned and indicated the image on the wall behind him. "Dr. Isaiah Bedan—a foremost scientist in the realm of biological warfare—is in the country, and six ounces of anthrax were stolen en route from Fort Detrick to the CDC. I don't believe Dr. Bedan's arrival in the States the same day the anthrax was hijacked is a coincidence. The two are undoubtedly intertwined and are being coordinated by Dr. Khaled Ebcid of the Islamic Cultural Institute of the Mid-Atlantic—a front for a vast terrorist network of sleeper cells here in the U.S.

"Thankfully, we have an incredible asset on our team," Declan said, his gaze falling on Luke. He indicated for him to step forward. "CIA operative Luke Gallagher is partnering with us." He gestured for Luke to take the floor as he took a seat in the first row.

Luke stepped to the front of the room. "I'm in full agreement with Agent Grey," he said. "We are facing our fiercest biological warfare terrorist threat on American soil yet." He looked back at Ebeid's picture—the man his world had centered on for years. "To give you some background," he continued, "we first learned of Dr. Khaled Ebeid's extremist ties and activities seven years ago—eight this coming May, to be precise."

He looked at Kate. Her expression indicated she understood this was the operation that he'd left for. Not that it'd make the fact of his leaving any easier to bear, but maybe she'd better understand what he believed he had been fighting—was still fighting—only now on U.S. soil.

"I was first assigned to a team focused on Khaled Ebeid in Ebil, Iraq. Back then, he was co-founder of the Iraqi Heritage Institute. The Agency flagged him when they discovered his loyalty and ties to Osama bin Laden. After bin Laden's death, Ebeid fled the country, moving, fortuitously for him, to Paris, where he took a position as the cultural attaché at the Middle Eastern Antiquities Museum.

"Five car bombings and one subway bombing occurred during his two-year tenure there. Upon deep investigation in conjunction with local authorities and Interpol, all suicide bombers tracked loosely back to Ebeid, and Interpol continued to work with us. Yet despite their thorough inquest into Ebeid, nothing concrete could officially tie him to the bombings, and again, with perfect timing, he moved. This time to Baltimore, where he set up shop. Though here on U.S. soil he has been more patient and far subtler in his terrorist actions—waiting, building, preparing.

"We, of course, alerted Langley to his presence and background, and the NSA has been keeping close tabs on him. While Ebeid has become less aggressive in his approach, at least on the surface, he's no less dangerous. I fear he's even more deadly a threat. He's still putting on a cultural attaché front, which suits his background and degrees, but he's using the cultural institute as a buffer for his continued terrorist activities and extremist ties. We know Ebeid has been bringing over young Southeast Asian recruits and forming a network of sleeper cells."

He cleared his throat. "As I'm sure you're all aware, Agent Grey had a direct encounter with one of these recruits—a man by the name of

Anajay Darmadi. Prior to that encounter, I had been following Anajay in Asia—first in Thailand, and then in Malaysia. I was tracking the funnel Ebeid was using to recruit and then smuggle the young men over.

"But all of this has simply been preparation for what is about to occur. As Declan said, yesterday Dr. Ebeid managed to smuggle Dr. Isaiah Bedan into the country."

Declan flipped the LED image to one of Bedan.

Luke nodded his thanks and continued. "Dr. Bedan is a U.S.-trained microbiologist at the top of his field, or at least he was until his fall from glory two years ago, when he recruited a young student to release anthrax into the air in Munich by dumping it from the top of a four-story building. Fortunately, a security guard noticed the man headed for the roof, and while he was unable to fully prevent the attack, he did intervene in time to keep the death toll to a minimum. Though six deaths, including the guard's, is hardly inconsequential."

"How do you know Bedan recruited him?" a female agent in the second row asked.

"Because the young man proudly confessed before he died from the anthrax he exposed himself to." Luke's jaw tightened, the defiance and lack of any remorse in that young man still tugging at him, filling him with righteous anger. Burning anger to protect the country he loved.

"After deeper investigation," he said, shifting his gait to the right, "we discovered this wasn't the first time Bedan conducted biological warfare. Horrifyingly enough, it appears Bedan had been refining what he refers to as 'his craft' by performing human biological warfare experiments for numerous years leading up to the anthrax attack in Munich."

Shocked expressions and gasps swept through the room.

Luke looked at Kate, whose eyes were wide and her shoulders squared—always ready to take on injustice.

A sea of hands rose like a wave spreading across the room. This was going to be a long and heavy discussion, though he had expected it and, to be fully honest, hoped for no less. The agents present were taking the threat as seriously as it deserved to be taken, though *serious* didn't come close to describing just how horrific Bedan, Ebeid, and their plans were.

Luke pointed to the hand farthest away and would work his way forward. Every agent had some form of note-taking device in hand, their full attention on him.

"You said Bedan is a *U.S.*-trained micro-biologist?" an agent with blond wavy hair cropped above his ears asked.

"Yes. Bedan's background is . . ." Luke exhaled. "I'll let you judge for yourselves. His family immigrated to the U.S. right after World War II, because his grandfather, Abel Bedan, an Austrian Nazi scientist, was part of Operation Paperclip."

"Seriously?" Declan said.

"I'm afraid so." Luke swallowed. "For those of you who don't know, Operation Paperclip was a decades-long covert program of the Joint Intelligence Objectives Agency. The program brought more than sixteen hundred German scientists, engineers, and technicians—mostly of the Nazi party—along with their families, to the U.S. in anticipation of the Cold War with the Soviet Union. One was Dr. Kurt Blome, who developed offensive and defensive capabilities to counter Soviet biowarfare activities. He had previously committed heinous human biowarfare and germ warfare experiments on concentration camp victims at Auschwitz, including injecting the victims with plague vaccines and exposing them to sarin gas. His right-hand man was Abel Bedan."

"Isaiah Bedan's grandfather?"

"Correct."

With a perplexed expression, the blond agent continued. "How does the Muslim connection fit in if Isaiah Bedan came from Nazi heritage?"

"His maternal grandmother was the daughter of Haj Amin al-Husseini, a mufti in Jerusalem. Al-Husseini lived in Germany from 1941 to 1945 before moving to Egypt. During that time, Abel fell in love with al-Husseini's eldest daughter, Ayla. They married and had Erich Bedan, who married Eva Shahid, a distant relative of Ayla's, and they had Isaiah, who has remained unmarried, fortunately. I pray that family line of death and destruction ends with him."

"I'm sorry," the young agent said, confusion marring his brow. "I still don't understand the Nazi-Muslim connection."

"Haj al-Husseini admired Hitler's beliefs and protocol, and in turn provided soldiers to Hitler. They were part of the Waffen-SS division Handschar, which was the German word for *scimitar*—the swords the Muslim soldiers used to fight for Hitler.

"Our greatest concern is that Abel Bedan was responsible for the disappearance of biological weapon research notes when Operation Paperclip ended."

"Excuse me?" another agent said, the possible magnitude of the result of such a theory clearly shaking him.

"Yes, though it is known by only a few key individuals, on a need-to-know basis, biowarfare research notes went missing after Operation Paperclip wrapped up."

"And you believe Isaiah Bedan is in possession of the research notes Abel took?"

"That is correct." Luke pulled up a stool and

sat, propping his shoes on the rungs underneath. "Isaiah Bedan is brilliant, naturally gifted in all STEM fields, highly adaptable, and his knowledge of biowarfare is frightening. His research appears to be very similar to what the Nazi scientists were barbarically working on using the Jews as guinea pigs in concentration camps."

An even younger agent—Luke was betting not long out of Quantico—raised his hand.

"Yes?" Luke said.

"So the Nazis did experiments with anthrax using concentration camp victims?"

"Absolutely."

The agent shook his head. "I'd heard about Mengele's experiments and most of what you just shared. . . ." He swallowed, his pronounced Adam's apple dipping. "But I had no clue the Nazis worked with anthrax."

"Yes, but as bad as the Nazis' experiments with anthrax are, the country most infamous for their work with anthrax was Japan. Japanese Unit 731 was a covert biological and chemical warfare research-and-development unit of the Imperial Japanese Army. They undertook deadly human experiments during the war, primarily with anthrax. The unit was responsible for some of the most atrocious war crimes carried out during World War II, but the Nazis had access to the same diabolical research."

"And Dr. Isaiah Bedan, who now has access

to an extremely lethal amount of anthrax, has specific records and research notes of these Nazi biowarfare experiments via his grandfather's stolen papers from Operation Paperclip?" the young man asked, looking rather peaked.

"I'm afraid that is correct."

"Based on that terrifying knowledge, where do you suspect Bedan might attack? From on top of another building here in Baltimore, or in D.C., perhaps?"

"I'm afraid Bedan has a far wider-reaching plan in mind."

9

"Special Agent Thornton, I'm Detective Griffin McCray, and this is my wife, Dr. Finley Scott-McCray. You and I spoke on the phone."

"Right." Thornton dropped his files on the desk and pushed back in his rolling chair, interlocking his fingers over his abdomen. "You flew all the way here to discuss Chelsea Miller's cold case."

"Hers and the other women like hers."

Thornton shook his head, pushed up on his armrests with a sigh, and stood. "Look, I know Burke was all bent out of shape over the theory of some serial killer—"

"Seven women across three states have been killed in a similar fashion over the past decade. I'd say that makes a pretty convincing starting point for an investigation into a common killer," Griffin said.

"And you're welcome to investigate all you like on your time and dime, but I've got a pile of active cases that I need to devote my time, energy, and the Bureau's resources to. I hate that those women's cases were never solved, but they have been deemed cold—even with what Burke brought to the table."

"You looked into his findings?"

"Of course."

"And?"

"In almost all of the cases, the police narrowed in on a suspect—boyfriend or lover the young lady was meeting for a late-night rendezvous, but she supposedly never made it to the meet-up or never returned home after it."

Like Jenna had disappeared on the way to meet Parker. "And reexamining the cases while considering that similarity didn't bring any new leads?" Griff asked.

"If anything, it only convinced me more that there isn't a single killer." Thornton exhaled. "Not with each case having a different lead suspect."

"So all the boyfriends were different? There was no possibility one of the guys met up with more than one of the women?"

"Nope. All different men, and after reassessing the cases, I concluded there was no evidence to warrant reopening any of them."

"What about Burke's key words?"

"Murders with similar circumstances occur all the time. It doesn't automatically indicate a single killer. Lots of women are killed with a large-caliber weapon. Lots are raped, I'm sorry to say. I'm sure you could search out each word singularly and you'd find hundreds of cases with hits."

Perhaps for one or two similarities, but the combination that repeated—meeting up with a man, bound wrists, rape, large-caliber round, dumped in water—could hardly be a coincidence. If one of the boyfriends wasn't the killer, then perhaps they needed to look at the circumstances differently. Maybe the fact the girls were meeting men late at night had sparked the killer's motive or interest.

"Look," Thornton said, raking a hand over his head, "even *if* there is one killer—which I highly doubt—the fact is, we have absolutely no idea *who* it could be or any concrete leads to follow."

His hardened expression softened as he leaned forward, resting his hands on the desktop. "I hate that those women are dead, and I hate that their cases are cold, but there's nothing more I can do at this point. I have too many *active* cases on my desk—boss's orders. Any further work is going to have to be on your end, but I should warn you, I honestly believe you're headed for a dead end."

As they exited the Houston federal building, Finley released a belabored exhale. "Well, that was helpful."

Griffin shook his head as he opened the car door for his wife. "I don't believe all the cases' leads are cold. With Burke's enthusiasm for pursuing them, there has to be *something* there."

Finley clasped his hand when he climbed into the rental car beside her. "Thornton may have given up on Chelsea and the rest of the women, including Jenna, but we won't."

He cupped her soft cheek and kissed her, then

pulled back and warmed at her smiling face. "Thank you."

Her nose crinkled. "For what?"

"Standing by my side and fighting as hard as I am to find Jenna's killer."

"We're in this together." She squeezed his hand. "And who knows, maybe we'll get more help from our other interviews."

"We can pray," Griffin said, starting the car and pulling out of the lot, headed straight for Eason and Hood's office about an hour and a half southwest. "Hood and Eason worked Ashley Carson's case—the one just prior to Chelsea Miller's."

Luke took the rear as their small group headed back to Declan's office following the task force briefing.

Everyone was stone silent, rocked to the core no doubt by the information Luke had shared.

Same with all the agents in the briefing room as he'd wrapped up. Stunned expressions blanketed their faces as they'd exited the briefing.

He wished he could say he hadn't meant to scare them, but he absolutely had. With Isaiah Bedan in the country, six ounces of anthrax at his disposal, and Ebeid's nearly unlimited funding, they should all be alarmed at what Bedan could concoct.

Something terrifyingly momentous was coming.

So far, they'd been unable to locate Bedan or the anthrax, and it was beyond frustrating that the FBI didn't have enough concrete evidence to arrest Ebeid, or at least to question him about his role in it all. Ebeid excelled at evading legal connection to his men, but the Bureau needed to take a lesson from the CIA and be willing to cut through the mounds of red tape. *Better to ask for forgiveness than permission.* At least that's what his overseas handler had always said before a mission. Luke had lived by that motto for longer than he cared to admit, but he wasn't in that world anymore. He had to keep that in perspective. He was on U.S. soil. He was home, though he doubted the word *home* still applied.

Once they were all inside Declan's office, Kate shut his door behind them. This would be *his* team until Bedan and Ebeid were stopped.

"Okay," Kate said, sitting on Declan's black sofa, one leg bent and hugged to her chest. "Tell us what you really think."

"Meaning?" He cocked his head as he leaned against the wood-paneled wall, arms linked across his chest.

"Meaning, as frightening as everything you laid out in there was, you're holding back."

He arched a brow, curious though not surprised. Kate was never one to beat around the bush. She told it straight and expected the same in return. "Why do you say that?"

She tilted her head to the side, her soft blond hair brushing over her left shoulder. "Because I know you, and I can still tell when you are holding back."

She was right on the holding back part, but could she possibly be right on the *knowing him* part? Was it even possible—after all the years, after the compromises he'd made and the shell of a man he'd become—for her to still *know* him? For that part of him to still exist?

"I have theories," he said, pushing off the wall.

"And?"

"Theories aren't concrete," he said, explaining why he'd kept silent on this. "This is the Bureau. They work on facts and evidence, not gut feelings or personal theories."

He looked at Declan. "Am I right?"

"Yes," he said slowly, grinning at Tanner. "But there are exceptions."

Tanner grinned back.

So Declan had changed from the strict, by-the-book idealist he'd been all through college—basically for the entirety of their growing-up years—and had at least some flexibility.

"So you're saying if I go to Alan with my theory, he'll listen?" Luke asked, not buying it.

"He'll listen . . ." Declan hedged.

"But he won't do anything about it?"

"Not when there are concrete leads to track down," Declan explained.

"Such as?" Luke asked.

"Such as discovering who Ebeid's inside snitch is. Is he or she at the CDC or Detrick? Until we find the mole, we're constantly at risk of another theft like the anthrax—not to mention compromising the confidential nature of the work being done at both installations."

Kate stood to pace. "You said Abel Bedan was brought to the United States after World War II?"

Luke nodded.

"Which means Isaiah Bedan grew up here?"

Luke nodded again.

"And I'm guessing he attended college . . . and grad school in the States?"

"Yes," Luke said. "He got his undergrad in biology at Stanford. Masters and Ph.D. through a joint program between UCLA and Cal Tech. Emphasis in microbiology and medical research in virology."

"And then at some point he left the country for . . . ?"

"Germany, right after he obtained his doctorate," Luke explained. "Though he grew up here, it seems Bedan never viewed America as his home, only a place to service his needs. Once he believed those needs were met, he went to work as a professor of medical microbiology and director of the Institute of Medical Microbiology and Epidemiology at Hanover Medical School."

"And his ties to Ebeid?"

"It appears Ebeid had been watching Bedan, admired his work, and soon after the Munich attack, the two met. Bedan needed to work off-grid, and Ebeid hired him to do so—and then smuggled him into the U.S."

Tanner sighed. "Unbelievable."

Kate stopped pacing. "But during Bedan's time in the States, particularly his time working alongside other scientists at Stanford and Cal Tech, perhaps he formed a friendship there. And maybe that friend now works for the CDC in Atlanta."

"Or here at Detrick," Luke said. "Smart, Katie."

She shrugged. "I have my moments."

Declan stood, striding for the door. "I'll have the techs start combing through the students attending Stanford and Cal Tech at the same time as Bedan, then cross-reference them with anyone currently working at the CDC or Detrick." He paused in the doorway and looked at Luke. "Then I want to hear your theories, concrete or not."

10

Griffin and Finley entered Detectives Hood and Eason's precinct. Finley took a seat in the waiting area while Griffin stepped up to the intake desk.

A few minutes later, a tall, robust man with a friendly smile approached.

"Detective McCray?" he said as Griffin stood.

"Yes."

"Detective Clint Eason."

"Nice to meet you. And this is my wife, Dr. Scott-McCray."

"I know it's a mouthful," Finley said.

"Nice to meet you, ma'am." He shook her hand. "Why don't you follow me back to my desk?"

He led them to a set of back-to-back desks in the center of the large room where another man, of similar build to Eason, sat flipping through a file. Phones were ringing, criminals in various stages of the booking process slouched in chairs, and Eason's and, presumably, Hood's desks sat smack in the center of all the commotion. How they could even think with all the noise was beyond Griffin, and yet hope sparked inside him for the first time since leaving Agent Thornton's office. Maybe they'd get a lead here.

"This is my partner, Detective Joel Hood," Eason said.

Hood politely stood. "Nice to meet you. I was just referring back to Ashley's file. Clint said that's why you're here."

"Primarily," Griffin said, sparking interest in the man's green eyes.

"Go ahead and take a seat. Make yourselves comfortable." Eason gestured to the two chairs positioned on the right side of the two old-school black metal desks. The chairs were old-school as well, metal frame with brown tweed upholstery on the seat and back. Griffin pulled one back for his wife, the metal legs grating along the cheap, clearance-section flooring.

"So you're here about Ashley Carson and . . . ?" Eason asked.

"And anything you might know about the other women."

Eason's face went slack. "*Other* women?"

"Didn't Federal Agent Burke contact you about Ashley's case?"

"Yes, Burke called asking about Ashley, but he didn't say anything about other women," Hood said, scooting his chair to better face them. "But you've definitely got our attention."

Griffin shared all the pertinent details, and Eason and Hood both sat back, shock plastered across their faces.

"I had no idea," Hood said. "Burke just asked about Ashley. Never said anything about a possible serial killer."

That was strange. Griff would have led with that had he been Burke, but perhaps he hadn't wanted to cloud the detectives' judgment while he obtained information about Ashley's case. Perhaps he wanted to know about each case individually before pursuing them as a whole—especially since Thornton was the one running that part of the investigation and it was in Bureau hands. Burke probably had zero desire to start a jurisdiction war.

"Are you looking into all the cases?" Eason asked.

Griffin nodded.

"And I assume you have a possible connected case you're working from your jurisdiction?"

"I'm afraid so." *Jenna.*

Eason and Hood filled them in on Ashley Carson's case and how her boss had been the top suspect since the two were having an affair. She'd disappeared after meeting him at a hotel one night, supposedly headed for the bus stop, but she was never seen again.

"I assume you considered the boss, but there wasn't enough evidence to make it stick?" Griffin asked.

"Yes," Hood said. "He said he stayed the night in the hotel. He ordered room service, and the attendant who delivered it a half hour later provided his alibi."

"And no one else came up?"

"Afraid not." Eason shook his head. "The case went cold quick. Stayed that way."

"Any chance these words mean something to either of you?" He handed them a list of Burke's code words.

Eason lifted the list, his eyes tracking across the words typed in Georgia font, size 14. He shifted forward, resting his forearms on the desk, and then handed the list to Hood, who read it aloud. "'Barn. Leader. Agent. Handcuffed. Glock. Wrists. Message.'"

"Those are key words Burke compiled," Griffin explained. "I believe they relate to the missing women's cases and work together to form the killer's M.O."

Hood flicked the paper. "I never thought about it being part of an M.O., but Ashley Clark had marks on her wrists consistent with handcuffs."

"And her body washed up on shore?"

"Yeah, three days after her reported disappearance," Eason said.

That was the one thing that bugged Griffin. Why hadn't Burke included the wash-up-on-shore factor to the killer's M.O.? Surely, Burke had to see that key similarity. So why not add it to the list? Unfortunately, with Burke's death, Griffin would never get to find out, or to thank the man for the first lead in Jenna's case in eight years.

Three days. That was quicker than with Jenna. Though even if each case shared similarities and were committed by the same killer, they were unique. Each young lady's case deserved individual attention and scrutiny. "My sister washed up after three weeks," he said quietly.

Distress clouded Eason's narrowed eyes. "Your sister?"

"My sister Jenna was killed in a similar fashion nearly eight years ago, when she was seventeen. We believe she was the killer's first victim."

"Oh man . . ." Hood swiped his brow. "I'm sorry. No wonder this case, these cases, mean so much to you."

Jenna, and all the other victims, deserved for their killer to be caught and justice served. It wouldn't bring them back or erase the pain, but it would, at least for Griffin, bring a measure of satisfaction that her killer was finally behind bars and paying for what he'd done.

"Do any of the other words apply to Ashley's investigation?" he asked, trying to keep his focus on Ashley and her case, but it was so hard not to allow thoughts of his sister to creep in.

"It's been a while." Hood exhaled. "But like I said, I pulled her file after your call this morning." He flipped the thin file open again, and his eyes scanned the pages. "Here's one. She was eventually killed with a large caliber round, like what you have found in other cases."

"Eventually?" Finley asked, biting her bottom lip.

He knew exactly why his wife was cringing, and the same queasiness swirled in his gut.

"Ashley was tortured before the sick b—" Eason cut off the word. "Before the sicko pulled the trigger."

11

"So let's hear this theory," Declan said to Luke as he reentered his office, but Kate's body language indicated she was the far more interested of the two. Kate was carrying this case the way she carried the weight of everything else, bearing the full burden of it. Oh, she handled it well, but even in the short time he had been back, he could see she still tended to carry the weight of the world on her shoulders, even when it wasn't hers to bear.

He was certainly no saint. He had years, choices, and actions to beg God's forgiveness and mercy for, but even *he* knew God never intended for anyone to shoulder such massive burdens. Christ had flat-out begged His children to hand over their burdens and take on His yoke instead.

Kate, he feared, still struggled in that area— *full dependence on God*—just as she had in college. She loved her Savior—always had and, from what he'd observed, still did mightily— but *loving* and *depending on* were two vastly different things.

"Your theory?" Kate said at his silence.

"I overheard a couple of Ebeid's men talking at the docks in Malaysia before one of his shipments left, and the captain said the weapons and *parts* had been loaded onto the vessel."

"If you knew the shipment contained weapons headed for the U.S., why on earth did you allow it to leave Malaysia?"

"I had orders."

"And you didn't have a problem with those orders?" Kate asked.

"There's a larger situation at play here. If we'd have stopped the shipment, Ebeid would have simply sent another one."

"So this way you give him what he wants with less effort on his part?"

"It's not that simple. It was far better to track the shipment, to see where it was headed. To try and physically tie it to Ebeid."

"Wow," she said, shaking her head in disappointment. "They've really changed you."

"Excuse me?" How had the little he shared resulted in that pronouncement? If that upset her, how would she respond to some of the other orders he'd heeded?

She linked her arms across her chest. "The Luke I knew would *never* have let that shipment leave port."

He swallowed. Perhaps she was right. The Luke she knew had been young and naïve. The world, unfortunately, worked far differently than he'd expected.

"Sorry to interrupt this fun exchange," Declan said, "but can we get back to the *parts* you mentioned?"

"I don't know for certain, but I believe Bedan is using those parts—whatever they are—to create a dispersal method for the stolen anthrax."

Declan's brows shot up. "Dispersal method?"

Luke rubbed his forehead. "I suppose it's best to start from the beginning." He moved to take a seat on the sofa. "Anthrax is a gram-positive, rod-shaped bacterium that infects people when the spores get inside the body. Anthrax is a Tier 1 bioterrorism threat because it produces the greatest risk with significant potential for mass causalities, which affects the economy and public confidence. It attacks on multiple levels and infects in one of three ways—via contact with skin, ingestion, or inhalation. It makes such a strong bioweapon because it can be released without anyone knowing—if done right, of course."

"Which would be how?" Declan frowned. "Other than putting the powder form in letters like back in 2001, or dumping it off a building like Bedan apparently so inelegantly attempted in Munich?"

"We know anthrax spores can't survive long in water, and I highly doubt they'd attempt to repeat the powder-in-the-mail scenario, as we have so many more precautions in place. I believe it far more likely that Ebeid and Bedan will attempt to contaminate the food supply."

"But I thought cattle and crops couldn't survive

long after being injected with anthrax?" Tanner said.

"You're correct, which means we're looking at fresh food at the packing stage. Food that must be consumed rather quickly following purchase. For example, they could infiltrate a meat packaging plant and contaminate the hamburger before it's packaged and loaded onto trucks headed for grocery stores."

"So the parts you referred to would be installed at a packaging plant?"

"Yeah. If they went that route."

"You also mentioned inhalation," Declan said.

"Correct. Anthrax is the most deadly when it is inhaled. If not identified and treated almost immediately, the results are lethal."

"How do you recommend we proceed?" Declan asked.

"You continue working to bust Ebeid." Though he doubted a man like Ebeid would ever be brought down through traditional legal means. "The NSA and Langley are scouring the country for Bedan, but I expect he's quite near."

"Why?"

"Because Ebeid likes to keep his team close, and if that's not possible, at least tightly knit together and overseen by only a select few worldwide."

"Bedan nearby is a terrifying thought," Tanner said.

Especially if it meant they were at ground zero for Bedan's impending attack. But surely Ebeid wouldn't have anthrax dispersed so close to where he was currently calling home. Although the man likely had no true concept of *home*.

To Luke, home had become far more than a physical dwelling. To him a home was where his heart resided, and *she* was sitting three inches to his right.

Even after all the years of attempting to suppress his feelings for her, one nanosecond back in Kate's presence and his pent-up feelings had come thundering back like a wave crashing over him.

"Where do we even begin the search for possible food contamination, especially without inciting mass panic?" Declan asked, thinking logistically.

Which is how Luke needed to be thinking. Not about Kate and how she made him feel. Rather, he needed to work the case as he'd been trained to do—with intense focus. "Send out a warning to fresh-food packaging plants to report any new illnesses or any suspicious activity," he suggested.

"That's a shot in the dark, don't you think?" Declan said, clearly wanting something far more concrete and actionable.

"I'm afraid that's the best we've got right now." Luke stood.

Kate frowned, tilting her head. "Where are you going?"

"To do my job." He had his own leads to follow.

"But I thought . . ." Tanner glanced between Luke and Declan. "Aren't you working with us?"

"Yes. As a consultant."

Declan raised an eyebrow. "But . . . ?"

"But I still work for the Agency." He had work to do. They were facing the very real possibility of an epidemic, and from all the intel that had been gathered thus far, they were running out of time to stop it. He couldn't just sit around.

Kate stood. "Fine," she said, slipping on her navy pea coat. "I'm going with."

Luke started to chuckle, then realized she wasn't joking. He hadn't planned to leave her side whenever possible, but taking her with him for *this?* He'd figured she'd be safe at the federal building for such a short amount of time— or staying with Declan and Tanner, if this took longer than expected. "I realize as a PI you're used to no rules, but . . ."

He frowned at her burst of laughter. Dare he ask? "What's so funny?"

"*I* have no rules, but a CIA operative does?" Kate continued to chuckle. "That's a good one."

He was ready to argue, but she was right. Rules in his world were ever changing, ever fluctuating, and somewhere amid the sea of compromise, he'd slipped into the murky gray.

There was nothing like living in the furnace to keep you dependent on God for survival day by day, and he kept God's Word close. Yet he'd never felt farther from his Savior.

Kate moved for the door. "You coming?"

He inhaled deeply. *Should* he bring her along?

She was a federal consultant on the task force and a private investigator. What he was about to do was off the books anyway, as he had zero jurisdiction on domestic soil. It couldn't hurt to have Kate along. Considering what he'd heard of her unique skill set, along with what he'd witnessed, she'd probably be a great asset. Besides, judging by the *Barefoot* explosion last night, it seemed Ebeid had already discovered she was his weakness. It wouldn't be long before another hit came. The closer he kept her to him, the better he'd feel.

And his family? How long would it take Ebeid to discover his parents and his brother's family?

Late last night, he'd confirmed with his Agency contact, Mack, that his folks, who'd recently retired to Florida, and his brother and family in Chesapeake Harbor were being watched for their protection. But Kate, no matter how good the detail, would pick up on other agents' presence and refuse their help. Refuse Luke's help.

He swallowed and grabbed his coat. With a quick wave to those remaining behind, he followed Katie to the elevator.

He waited until they stepped inside the elevator and the doors slid shut, leaving them alone, before he moved for his secondary gun. He pulled it from its ankle sheath and offered it to Katie. "If you're going with me, you aren't going unarmed."

"Not a problem." She lifted the back of her shirt, giving him a quick glance at her Sig Sauer P938.

He choked out a laugh. Why wasn't he surprised?

12

Kate climbed in Luke's rental car, remembering his red soft-top Jeep and all the adventures in that beat-up thing.

Luke started the engine and pulled out of the lot, the black Ford Focus not suiting him at all—both the Luke she'd once known and the man behind the wheel beside her. It almost bordered on comical. She kicked her shoes off, her fuzzy, polka-dot socks pressed up against the lower heating vent. She hated shoes, even when the temperatures dropped. They were so restrictive. "Where are we off to?"

"To do a little recon," he said, speeding down the on-ramp to 695 West.

"Let me guess . . ." She wiggled her toes as Luke merged in with the flow of traffic. "Ebeid?"

Luke glanced over at her. "Not directly."

She toyed with the notion of pressing him for more details, but what was the point? She'd see for herself when they arrived at whatever destination he had in mind.

Rays of sunlight streaked through the patchy blankets of clouds swirling across the wind-tossed sky, warming her skin through the windshield.

Traffic was on the lighter side at the late-morning hour, but when it came to Baltimore traffic, nothing was a given. Unsure of the duration of their ride, she settled back in her seat. Would she ever be settled fully in Luke's presence? She never had been, which, truth be told, had been a huge part of her initial attraction to him. He'd unsettled her in a way she couldn't explain. He unsettled her still, and something about it was still very enticing. Like anything could happen at any given moment. Luke was the embodiment of unsettling adventure, and she felt as if she could never get enough of him.

It wasn't fair. After what he'd done, he deserved to have zero hold over her, but much to her frustration, his grip on her heart held firm. Foolishly, she still loved the man—still loved the man who'd deserted her.

She wondered if he'd thought of her as she had of him over the years— daily, nearly hourly. His kiss the first night back . . . She exhaled, shifting in her seat. It'd been some kiss.

Frustration seared through her. She was a strong, independent woman, but somehow he frazzled her brain and muddled her thoughts. Somehow she'd regrouped after he'd left, focusing all her energy into finding him. Now that she had found him, or rather he'd found her, what did she do with all the energy coursing through her? With all the emotions rattling inside?

It crushed her when he left the first time, and he'd surely made no promise to stick around this time. How would she handle his leaving again?

She had weathered the crushing blow of his disappearance, but it'd nearly killed her. She had no desire to go through that again.

Her chest tightened, her breath constricting.

"You okay?" he asked, glancing over as he shifted lanes.

"Fine. Why?" The nanosecond the loaded question left her lips she knew she'd screwed up. *Fine. Always leave it at fine.*

He studied her before turning his eyes back to the road. "You look a little flushed."

"I'm fine." This time she left it there and shifted her focus out the window for the remainder of the ride but felt her eyes widen as they pulled into a tattoo parlor lot.

Kate furrowed her brow. "I don't understand."

Luke pulled the keys from the ignition. "I'm getting a tattoo."

She frowned. "What does this have to do with the case?"

"My local handler informed me that the guy who runs this place, Hank, also rents out his vehicles to Ebeid's and Stallings' men."

"Oh." Declan had recently discovered that Max Stallings and Ebeid used the same cargo ship to smuggle in their contraband—Ebeid for weapons, parts, and most frighteningly, terrorists. Max smuggled weapons, but even more horrifyingly, modern-day slaves.

There was no point in Luke's going directly to

Max or his man Lennie—neither of them would talk. Declan had tried and couldn't get anything out of them. A tattoo artist was often like a barber. They talked while they worked. And if Luke played the role right and asked the right questions . . .

Luke stepped from the car and walked around it, opening the passenger door for her. "By the way, I'm Garrett Beck, and you're my girlfriend, Jasmine. If you get the opportunity, casually ask if you can get a consult with Tanya. She's the owner's wife. You might be able to get something out of her."

He took hold of her hand as they strode across the paved parking lot to the set of glass double doors painted in fantastic, colorful mandala patterns. His skin felt so good pressed to hers. She struggled to breathe.

"Just say you aren't sure what you want, but you've heard she's great at custom designs."

She nodded. "Got it," she said, trying to ignore his touch. She already had a tattoo in mind, had for a while. She'd just never taken the step to get it.

"Oh, and one more thing," he said before opening the door.

"What's that?"

"Remember we're in love." He pressed a kiss to her lips.

Heat rushed through her limbs. *What* had she gotten herself into?

13

"Detective Crest?" Griffin asked the man before him.

The tall, slender man about Griffin's age looked up from his desk. "Yes?"

Griffin extended his hand. "Detective McCray," he said. "We spoke on the phone."

"Right." Crest stood and shook his hand. "Your timing couldn't be better."

Griffin arched a brow in confusion. "How do you mean?"

"I just got a call. Two women out walking along the river discovered human remains."

"Do you think it's our killer?"

"Let's go see."

Griffin and Finley rode with Detective Crest to the crime scene. The poor woman, what was left of her, was a ghastly reminder of seeing his sister's remains washed up on shore. Oh, the police had tried to keep them all away, but he'd reached the site before her body could be covered and the ME could finish his on-site examination, the beach being too narrow to effectively block anyone's view.

He swallowed the bile burning up his throat as Finley clutched his hand.

"Crest." The ME looked up from his kneeling

position near the body, or rather the remains, and acknowledged his presence.

"You beat us here?"

"Was teeing off on the golf course around the corner when the call came in."

"Thanks for coming so quickly." Crest looked around at the gathering crowd. "The faster we can speed this along and get her covered up, the better."

The ME nodded. "I understand."

"This is Detective McCray and Dr. Scott-McCray, a forensic anthropologist out of Baltimore."

"Dr. Scott"—the ME nodded—"your reputation precedes you."

"Scott-McCray now," Finley said and then turned to smile widely at Griffin. He clutched her hand. She had been called in to work a case in Houston some time ago, which resulted in a twenty-year-old cold case being solved. No wonder her reputation preceded her.

His wife was as talented and gifted as they came.

Crest slipped on his gloves and bent over the remains. "Please don't tell me we're looking at a second victim of our killer."

Second victim? So Burke hadn't mentioned his belief in one common killer to Detective Crest either. He must have wanted to see the cases as they were and as the detective in charge saw them. Presumably, Burke would have eventually shared his theory about a serial killer, but he'd been murdered before he could do so.

"There isn't much left to work with," the ME said with a shake of his head. Some animal had definitely gone to work on the remains. He pointed at the gunshot wound to the skull. "It looks consistent with a large caliber round, but I'll need to get her back to the autopsy room to do a thorough examination before I'm comfortable confirming anything." He shifted his gaze to Finley. "Dr. Scott-McCray, given the state of decomposition and your expertise, I'd be honored if you'd assist with the examination."

Crest looked to Finley. "Are you up for it?"

Finley nodded. When it came to helping identify a lost loved one, she was always in.

"Which one you want, hon?" a tall, slender brunette with tat sleeves asked Kate as she flipped through the sample display.

"Actually, I was wondering if Tanya was in. I've heard she does incredible custom work."

"That'd be me." The brunette cracked her gum and smiled. "And you heard right."

"Oh, cool. Nice to meet you. I'm Jasmine, by the way. My guy is getting a tattoo with Hank, and I was hoping for a consult."

"No problem," Tanya said. "Come on back. I always like original ideas. You can only see so many hearts and roses, if you get my drift. It's fun doing something unique."

Tanya led her around the corner and down the back hall, past cubicles with neck-high dividing walls. Luke was in the third stall. He'd been taken back by Hank a half hour earlier and was lying on his stomach as Hank worked on his back, which was a mixture of scars and tattoos. She nearly tripped in shock at the scrolled tattoo of her nickname on his right shoulder blade. How had she missed that when he was doing his chin-ups last night? Maybe because she'd been too focused on his muscles to notice anything else.

"Hey, honey," Luke said, lifting his head. "Having that consult?"

"Yep." Though if Tanya had time, she wasn't just getting the consult. She was going for it. She knew what she wanted, had known for a while, and there was no time like the present. Though she still couldn't wrap her mind around the fact that Luke had *Gracie* tattooed on his back.

Grace was the nickname given to her by her dad when she was young for her lack thereof. She'd been the tomboy climbing and, in accordance with her nickname, falling out of trees, rather than doing perfect pirouettes in the ballet studio like her sister, Beth.

Luke had taken the name and altered it to Gracie to fit her better. The new nickname was based off Sandra Bullock's tough yet endearing

FBI agent character in *Miss Congeniality*, a movie she loved.

And he had it on his back. Permanently.

"I know your man is hot," Tanya said, "but you gonna stand there and stare all day, or are we going to do this?"

Heat flared in Kate's cheeks, and she quickly hurried down the hall after Tanya, mortified.

"Seriously, Tanya, hot?" Hank hollered at her before she entered the cubicle in front of her.

"You know I'm just messing with you, baby," she said as she blew him a kiss. "You know you're the hottest." She winked and he smiled.

The two rough-around-the-edges tattoo artists had a surprisingly playful side that didn't fit at all with what Kate had anticipated. But like Grammie always said, never judge a dish by the way it looks. Some of the yummiest food looked the messiest. And that was certainly true of her gram's mud pies. They always came out lopsided and indented in the center, but there was nothing better on earth. Man, she missed Gram. Sweetest little Irish fighter of a lady she'd ever known. She'd inherited so much from her.

"So," Tanya said, indicating for Kate to take a seat as she grabbed a sketchpad and cup of colored pencils from her desk. "What'd you have in mind?"

"Something that symbolizes my love for the sea. One thing I definitely want included is a starfish, but other than that, I'd love to see what you come up with."

This tattoo would be a reminder that God was with her through deep waters. He had been these last seven years, and she was so grateful. He was with her now as her heart was both elated at Luke's return and torn apart. The starfish would symbolize her unending love for Luke, reminding her of the starfish ring he'd given her back in college. One she still wore to this day. Thank goodness she'd been wearing it when the boat exploded or it, too, would have been lost along with everything else.

"Cool," Tanya said. "What size are you thinking, and where do you want it?"

Kate indicated her left shoulder blade. "This general area, and I'd say about a handspan."

"Okay." Tanya smacked her gum again, the smell of grape Bubblicious filling the air. "Cool." She started sketching while Kate surveyed the ten-by-ten-foot space. Pictures of Tanya and Hank hung on the wall, sat in frames on her desk, and were clipped or pinned to various surfaces throughout the office. Tanya clearly loved her husband.

Kate wondered if she knew the type of men her husband associated with on the side. Instead of jumping right into questioning her, she'd play it cool and wait for the right timing. If she came on too strong, Tanya would retreat.

Fifteen minutes of small talk later, Tanya turned the sketchpad around. "How about this?"

It was a beautiful conch shell with a starfish nestled inside.

"It's perfect."

"Glad you like it. My eleven o'clock canceled. Wanna go for it?" she asked.

"Absolutely." Not only was it perfect, but the time spent with Tanya would provide the opportunity to toss some questions her way.

To Kate's horror, Tanya led her to the cubicle next to Luke's. The last thing she wanted was for him to see her getting a tattoo of a starfish. He'd know the depth of meaning it held straightaway.

"You nervous?" Tanya asked, picking up on her vibe.

Kate swallowed as her gaze connected with Luke's. "Nope." *Terrified.*

Luke cocked his head up a notch. "Whatcha doing, babe?"

"She's getting a gorgeous tat," Tanya said, moving to show him the sketch.

"Oh, wait," Kate said. "I want it to be a surprise."

Tanya turned back around. "I got ya." She winked. "Go ahead and lie down. Slide your shirt off your shoulder. It's loose enough—you shouldn't have to take it off."

Thankfully she'd worn a loose, scoop-neck top with a bandeau underneath.

With a tight swallow, she made herself as comfortable as possible on the sheet-draped tattoo table.

She could practically feel Luke's curiosity radiating through the neck-high wall separating them. She was *abundantly* thankful for that wall.

"First tattoo?" Tanya asked.

"Yep."

"You'll do just fine. You're strong. I can tell." She was, except when it came to Luke, and it irritated her that he still possessed that weakening effect over her emotions.

Tanya laid the cool stencil on her back and got started. Kate tensed slightly as the needle pricked in and out of her flesh. Tattoos did, in fact, hurt. But it was nothing she couldn't weather.

She made small talk with Tanya while Luke did the same with Hank. A half hour later, Luke was done and offered to buy Hank a drink at the pub next door while Tanya finished. Hank readily took Luke up on the offer, and the two left. Now she could really start asking questions. Without Hank there to overhear, perhaps Tanya would grow even chattier.

Hedging her bets, she went with her gut instinct. "Did you see that gorgeous white Escalade in the parking lot?"

Tanya beamed.

Bingo.

"It's mine," Tanya said, lifting the needle,

wiping it, and dipping it in the yellow ink before returning to Kate's shoulder blade.

"You're kidding. Man, I'd love a vehicle like that."

"Hank bought it for me last week for our tenth anniversary."

"Wow! I wish Garrett could afford gifts like that. I had no idea owning a tattoo studio paid so well. Maybe my guy should switch professions." Using the term of affection she'd used so often for Luke stung more than the bobbing needle. He was no longer *her guy,* despite the scenario they were playing today.

"It pays the bills," Tanya said with a disinterested shrug.

The needle continued pricking her skin like a bee stinging the same area relentlessly, making the area raw and tender.

"Sometimes you need to find other ways to supplement your income," Tanya finally said.

"Like selling Mary Kay?" she asked, trying to play the fool.

Tanya laughed. "Not exactly."

Kate frowned.

Tanya looked over her shoulder, then lowered her voice. "Let's just say you find a need—one that people are willing to pay high dollar for in exchange for their autonomy."

"Like what? Jewelry? I have a friend who works for Ross-Keller as a jewelry rep. She throws parties in her home. Last year she even won a car. . . ."

Tanya chuckled. "Hon, there's a lot easier ways to make money. You just gotta be willing to take the risks and, no offense, but your boyfriend doesn't exactly look like the high-risk type."

Kate swallowed her laughter. If Tanya only knew.

He had been young. It was so long ago, before he was exposed to the cruel truth. And she had been beautiful—long, blond hair, vibrant green eyes the shade of the Aegean Sea—and so kind and attentive. He was a college student on exchange and boarding in her home. She was a professor at the Sorbonne, and seven years older than him, yet she treated him like a man. Something his father had never managed to do.

They'd talked—oh, how they'd talked—long discussions about his love for history, archaeology, and the great antiquities of the world, how he longed to dig some forgotten artifacts out of the ground with his own hands one day.

And that's when it began. *That moment.* It was so clear in his mind, his hand even tingled the way it did that day so many years ago, when she took it in hers and led him to her bedroom.

On that day, she became his lover. For nearly six months, it had been idyllic.

119

His parents never would have approved, but they'd never approved of anything about him. He hadn't joined their crazy, extremist faith. He was open to all cultures of the world.

He'd studied ancient art rather than the Quran. He would never be an extremist like his father . . . or so he'd thought.

A knock rapped on Khaled Ebeid's door, pulling him from days long past.

"Sir." Brandt, his new right-hand man, stuck his head in.

"Yes? What is it?"

"She's here."

"Perfect. Show her in." Now to offer a contract fee high enough to entice her to take the job.

She entered the room with a cold, calculated expression on her beautiful face. "Let's make this quick. I have somewhere I need to be."

"With pleasure." He liked a woman who got straight to the point. "We just need to agree on a price."

She wrote down a number on a pad of paper she pulled from her purse.

Khaled read it and then slipped it into his jacket pocket. "Looks like we have a deal."

She smiled. "I'm going to enjoy this one."

14

"How did it go?" Griffin stood as his wife exited the autopsy room.

"There are dentals there, so an identification will be made. It'll just take time."

"I was speaking with Crest while you were in there. He went back through the missing person's database and two young women who share similarities with other victims popped up. I'm betting she's one of the two."

"Two missing persons?" Finley asked.

He nodded.

"So we may be dealing with more victims than we realized?"

"Yeah, I suppose we should have assumed not all the victims would wash up on shore. What is the likelihood the remains you just examined belong to a victim of our killer?"

"Based on the evidence, I'd say it's very likely she was a victim of our killer. The 'Shore Killer,' according to the ME."

"The Shore Killer?" Griffin shook his head. "I suppose it fits." He grimaced. "It looks like we are indeed dealing with a serial killer, and one who's still very active."

"Agreed."

"How long was she in the water?"

"We're estimating a couple weeks."

"She had a lot of damage to her remains for so short a time."

"Something large fed on her," Finley said.

"But you were able to determine she fit our victim profile?"

"She was in the same age range—late teens, had the same build. She was killed by a large caliber round at close range and had endured torture—broken fingers and deep knife wounds that abraded her ribs."

Finley shook her head. "The increase in his killing is flat-out frightening. One in Maryland, two in North Carolina, five—and now what appears to be a sixth—in Houston, and maybe a seventh, if the other missing girl was his victim. My experience with serial killers tells me there comes a time when they lose control over their compulsion."

Griffin exhaled. "I'm afraid you're right, but as his compulsion increases, it also means the likelihood of him making a mistake increases. He needs to kill more often, and that's when killers get sloppy."

Griffin stopped and considered a possibility, something they had not factored in. "The killer had control over many aspects of the crime— the type of women he hunted, how he abducted them, how he tortured and killed them, and even where he dumped the bodies—but he didn't have complete control over what happened to those bodies after he dumped them in the water. It is likely some stayed put and might never be found.

"We need to run a new search in the three states for all missing women who fit the other factors of the profile. Not looking for women who washed up on shore but for those who fit the other parameters. We may have way more victims than we realized."

"Well, if the profile—"

"Profile . . . Shoot!"

Finley frowned. "What's wrong?"

"I had Agent Evans at Declan's office write up a profile on our killer as a favor. I was so engrossed in reading Burke's files on the plane, I totally forgot he'd given me the report. What if there is something in Evans's profile that could have been helpful in our previous meetings?"

"We can always call or revisit Agent Thornton or the detectives."

"Very true." He wondered what was in that report. He prayed it would include something to draw them even closer to the killer.

"Let me see your tattoo," Luke said as he and Kate stepped into the brisk and windy October day.

"It's covered with Saran Wrap," she said, thrilled with the work but not at all wanting to share it with Luke. Not when it held so much meaning involving him.

He chuckled. "Saran Wrap is clear. I can see the tattoo through it."

"True, but you can see it later." She climbed into the car.

He stood over her door, his arm draped along the roof of the car, and arched a playful brow. "Why the secrecy?"

"What can I say?" She shrugged, regretting the movement with the site still tender and tight. "I'm a private person."

"Uh-huh," he said, striding around the car and climbing in the driver's side.

She'd become a far more private person after he left. His leaving taught her a vital lesson—guard your heart well, even from those you love most. *Especially* from those you love most, because they hold the power to wound you the deepest.

A few minutes into the drive, he glanced over again, this time tapping the wheel with his thumb. "So you're really not going to let me see your tattoo?"

He was pushing her, and she didn't like it. "Why is it such a big deal?"

He narrowed his eyes. "You tell me."

She bit the inside of her cheek. Because if he saw, he'd know. "I want it to heal up." It sounded like a good excuse, but it was also true. Not the healing of the tattoo, but the healing of her heart. When it healed, then he could see her tattoo.

"Where to next?" she asked, attempting to switch topics.

"I need to meet up with my local handler. But I'll drop you at Declan's office first."

"That's not necessary. I'll come with you. I can always sit in the car."

He was poised to argue and then realized arguing with Katie was useless. Her determination was impressive. The lady was full of fire, and while the flame in her eyes was dimmer than it had been in the past, it still flickered. How he longed to see it spark fully back to life.

Father, it breaks my heart to see the woman I love suffering, especially knowing it was, in large part, my doing. I just want to see her happy again. Please help her sadness abate, and equip me to let her see how desperately sorry I truly am and that my leaving was no reflection on her. It was my own stupid, young idealism and selfish need for what I thought would be a short, albeit grand, adventure. Help me to make this right, if that's even still possible. Amen.

He swallowed, wondering how God felt about him. Did He even care about Luke's prayers after the life he'd been living? Compromising, blurring the line between right and wrong? Even if it was in service to the country he loved? He'd taken lives. He'd played more roles and told more lies than he could count.

Could God really forgive a sinner like him? It

seemed impossible, and yet he felt God clinging to the fraying thread of his faith, refusing to let go or give up on him. God was abundantly more gracious and merciful than Luke deserved.

He glanced over at Katie, dying to know what tattoo she'd gotten, and it vexed him that she wouldn't let him see it.

He'd caught a very quick glimpse as he'd followed Hank out of his cubicle. It looked like a seashell, perhaps, but the way Tanya had been hunched over Katie, working on the tattoo, it wasn't readily visible.

At least his time with Hank had been profitable. The intel on Hank's transportation services was correct, and Hank had extended an invite for Luke—or rather Luke's alias, Garrett Beck—and his lady to join him that evening at a local establishment called Jiffers. Hank had said he wanted Luke to meet the crew, and his girl could hang with Tanya. Hank hadn't talked specifics, but he'd said he might have a position for a guy like him and that they'd discuss it more at Jiffers. Luke was thankful for the opening.

He wondered what, if anything, Katie had gleaned from her time with Tanya. Hank's wife was a talker and liked to boast about her and Hank's possessions, so Kate had probably learned something. But if she had learned something significant, she probably would have filled him in the moment they got in the car. Since they were approaching the mall, he decided to wait until after his meeting with Mack to ask her about it.

Weaving his way up the parking garage ramps at Towson Town Center was an adventure, with traffic flowing the opposite direction along the winding and narrow path. Finally locating a spot, he pulled in and took a moment to survey the garage.

"You better come in," he said to Kate, slipping on his Orioles baseball hat.

She frowned. "But I thought . . . ?"

"It's not safe for you to stay out here alone. Pick a shop to browse in while I meet my contact. It's safer than having you alone out in the car. I won't be long, and if you need me press nine on this phone." He handed her a burner cell.

She took it from him, curiosity dancing across her delicate brow.

"Meetings like this last two minutes, max." The shorter, the safer for all involved.

"Okay." She nodded, slipping the phone in her pocket.

He followed her into the mall, where she chose a store called Anthropologie to hang in. A glance about showed him it was the kind of shop where she could get into some serious trouble, a place her mother would no doubt frown upon but that suited Kate perfectly. Kate was free-spirited and eclectic, while her mom was prim and proper, vastly different from Kate in just about every way possible other than her looks. Kate had her mom's blond hair and blue eyes.

The thought of parents—his own in particular—made him waver. He'd lost so many years with them, caused so much damage in so many lives. The only thing that brought an inkling of solace was the certainty that he'd been serving his country, thereby protecting those he loved from men like Ebeid.

After leaving Kate in Anthropologie, he made his way to the food court down one level and off to his left.

Mack sat in the second-to-last booth.

Luke ambled over, scanning his surroundings. Finding them clear, he slid into the last booth, his back to Mack's.

He remained silent, waiting for Mack to begin, as he always did.

"How'd it go with Hank?" Mack inquired.

"It took a couple drinks at the pub next door to his tattoo parlor to wriggle my way in, but I mentioned I was looking for a job, being new in the area.

"He asked what I did. I told him I had my CDL, and he said he might know of something. Asked me to meet him tonight at a place called Jiffers. I'm sure he's running my legend now. Checking me out before he invites me any further in."

"No worries. Garrett Beck's legend is perfectly in place."

He knew it would be. Mack always had his back.

In more ways than one. "We've got one hiccup."

"Oh?"

"He expects Katie—aka my girlfriend, Jasmine—to be there."

"So bring her along."

"I don't want her in the middle of all this."

"Too late for that."

He swallowed, knowing Mack was right, and it was his fault.

"Check in again after tonight's meeting," Mack said.

"Okay." Luke stood to go.

"One more thing . . ."

Nervousness tracked through Luke, immediate concern for Katie filling him. "Yeah?"

"Malcolm's incensed."

"I don't care." Especially now that he was home and surrounded by those he'd walked away from. It had been *his* choice, and he had to take full responsibility for that, but looking back, it was obvious Malcolm had been grooming him, manipulating him throughout his college years. The mentor Luke and his friends had admired so much had been molding Luke into the agent he wanted him to be since his first day in Malcolm's criminal justice class. Luke had looked up to Malcolm, respected every word that came out of his mouth. So when the invitation came . . .

"I'll be in touch." Without a glance in Mack's direction, he walked away as quickly as he'd come.

15

"Would you mind grabbing my bag off the back seat?" Griffin asked as they pulled out of the lot. "The profile's in it."

"Sure," Finley said, leaning back. But it was just out of reach, so she unbuckled. Making him nervous as all get-out, she rustled around and grabbed the bag. Thankfully she quickly returned to her seat, clicked the buckle back in place, and set his bag on her lap.

"It's in the zippered, middle compartment."

She nodded, and metal teeth rasped as she slid the zipper open and pulled out the document. "Got it." She set his bag on the floor to the left of her feet.

"Don't set it on your left, love. You'll block the heating vent, and I want your feet staying warm."

Finley had an autoimmune disorder known as Raynaud's, which affected her circulatory system and restricted blood flow to her extremities. When she got cold, which happened to her far easier than to the average person, her feet and hands turned purple. He knew it was painful, and the last thing he wanted was his wife in pain.

"It's in the upper fifties. I'm okay, but I appreciate your concern."

"It doesn't take much to give you a chill." He smiled softly at her. "Humor me?"

"Okay." She moved the bag over to her right. "But only because you're looking out for me and because you humor me as well."

At the red light, he leaned over and brushed his lips across her soft cheek before planting a kiss on it. "I love you."

"I love you too. Now focus on the road, Mr. McCray."

"Yes, Dr. Scott-McCray."

"It really is a mouthful, isn't it?"

"A beautiful mouthful, if you ask me."

"You're still not focusing on the road." She smirked.

"It's hard to focus on anything besides you when you're present, love."

Her gorgeous smile, which lit up a room, widened. He couldn't wait to get back to the hotel and curl up with his wife—she was the greatest blessing in his life.

"Okay, flirty, let's get back to it." She indicated the document.

"Right." He exhaled, knowing he needed to hear it, but tensing at the thought of what he might learn about his sister's killer.

"Would you like me to read the full report or summarize it?"

"I'm anxious to hear what Agent Evans came up with, so I'd like to hear the full report. But feel free to summarize or interpret as you see fit."

Finley cleared her throat, her eyes tracking across the page.

"Adult male. Caucasian. Comes from money. Feels entitled. Single or divorced. No children. Early thirties to early forties. Athletic, as he's able to move women's bodies to the dumping sites."

Finley winced. "Sorry for the cold term."

"It's okay, babe. You're just reading what he wrote." Besides, he already knew the cruel truth that his sister had been "disposed of."

"He's got above-average intelligence. Works in a job that suits his needed façade of a certain lifestyle and most likely provides him with either access to victims or the ability to hide behind it. However, his profession hardly stimulates him intellectually.

"He has limited family and limited contact with them. Most likely an only child. Very possibly had an overbearing mother or woman figure in his life.

"He methodically plans his abductions and murders. He stalks and studies his victims ahead of time. They aren't chosen at random, nor are they abducted at random. The killing fulfills a hunger inside him.

"It is possible having the bodies wash up on shore is his attempt at sending a statement. Perhaps that the victim was . . ." She hesitated, biting her bottom lip.

"It's okay, babe. Go on."

"That the victim was garbage or waste to be dumped. Or perhaps the water holds a far deeper significance."

Griffin sharply inhaled his anger, then slowly exhaled. Listening to the report was painful, but he knew what he was getting into when he vowed to find Jenna's killer. He'd suffer through the pain, anger, and helpless feelings if it meant finally putting her killer behind bars.

"The profiler believes that the killer avoids detection by moving about the areas he's in, and moving often, but now he clearly feels untouchable in the Houston area, as he's been killing there for five years. The question is why? What is making him feel so comfortable despite the rising body count?"

Griffin was thankful for the information. He needed to understand Jenna's killer to catch him, but in no way did he want to live in the sicko's twisted mind. He'd heard enough. "I definitely believe we've missed other victims who haven't surfaced. I hate to think how many there could be."

"Should I call Kate? She's the best at tracking missing people."

Luke included, Griffin thought. "She is the best, but I'm sure she's got her hands full with the terrorist case. I'll give Jason a call." His partner would be happy to run the search, and he'd planned to call him anyway. A partner should know everything, even if Griffin had taken personal leave to work this case and it wasn't officially theirs.

"Oh, wait," Finley said, her eyes darting to the bottom edge of the page. "The profiler noted some comments at the end. He suggested the killer's movements could be related to areas he is comfortable with or areas he received a job promotion to."

"Excellent point. Once we narrow down his possible professions, we could search for people transferred between our three states—Maryland, North Carolina, and Texas."

"Agent Evans also listed some ways Burke's key words could point to what's fueling his need to kill."

"Such as?"

"The binding of the wrists, most often with handcuffs, shows he wants to feel in control of his victims but deep down he doesn't, and that fuels his anger toward his victims, his need to torture them. He's punishing them, which suggests there was a significant woman in his life that he felt very inferior to or dominated by."

Luke stepped into the store he'd left Kate in and stopped short at the sight of her conversing with Lauren Graham.

What was *she* doing with Kate? Had Malcolm

sent Lauren to try and insert herself into Luke's life, or was this one of Lauren's sick games—the only kind she liked to play?

"Luke," Kate said, looking past Lauren at him, "this is . . ."

Lauren smiled, cold and calculating.

"I'm sorry," Kate said, turning to Lauren. "I didn't catch your name."

"Margaret Anderson." Her smile widened.

One of Lauren's most often-used legends—the one she'd gone by when in charge of him, when she'd tried to seduce him. He'd nearly fallen for it, but it hadn't taken long for him to realize what kind of twisted woman she was.

"And Luke and I are well acquainted," she said, rubbing his shoulder.

Kate's eyes widened, and he quickly removed Lauren's hand from his body.

"We used to work together," he said as Kate's gaze quickly flashed between the two, trying to ascertain just how well they knew each other.

"Oh, come now," Lauren said with a laugh. "We did much more than that."

"Hardly," he said, reaching for Kate's arm. "Now, if you'll excuse us."

"Leaving so soon?" she said. "Are you sure you don't want to catch up over a cup of coffee? No cream. Two sugars. Right?"

Kate looked over at him. She was falling for Lauren's bit.

He kept his hand on Kate's arm and headed for the door.

"Don't worry. I'll be around anytime you're ready to catch up," Lauren called after him, her voice raking along his nerves.

Kate swallowed. "So . . . you two . . . ?"

"Worked together, and that's it."

Kate's cheeks flushed. "Certainly didn't get the impression work was all you two did."

"You can't believe a word that comes out of Lauren's mouth," he whispered through gritted teeth, his blood on fire.

"Lauren?" Kate said as they entered Macy's en route to the parking garage. "She said her name was Margaret."

"My point exactly."

"Wait." Kate pulled to a stop.

He looked over his shoulder, surprised Lauren wasn't following them, but teasing was more her game. "I'll explain in the car, I promise, but for now we need to—" He dropped her arm and ducked behind the bedding displays, his heart pounding. Luke's older brother, Gabe, was standing ten feet down the aisle.

"Kate!" Gabe called.

Kate stared at him, her heart racing, and then she scanned the area around her. How had Luke disappeared so fast?

"Miss Katie!" Trevor, Gabe's five-year-old son, ran to her.

Travis, the toddler, waddled behind his brother.

She bent, giving the boys big hugs. "Hey, kiddos, what's up?" She tickled them and the boys giggled.

"Just shopping with Dad."

She looked up at Gabe. "Where's Mara?"

"I gave her a day off from mommy duty."

"That's nice."

"She deserves it with these two always bubbling over with energy." He swooped his boys up in his arms, pressing zerberts to their cheeks. They wiggled and squirmed, and sweet laughter filled the air.

She glanced around again, getting back to her feet. Where had Luke gone?

"How are things with you?" Gabe asked, his gaze a bit too appraising. He shared Luke's gift for quickly sizing up people and their emotional state.

"Good. Busy, but good."

"We're headed for the food court and Chik-fil-A. Care to join us? It's been a while since we've caught up."

"Thanks," she said, "but I've got to be going. I'm meeting a friend." She swallowed.

"No worries. You'll have to come down for a bonfire dinner soon. It's been too long." Gabe and Mara threw the best bonfire cookouts on the Mid-Atlantic coast. She had been so thankful when Luke's family insisted on keeping in touch after Luke's disappearance. She supposed it had partially been their way of keeping the hope of his return alive, but she also believed they'd already considered her family—and she felt the same way about them.

"That would be great," she said, inching toward the exterior door. Perhaps Luke had darted out to the car.

"I'll have Mara call you," Gabe said, his furrowed brow indicating he knew she wasn't herself.

"Great. Thanks," she said, hurrying outside.

The cold, exhaust-filled air of the parking structure wafted over her, and she jumped as Luke's hand clamped on her arm.

"Where did you go, and how . . . ?"

He remained silent, striding purposefully for the car. He held her door open, shut it behind her, and jumped in. Starting the engine, he streaked out of the spot.

Kate caught a glimpse of Margaret or Lauren or whatever her name was as they rounded the bend. The woman stared at them like a cat watching its lunch fluttering around the cage in front of it.

She turned back to Luke. "What is going on?"

Luke's chest constricted, his breaths short and shallow. Why was he so hot? He cranked down his window an inch. He needed some air.

His brother.

His nephews.

Mere feet away.

And Lauren, not surprisingly, waiting for them around the bend.

"Like I said, Lauren Graham—which I believe is her real name—is dangerous. You can't trust her, can't trust anyone new who enters your life right now. People often aren't who they seem, at least not in the arena where I live and work."

He was truly terrified of what Lauren intended to do to Kate. She'd never taken his rejection well. She'd had it out for him ever since that night in Paris. Ever since he'd walked away from Lauren sprawled on her hotel room bed, beckoning him to join her. He'd been gone long enough to know he wasn't going home anytime soon. He'd left his old life behind, and Lauren was gorgeous, brilliant, and inviting, but God had given him restraint when he needed it most. And Lauren had never forgiven him for it. Apparently, he was the only one to turn her down, and she clearly didn't handle rejection well.

Kate braced her hand on the doorframe as he left tire marks in their wake, screeching down the parking garage ramp. "Is that how you've had to live the last seven years? Not trusting anyone?"

"I trust you," he said as they skirted another corner, nearly colliding with an oncoming SUV.

"Luke! *Seriously*. What's going on?" she demanded, her voice and posture tense.

He swerved onto Dulaney Valley Road,

heading for Lock Raven Reservoir. The reservoir contained plenty of winding back roads for him to lose Lauren. Roads he'd spent a great deal of time racing around during his college years.

Glancing in the rearview mirror as he ramped onto the freeway, he spotted Lauren three cars back in a black SUV.

"Lauren is dangerous. She's targeted you." He'd repeat it as often as needed to get his point across.

"Why? I don't understand. If you worked together, isn't she on the same side?"

"Lauren's on her own side. Always." It had nearly gotten him killed, less than a week after he'd turned her down. Either it was a vindictive attempt at payback or a huge coincidence that she'd made her first and only mistake in the field. And that was why she'd been reassigned. They'd crossed paths many times over the years, but they'd never been assigned to the same team since.

Kate shook her head. "I'm usually so good at reading people. She seemed decent."

Decent was the last word to describe Lauren Graham. "She's an expert at playing roles. Margaret Anderson is her friendliest role. The one she takes on most often."

"How can you work with someone like her?"

"We're in the same agency, but I most definitely don't work *with* her." The woman was flat-out unstable.

"Then *why* is she here, and why are you so upset?" Kate's eyes narrowed. "Did you two . . . ?"

"No. *Never.* Despite what Lauren attempted to make you think, we only worked together."

Kate appraised him, her expression suspicious.

He swallowed. "She came on to me one night. I turned her down. She didn't take it well."

Kate nodded. "You two must have spent a good amount of time together for her to make an advance."

"There's nothing there, Katie. Never was."

"Then why is she here?"

"Malcolm brought her in."

"Why?"

"To make sure I stay in the fold—that I don't get distracted."

"Oh." She shifted, looking at Lauren's car still several car lengths behind them. "And if you do?"

He gripped the wheel. Malcolm would never harm Katie or order anything of the sort, but he would order Lauren to play interference. And Lauren would, no doubt, love nothing better than to bring harm to him or, even more so, someone he loved.

"Lauren's a wet work asset," he said.

"Wet work asset? As in . . . assassin?"

Luke nodded.

"Okay, but she can't legally hurt me. CIA operatives have no jurisdiction on U.S. soil, and I've done nothing wrong."

141

"True, but Lauren doesn't play by the rules."

"If that's the case, why would the CIA keep her on?"

"Nothing's been proven, and she does the work they require with startling speed and accuracy."

Luke banked onto the off-ramp and then onto the back-road maze he was about to take Lauren through.

"But if she's in the Agency, like you, surely she can't—"

"She's in the Agency, but she's *nothing* like me." Or at least he prayed deep in his soul he was nothing like Lauren, or Margaret, or any of the legends she'd gone by.

He shifted gears and pressed the gas pedal, practically flying around the sharp bend. Orange and yellow leaf-blanketed trees followed the curved lines of the road.

"You *really* think she'd try to kill me?"

"Without hesitation." He hated to upset Kate, but better she knew what she was facing than get blindsided. Lauren took lives as casually as one flicked lint from a sweater—without a second thought. And now she likely had her sights set on Kate. "Lauren possesses a certain skill set."

"Seducing men?"

He choked at Kate's quick wit. "She does that with some. Not me. But I was referring to her unique methods of accomplishing her assassinations."

"Such as?"

"Let's just say Lauren takes great pleasure in putting other people through pain, even if it's only momentary."

"So what are we going to do?"

He loved the sound of *we,* though Lauren was the last person he wanted Katie involved with.

"Two more turns and she's gone."

"And then what?"

"I talk to Malcolm."

16

Luke grabbed his cell phone while still driving like a NASCAR racer, but driving fast and skillfully seemed to be second nature to him. Kate imagined defensive driving had been a part of his Agency training, but she was curious who he was taking the time to call. Perhaps Malcolm?

"Hey," he said into the phone. "I'm bringing Kate to you."

"Bringing me to who?" she said, stiffening.

"Hang on," he said to her. "Please."

She swallowed and waited, not happy she was being discussed as if she were an asset.

"Lauren showed up in the store with Kate. Where are you? Okay. See you there in twenty." He hung up.

"See who? When?" She wasn't a child to just be dropped off.

"My local handler, Mack. He'll keep you safe while I pay Malcolm a visit."

"Mack? . . . As in Declan's friend Mack?"

"Yeah, turns out they became friends over the years with Mack being Declan's contact at the Agency."

"No offense, but if Lauren, or whatever her name is, was Malcolm's doing—the Agency's doing—do you really think leaving me with your handler is the wisest option?"

"I trust Mack. He's safe."

"Aren't you the one who just told me not to trust anyone new who enters my life?"

"Because I *know* Mack. He's been my private contact and source of information since I left town."

Her eyes narrowed "What kind of information?"

He glanced over, his expression conveying a world of hesitation. "About you and the gang. And family."

"You had him spying on us?"

"No. I had him checking in on you. He let me know you were safe and gave me updates."

"What kinds of updates?"

"Like when you left the Bureau and started your private investigation firm."

"He's been keeping tabs on me?"

"On all of you."

"And you don't find that . . . what's the word I'm searching for? *Intrusive?*"

"No more so than the PI you had watching me."

"That was to see if you were alive, not find out details of your life."

He looked at her with a knowing tilt of his head.

Okay, so she had been curious about his life beyond her contact simply finding him. Perhaps he was making a decent point after all, and she liked that he'd been concerned for her and cared about her enough to keep tabs on her. She just wished he'd loved her enough not to leave in the first place.

Fifteen minutes later, they pulled down a long gravel drive and finally stopped in front of a house with a man she assumed to be Mack standing on the porch. He was about Luke's height—a little over six feet and built—muscular and toned but not bulky. He had similar brown hair, but unlike Luke's vibrant blue eyes, Mack's were a honey brown.

"Mack, this is Kate."

He smiled. "Nice to finally meet you."

"Yeah, Luke was just telling me you've been keeping tabs on me."

Mack's cheeks flushed.

"Okay," Luke said. "I'll be back in an hour." He moved for the car.

She bounced her right leg, anxiety tracking through her. "I don't need a babysitter," she called after him. Despite her unusual unease, she could take care of herself—had for over seven years.

Luke turned and strode back to her as Mack stepped to the edge of the gravel driveway, offering them a smidgen of privacy. "I know," Luke said. "But I'll feel a whole lot better knowing you're with Mack."

She shoved her hands into her weathered jean pockets. "And how do you think *I* feel?"

"Protected?" he offered with a charming smile.

She rolled her eyes. He was such a smart aleck. "More like a child who needs watching."

"I know you can handle yourself, but Lauren . . . You have no idea how dangerous she is. Please just hang with Mack for an hour."

"Seeing as I have no car, it doesn't look like I have much say in the matter."

"Mack's great. You'll like him, I promise. He's a Caps fan."

At least the man had good taste in hockey teams. With a bracing exhale, she turned to glance in Mack's direction and heard Luke pulling away before she could turn back around.

"Come inside," Mack said, indicating the cabin-style home perched on a hill overlooking a portion of the reservoir.

"No offense, but if Lauren knows Luke, she probably knows your connection to him, which means she knows or can discover where you live."

Mack smiled. "You catch on quick, but don't worry, this isn't my house."

"Then what is this place?" she asked as she followed him inside.

The cabin was cozy and welcoming, but she had a strong feeling it wasn't often used for cozy and warm purposes.

"It's a safe house I use occasionally. One of several."

"Does Malcolm know about it?"

"Not this one," he said, exuding an air of steadfast confidence.

"Why not?"

"Because this is my own."

She arched a brow, curiosity creeping through her. "You have your own safe house?"

"A couple." He set a black case on the entryway table and took off his coat, draping it over the coatrack. "I may no longer be in the field, but how you function in the field, your training and tactical skills, never leave you, or at least that's been my experience."

She wondered if that'd be true of Luke if he left the Agency.

"How come you're no longer in the field?" she asked, scanning the books on the corner case. Gram had a similar corner cabinet—though hers was white and this was pine, like the rest of the wood furniture and flooring in the room.

"Injury," he said.

"Oh." She hadn't expected that.

"No worries. I've adapted."

She was curious, but it'd be extremely inconsiderate to ask.

"My hearing was compromised in an explosion," he said, clearly sensing the question forming in her mind.

"I'm sorry." That sucked.

"It's okay. I still hear fine for most situations,

but in the field, compromised hearing can get you killed. Here, I'm able to make adaptations." He pulled a small hearing aid out of his right ear and then popped it back in place. "I used to be able to hear long range. Now, not so much, so I take other measures. I have triggers in place to alert me if anyone comes near my property. Like I said, operative training never leaves you. Once an operative, always an operative."

She got that. She could never quell the curiosity and observational skills she used as a private investigator. She spotted inaccuracies in conversations, observed illicit liaisons before they fully occurred, and had a knack for sizing people up. Though she'd apparently completely blown it with Lauren.

"So how long were you in before your injury?" Might as well ask since he'd brought it up.

"I went in nearly eight years ago. Luke and I went through training together and then were sent into the field. Our second op in, there was an explosion. Thanks to Luke, I only lost some hearing."

"What?"

"He saw it coming before I did and raced toward me, signaling me to get back. It wasn't quite enough to preserve my ears, but Luke flat-out saved my life."

"What about Luke? No injury?"

"He was still far enough back that he came through with just some gashes and flash burns."

Flash burns? She wasn't even going to ask what had caused that explosion because there was no way Mack would be able to tell her.

A thought occurred to her. She felt terrible even pondering it, but she wondered how things might have been different if it were Luke who'd gotten sent back home and Mack who'd stayed in the field. Of course she wouldn't have wanted Luke to suffer hearing loss, but she'd rather have had him home with his hearing slightly impaired than not have had him home at all.

So that's why Luke trusted Mack so much. He'd saved Mack's life.

"You know," Mack said, taking a seat on the tan microfiber sofa, "Luke loves you. He doesn't say it outright, but I see the hope in his eyes when he looks at you."

"Hope?"

"For a different life. One at your side."

Kate exhaled.

"He checks in just to know you all and his family are safe, and I update him on anything I notice."

"Such as?"

"I check in monthly or whenever I'm in the Fell's Point area with Declan. I observe things, like that your investigation firm is doing well, or when Griffin married Finley. . . ."

"Dude, you've got to admit that's kind of shifty."

150

"How is it any different from the people you're hired to observe?"

"That's different."

He lifted his chin. "How?"

"Because I'm doing my job."

"So am I. I'm doing my job for a colleague who saved my life."

When he put it that way . . .

"I know it feels like an invasion of privacy"— at her smirk, he had the decency to look a bit sheepish—"and it is. I apologize for that, but I can't say no to Luke. He is fiercely protective of the people who are important to him—of you, in particular."

"Yeah, I got that."

"It's because he loves you so much. I heard the fear in his voice when he said Lauren was with you, and I've never heard that kind of fear in his voice before."

"So she's pretty awful?"

"She makes Black Widow look like a saint."

And she was coming after her. *Lovely.*

Luke banged on Malcolm's locked office door, knowing he was inside. He'd spotted him through the window as he stood over the couch. Was he talking with someone?

He banged harder.

Malcolm opened the door, and Luke rushed in, closing the door behind him.

"Why'd you do it?" he asked, getting straight to the reason for his visit.

Malcolm frowned. "Do what?"

"Have Lauren introduce herself, or rather Margaret Anderson, to Kate."

Malcolm's eyes flickered. His "tell" said he had no idea. "What are you talking about?"

Luke exhaled, now wishing Malcolm had ordered her to make contact. It was the less dangerous option.

"I didn't order her to meet Kate."

Luke raked a hand over his head. "Whether you ordered it or not, tell her to keep her distance. Better yet, pull her out. She's not needed."

"*I'll* determine who is and who is not needed on this op."

"You only called her in to cause trouble."

No flicker. Unfortunately, Luke was right on that one because she was already causing trouble, but he feared with someone as unstable as Lauren, matters could escalate from trouble to downright danger in the blink of an eye.

Lauren stepped out of the bathroom as Luke shut the office door on his way out. "Well, seems my visit definitely got under his skin." She glanced at her red French manicure, checking for any chips or imperfections. She hated imperfections. "He must actually love her." Why, she had no idea. The woman, while beautiful, was nothing special. Yet Luke had dismissed her advances as if she were a pesky fly and was protecting this Kate person as if she were a precious princess. It was revolting.

Malcolm tilted his head. "What were you thinking? I told you to keep an eye on Luke. I said nothing about engaging Kate."

"Oh please. I was just scoping out the situation. If you want to make sure Luke stays in the fold, I'm going to have to keep the two of them apart, or at least have Kate questioning Luke's and my history."

Malcolm swallowed. "Under no circumstances is Kate to be harmed."

Not him too. What was up with the protected princess? Exhaling, she grabbed her bag. "I know how to do my job, so let me do it."

"No harm is to come to Kate Maxwell."

Or what? Did the old man really believe he held any sway over her?

17

Griffin and Finley rounded the corner and located their room—403. At the end of the hall, right next to the exit stairwell, just as Griffin had requested. Always good to be next to an exit route.

He swiped the key card over the lock and it flashed green. He opened the door for Finley and stepped in behind her.

The room was dark, the curtains drawn. Perhaps they'd received turn-down service, but typically a light was left on.

Fumbling her fingers along the wall, Finley found the light switch. Flipping it on, she gasped. "What on earth?"

There in the center of their bed, atop the fluffy white duvet, lay a pair of handcuffs and a printed-out note attached with a satin red ribbon.

Looking at each other, they stepped closer and bent to read the small font.

Go home before your wife becomes my next victim.

The crime-scene investigator's camera flashed as he processed the scene.

"Again, I am profusely sorry, Detective McCray," the hotel manager on duty, Bryson James, said. "I have no idea how anyone gained access to your room, but I do have the camera footage of the hall ready for you to watch."

"Great," Agent Thornton said.

This most definitely tied to their common case, unless it was just a horrid prank. Griff prayed that was the case, but his gut said otherwise.

But how had the killer known? Known they'd be in town? Known they'd be staying at this hotel, in this room? Did he have someone inside the Bureau or one of the police precincts they'd visited?

Agent?

Griffin swallowed. Was it possible the killer was a federal agent? Could he be Agent Thornton? Was that why Burke had kept his key words hidden, or why Agent Thornton was on the gruff side when it came to their questions, or why he'd shut down Chelsea Miller's case within such a short time of "looking back into it"?

He prayed the video footage would give them an answer.

Griffin kept his hand securely on the hollow of Finley's back as they made their way down to the security office where two armed guards sat.

"I've got your footage right here, sir," the guard informed Mr. James.

The hotel manager nodded, and the guard let the footage roll. "I started checking the footage at the time you called the front desk to report the incident, and then scrolled back from there. About a half hour before you arrived, there was a man. . . . There he is." He pointed.

The man was wearing a hooded sweatshirt pulled tight and low over a baseball cap. He never looked up. He knew where the cameras were and how to avoid them, unfortunately. He wore long sleeves, black pants, and black leather gloves, but he was tall—six feet three, at least—and slender. Not the build of anyone they'd spoken with today.

The man came straight from the stairwell door at the opposite end of the hall, striding quickly down the corridor toward Griffin and Finley's room. He swiped a key card in front of the lock, which gave them all pause. He let himself in, and after a minute and twenty seconds—Griffin timed it—he exited.

"Any other footage?" Bryson asked the guard.

"I got him coming in the east entrance, taking the east stairwell up, and exiting the same way."

Bryson winced. "The side doors aren't locked until after ten for guest conveniencc."

How about guest security? Griffin thought.

They had a height and build to go by, but none of the stairwell footage on the way up gave them a better glimpse of the intruder's face. On the way down, however, the intruder bumped into a woman coming up the stairwell. He quickly maneuvered around her and kept his head down.

Within seconds, he'd passed back out the exterior door.

"Who is that woman?" Griffin asked. "We need to question her now." She'd seen him up close. What details might she be able to provide?

18

Jiffers was part sports bar, part carnival games. It was in the enormous Arundel Mills Mall, and Luke was surprised Hank had picked this place over the casino next door. Hank greeted him with a lift of his chin, and Luke took the invite to join him at the high table as Hank ordered drinks.

Tanya grabbed Kate and pulled her over to the table catty-corner to them for some girl talk.

After introducing Luke to the two men at the table, Hank dismissed them, and didn't take long to get to the point of the visit. "You said you were interested in making some cash under the table?"

Luke nodded. "Not gonna lie, my current HVAC gig isn't bringing in the money I hoped it would."

"You mentioned you had your commercial driver's license?"

"Yeah. I used to run delivery trucks for FedEx and some off-the-books family-owned businesses."

Hank chuckled. "This would be a bit different than FedEx, but perhaps not so different from your other gigs."

"Okay." He didn't question. *Never question.* Let Hank share what he wanted, especially since this was only their second meeting.

"You'd be making deliveries for me from my warehouses to the addresses I provide. Most of the time it's simply delivering the trucks themselves with a runner to transport you back."

Luke shrugged. "Sounds easy enough." He purposely didn't ask what he'd be transporting.

Hank smiled. "I knew you were my kind of employee."

"Why's that?"

"You're eager to work, I have a feeling you're a hard worker, and best of all, you don't ask questions."

Luke signaled the waitress for another round. "On me."

Hank laughed and draped his arm across Luke's shoulder. "I knew I liked you."

"When do you want me to start?" Luke asked.

"I need drivers now."

"I'm ready."

"Unfortunately"—Hank exhaled—"I'm short on trucks. Had to lend some out."

"Yeah, what does Stallings' mysterious friend want with delivery trucks anyway?" Tanya asked as she approached, spilling the small amount left in the bottom of her gigantic margarita glass.

Hank growled—actually *growled*—at her.

She shrugged with a drunken giggle. "What?"

"You talk too much. Go do something."

She narrowed her eyes. "What?"

"You heard me. Go."

"Fine." She wobbled. "Me and Jasmine will have our own fun. We don't need you two."

Kate looked at Luke, clearly trying to hide her excitement over the gigantic lead Tanya had just blurted out. No doubt Stallings' mystery man was Ebeid.

Kate followed Tanya to the token machine.

Luke watched them fill up their cups with gold coins and head for the Skee-Ball section. Nearly every guy's head turned as Kate passed by. It wasn't unexpected, but he didn't have to like it. On the plus side, she never glanced back at any of them.

The waitress returned with their drinks, sidling up to Luke. "Poor baby. Your gal leave you? Someone as fine as you, I'd never leave. If you get lonely . . ." She slipped a folded piece of paper in his shirt pocket.

Kate was watching from the Skee-Ball lanes and rolled her eyes. So neither liked the attention the other received. Luke smiled as he took a swig of his drink.

Interesting . . .

"I'd say *dumb blonde,* but Tanya's brunette," Hank said. "Dumb either way. Broad doesn't know how to keep her mouth shut once she's had a few in her."

From what Kate had said, it didn't take anything to get Tanya talking—just opportunity. On the way over to Jiffers, Kate had told him that

160

although Tanya had been talkative at the tattoo shop, she hadn't spilled anything of significance. But now her loose lips very well might.

"Like I was saying . . ." Hank picked their conversation back up.

"You need drivers."

"Right, but I had to lend some trucks out, so I don't have any open for you now. If he keeps them much longer, I'm going to rent some U-Hauls. I'm not going to let my business suffer because he's using my trucks and warehouses."

Warehouses? Was Ebeid keeping Bedan holed up in a warehouse? Or was he simply using it for storage? Either way, it took all the restraint Luke possessed not to jump on that lead. Any questions would surely alert Hank—who Luke, at present, had in his very good graces and wanted to keep that way.

Tanya hurried back over with a stuffed Taz from Looney Tunes in her hands and squealed, "Look what I won for you, baby." She offered it to Hank as Kate stepped beside her.

"Thanks, babe."

She nibbled her bright red lips. "I'm sorry about earlier."

"It's done. Go back and play some more games while we finish talking, and then you and I will have some fun."

She kissed him, and Kate turned, following a giddy Tanya back across the crazy, psychedelic-patterned carpet to the arcade section. Kate took up residence at Ms. Pac-Man.

Luke exhaled. They were going to be there a while.

Hank pinned a very serious glare on Luke. "You didn't hear what Tanya said—especially the name. Got it?"

"What name?"

Hank nodded. "Good. The man pays well, but when he wants something, he takes it, and not just for himself. He's got some mystery man he's got to keep happy. No clue who the dude is, but he must be someone big."

"Sounds like you should branch out on your own."

"Don't think I haven't thought about it. I'm just waiting for the right timing and enough collateral to make the move." Hank appraised Luke. "You know . . . while I wait for the trucks to be returned, you could help unload shipments. If you're interested in starting now."

"Sure. That'd be great."

"It's settled, then." He reached for the waitress passing by. "Hey, hon, you got a pen on you?"

"Sure thing."

"Thank you, darling." He grabbed a cocktail napkin, scribbled an address, and handed it to Luke. "Be at this address tomorrow at eight a.m."

Luke slid the napkin into his shirt pocket. "Got it, and thanks."

"I knew I liked you. You know not to ask questions, and you thank me for the job."

"That's my motto—do the job well and don't ask questions," Luke said, before taking another sip of his drink.

"You're going to work out just fine. And speaking of fine . . ." Hank stood. "I'm going to go make up with Tanya." He winked.

Khaled Ebeid sat back with his cup of coffee. His mind, as it often did during his few moments of stillness, drifted back to her. *Caroline*. The woman who'd changed him and everything he stood for.

His hand tightened on the handle of his mug, and he exhaled through gritted teeth.

Their love had seemed so real and pure. Perfect. He'd even stayed on after the spring semester, taking a summer session just to be with her—until August 8, 1990, changed everything.

The Persian Gulf War began, and men raided his family's home, taking his father. He never saw him again. Only later did Khaled learn the CIA had taken his father to a secret location for interrogation. He'd been killed during an "escape attempt."

Prior to his capture, the family all believed his father had flown under the radar with his extremist ties. On the surface, he sold rugs. How had they known to come for him?

Unfortunately, that question had been answered quickly. The very day he got word of his father being taken, Khaled ran to Caroline, only to find her gone. Her apartment, other than his belongings, was empty. Suddenly her interest in his family, her curiosity about their life, about his father, hit him like a cold slap of Alaskan air.

She'd *used* him to gather intel. It was a certainty confirmed later, after he'd taken up the path his father had been forced to leave behind. Eventually, he discovered Caroline Ladew wasn't her real name. It was her legend. Her real name was Jennifer McLean, and she was a field operative for the CIA.

They'd known about his father. Known Khaled was heading to Paris. They'd targeted him, used his desire to attend the Sorbonne exchange program and set "Caroline" in place as his host. All their talks, all their intimate time together . . . It had all been a lie.

Khaled balled his hands into tight fists. He'd been too young and naïve to realize it at the time. But the day his father was taken changed the trajectory of his life, up to the man he was now.

He'd immediately returned to Iraq, turning to the one true faith, working with his brothers-in-arms. He'd trained hard, gained knowledge, and developed skills, all while under the cover of being an antiquities expert and cultural attaché. His cover positioned him for the revenge he'd one day wreak on the country that had used him and murdered his father. But during his years of investigation, he'd learned that Caroline's betrayal was so much worse than he'd thought. She'd—

"Sir, please forgive my interruption," Brandt, his new right-hand man, said. He'd be using Brandt for most of his needs, but for Beck and the woman, he'd hired a consummate professional— one far above a mercenary's level.

He set down his cup and cracked his knuckles. "What is it, Brandt?"

"I had Aman keep an eye on Beck, like you ordered, and you're not going to be pleased by who he met with."

Ebeid signaled Brandt to enter fully with a waggle of his fingers. "Go on."

"Beck and his lady friend were at an establishment called Jiffers with Hank and Tanya."

Heat flooded Ebeid's face. Hank had better have kept his mouth shut. He inhaled sharply and released it in a *whoosh*.

"I'm afraid Hank revealed that he lent out trucks and a warehouse. He refrained from saying to whom, but Tanya—"

"Let me guess. She imbibed too much, as usual, and spoke to her detriment?"

Brandt nodded. "According to Aman, she blabbed. Beck knows Hank rents trucks out to a couple higher-ups, and she even mentioned

Stallings' name, probably trying to impress Beck's lady."

Anger burned through Ebeid, his wrath groaning to be released. Agent Grey had figured out that he and Stallings worked together at times, so it wouldn't take long for Beck to do the same, if he wasn't already aware. On the surface, it wasn't a lot of information, but with Beck's intelligence, it could end up leading Garrett Beck to his door, especially if he worked a little longer on Hank and Tanya. Better to cut that information off at the knees.

"You know what to do."

Brandt bowed his head. "Consider it done."

19

Griffin had found the hotel guest who'd bumped into their intruder on the stairwell. Her name was Adelaide Henry. She was in her upper thirties and had been returning from the hotel gym following a workout. Unfortunately, she said her short encounter with the man had basically been him bumping into her, not bothering to apologize, and racing around her to continue down the stairwell. She hadn't seen his face—other than a quick flash of a portion of his profile, nose to chin—and he hadn't spoken a word.

Thornton brought in a sketch artist all the same. An image of any part of the intruder's face could be helpful.

The man had not parked in the lot, so they had no video footage of his vehicle, only him skirting the video camera's viewing area as he made his way to the east door.

Switching hotels, Griffin felt reasonably sure they were safe, but he hadn't been able to settle down enough to sleep yet. Instead, he was still sifting through Burke's files, but seeing as it was nearly two in the morning, he needed to try to at least get some rest. They had a full day of interviewing the remaining two detectives and the victims' families ahead.

He climbed into bed and curled around his wife, her hand pulling his arm tightly about her. He reached back, clicked off the light, and pressed a kiss to her head.

She'd asked him to leave the curtains open a smidge so she could fall asleep under the gorgeous harvest moon outside their window.

He closed his eyes, but the case still tramped through his mind. The correlation between the victims' killings and the key words *leader, agent,* and *barn* was downright bugging him. Three key words, *handcuffed, wrists,* and *Glock*—given all the murders were conducted with a large-caliber round, which could be used with a Glock—applied to all the murders so far, but what about the rest? And what was his *message?* Dumping the women in the water?

Finley snuggled deeper into his hold, snoring softly. More a humming noise than an outright snore, and he found it adorable.

He exhaled, praying for sleep to come, but the more perplexing key words continued to dance through his mind.

Agent. Leader. Barn.

Perhaps the killer took his victims to a barn somewhere outside of whatever town or city they were near to torture and kill the girls before driving to a body of water and dumping them. But how had Burke discovered that?

Leader and *agent* most likely referred to the

killer's position or job. Both titles could apply to so many different careers, it was nearly impossible to narrow it down. And that was if he was even correct in assuming the words applied to a profession. They could apply to an area in which he volunteered or to a hobby. But professions seemed the strongest possibility, so he let some run through his mind—travel agent, customs agent, ticket agent, life insurance agent. Leader of his team at work? Or leader of a volunteer group, fitness class, or even the principal player in a musical group? The word *leader* could also refer to a blank section at the beginning or end of a reel of film or recorded tape.

What if the sicko was videotaping or audio recording his time with the girls?

The thought disturbed him beyond measure.

He shifted against the concrete parking barrier he was leaning over for purchase as he studied the detective and his wife asleep in their bed in their hotel room across the alleyway. So they'd gotten his message and thought switching hotels would be enough to get beyond his reach. There was no place far enough for that. Not even death. All his girls learned that. He *owned* them. Whether they surfaced mattered not. They were his.

He watched the shafts of moonlight streak across Finley's soft cheek through the opening in the drapes and the urge to take her grew, but the detective started to stir, and he couldn't risk exposure. Not now. Not yet. Not under these circumstances. No, he needed to draw them away from other people and have his time with them. The detective he'd kill quickly, but the wife— he'd take that nice and slow.

The patrol officers struggled to keep everyone at bay while setting up a perimeter around the crime scene.

"How long until the homicide detectives arrive?" one of the officers asked.

"Said they'd be here in ten," another officer answered.

The first nodded.

Word of a body found along the shoreline had spread like wildfire that warm May morning in Chesapeake Harbor.

Griffin approached the sand's edge with dread weighing heavy in his gut. What if it was Jenna? She'd been missing three weeks.

Parker rushed forward, tears in his eyes.

Tears?

Declan and Luke were racing down the street to be at his side in case . . .

The four of them stood there, looking beyond the officers to the body washed up on shore by the morning's tide. Her hair was dark brown. She was the right build, though her skin was puffy and missing in places.

Griffin fought the urge to hurl.

An unmarked police car with sirens wailing arrived. Detectives stepped out, conferred with one of the police officers, and then approached the body. The crime-scene investigator took photographs, his camera snapping over and over until, finally, they rolled her over. . . .

Griffin swallowed the bile rising up his throat.

Jenna.

Sobs threatened to wrack his body as hot fury engulfed him.

Griffin shot up in bed, sweat clinging to his brow.

He hadn't had that nightmare in years. Now that they were so close to catching her killer, it had returned, plaguing his sleep with the horrible image of Jenna washed up on shore.

He stood and moved to the window, pulling the curtain farther open so he had an even better view of the moon.

His gaze shifted to the parking garage across the alleyway, a warning sensation darting up his spine.

Something was wrong.

His gaze raked over the structure, and the clear shadow of a man shifted on the level directly opposite him.

He grabbed his gun and opened the sliding door. Finding a corner pipe only a foot to his right, he climbed over the balcony rail and lunged for it before shimmying down. Reaching the ground, he raced for the garage, but a dark car roared out the opposite end, speeding for the end of the alleyway. Griffin ran barefoot along the uneven gravel, but the car—license plate covered—peeled around the corner, and by the time Griffin reached the street, the car had disappeared.

Griffin stood there, the cool of night wrapping around him, adrenaline coursing through his veins. The intruder had come closer still, as if taunting him, declaring they weren't out of his reach.

Finley leaned over the balcony. "Griffin! Are you all right?"

"I'm okay, but I think I'll use the front door to come back up. Shut the sliding door, lock it, and pull the drapes closed."

She nodded and did as he'd asked.

When he returned to the room, Finley insisted on helping clean up the scrapes on the soles of his feet.

"Do you think it was him?" she asked.

He nodded. "It's just now registering, but the shadow I saw was too short to be the intruder who left the message in our other hotel room earlier." He was about Thornton's height.

"Might there be two of them?"

Could there be two killers, working together? It went against everything in the profiler's assessment . . . and against Griffin's gut.

He swallowed, the dream he'd endured kicking back the flood of emotions he'd felt at the sight of poor Jenna's face upon finding her.

"Hey." Finley rested her hand on his arm. "You okay?"

"Yeah. Just thinking." He raked a hand through his hair. What *had* he been thinking right as he drifted off to sleep, before the nightmare took over? He'd been envisioning a barn, wondering why . . . "Why did Burke keep the key words hidden in code in a book?" he said.

She frowned. "What?"

"Think about it. The only people who know we are here are cops, federal agents, the ME's office, and the victims' families. And I keep wondering why Burke hid the key words."

"It's a good question." She finished cleaning out the last scrape, and with a thank-you kiss, he planted his feet on the floor, ignoring the sting.

"Do you think he suspected the killer might be someone he knew?" she asked.

"It could have been."

"Someone in the Bureau? Someone he worked with?"

"Yes. Or possibly someone he'd talked to during his investigation?" Maybe Burke had an idea who the killer was or feared the killer was paying attention to his investigation. Maybe, until he figured out who the killer was for certain,

Burke had decided to play it very close to the vest.

A chill raced up Griffin's spine at the thought. Had they already talked face-to-face with Jenna's killer—or were they about to?

20

Hank's warehouse was eerily quiet, still.

Luke swallowed. *Ungood.* "Wait here," he said as he opened his car door.

Kate pulled out her gun. "What's wrong?"

He surveyed the dozen or so vehicles in the parking lot. "I'm not sure." But something was definitely off.

A crow cawed as he climbed from the vehicle, his gun drawn. He never should have brought Kate in the first place, but once Tanya learned he was coming in to work for Hank, she'd jumped at the chance to scoot out of the office for a mani-pedi with her new buddy, Jasmine.

Kate climbed out, mirroring his movements.

He frowned at her. *Seriously?*

She ignored his silent protest to stay put and continued moving for the half-open warehouse door.

Knowing arguing was futile and would only alert whoever was inside to their presence, he tilted his head for her to come closer to him as he prepared to enter the building.

Taking a steadying breath, he fully opened the door with his foot and stepped inside the entryway. His back to the wall, his gun at the ready, he surveyed the narrow hall before him.

Lights were on and music played faintly, but otherwise, no talking, no machines running, no footsteps. Just absolute silence.

Luke indicated for Kate to follow at his six, and they moved unsurprisingly in sync down the hall, pausing at the corridor's end before entering the warehouse proper.

He took two steps forward and turned to block Kate.

Her eyes widened at the half dozen or so bodies strewn across the bloodstained concrete floor.

Yanking her to his side, he continued moving deeper into the warehouse, his eyes scanning the perimeter. More bodies littered the ground around them.

"Sweet Home Alabama" was playing in the office at the end of the hall. Luke entered to find Hank dead in his desk chair, a shot to the head and chest.

Kate stopped behind him and muffled a gasp. He longed to do nothing more than pull her into his arms and comfort her, but someone was still present. He could feel it, could smell the woman's perfume. Thankfully not Lauren's Chanel No. 5. This one smelled cheap. Whoever it was had attempted to smother her own gasp as they'd entered the office.

He held a finger to his lips and pointed to the wall across from them.

Kate's brows knit together, but she held still as he moved to investigate.

He studied a faded mark on the floor, tapped the wall, which echoed back hollow, and then flipped the light switch to the right just above the file cabinet's edge. Nearly concealed, but not quite. A hidden door popped open to reveal a quivering Tanya, balled up on the floor, her hands up to protect her face.

Luke slid his gun into the back waistband of his pants. "It's okay, Tanya. You're safe."

She cautiously lowered her hands. "Garrett?" Mascara streaked her tearstained cheeks. She looked past him at Kate. "Jasmine?"

Luke reached in, helping Tanya to her feet.

"Who did this?" Kate asked.

Tanya shook her head. "I don't know. Hank and I were in here. Next thing you know we hear gunfire, and Hank shoved me in the secret compartment and told me to be quiet. I heard his chair wheels move, him probably reaching for the .45 he kept under his desk. Within seconds, the office door kicked in, and I heard a . . . *thwack.*" Tanya glanced toward Hank and sobbed.

Luke looked at Kate. *Silencer. Professional hit.*

"Ebeid?" she mouthed so only Luke could see her.

He nodded. "My best guess."

Tanya looked back and forth between the two of them, confused. "What happened?"

"It's gonna be all right," he said, moving for his phone.

She looked at him as if he were crazy. "All right? Are you insane? Hank's dead."

Kate moved to Tanya's side. "We're going to get you out of here."

"If it was Stallings or, worse yet, his mystery man, I need to get out of here—fast." She trembled beside Kate.

Luke called Declan and explained the situation, along with his extraction wishes for Tanya.

Tanya stumbled back, her gaze wary. "Who *are* you people?"

"I'm Kate and this is—"

Luke shook his head. She could share her real identity if she chose, but he had to keep Garrett Beck in play.

"Names aren't important," Kate said, "What's important, what matters most, is getting you out of here."

Luke ended his call with Declan and waited a few minutes before alerting Mack, trying to buy Declan time to arrive before the Agency's sweeper team came in and whisked Tanya away. Her safety depended on Declan reaching them first, and having her placed in witness protection. But for Declan to provide that, Tanya had to give them something of value.

"I don't understand," Tanya said, her voice quavering.

"I'm a private investigator working with a task

force to bring down the person who we believe is your mystery man," Kate explained.

"You lied to us?" Tanya's eyes narrowed. "*This* is because of *you?* Is Hank dead because of you?" She angrily waved her finger at her husband slumped back in his chair. "They thought we told you something!"

They had talked—*a lot*—and Ebeid, no doubt, had gotten word of it. If only they could tie him directly to these hits, but Ebeid was far too careful for that.

Luke strode to Tanya. "I need you to tell me everything you know."

She retreated so quickly, she bumped into the wall and nearly tumbled to the ground. "I'm not saying a word. They'll kill me. Besides, I don't know nothing. Hank made sure I was protected in case anything went wrong."

She did know. She'd shared enough last night to get them all killed, and it had nearly worked. "They're going to kill you if you don't talk."

"What? Do you think I'm a fool?"

"To put you in witness protection, you need to give the FBI agent who's on the way here right now some information of value, or he'll be forced to let you go—and out there, you're dead."

"I'll go to my sister's place in upstate New York."

"You think the man who did this"—Luke pointed at Hank—"can't easily find you at your sister's? It's one of the first places they'll look, and then you'll be endangering her too."

Tanya nibbled her chipped, red-polished nails. "I don't know anything." Tears streamed down her face, her makeup running with them.

"Just think," Luke said, using a calming tone. "I'm sure there's something. . . . Hank said someone was using a handful of his trucks. You think he's connected to Stallings. Any idea who he is?"

"No, but he was foreign. Moved here a few years back. Started working with Stallings. I saw a couple of his guys once, and most were Middle Eastern or Asian."

"You guys also mentioned he was using a warehouse. Any idea where?"

"No. Hank didn't say."

"Who picked up the trucks?"

"I don't know. It happened late at night. Hank was told to be here—alone, with trucks ready."

"When was this?"

"Late last week."

Luke knelt in front of Tanya, trying to direct her focus. "And Hank never mentioned who picked them up?"

"No. He said he knew they were for Stallings' mystery man, but it's not like the man would actually pick up the trucks himself."

Right. He'd send his men. Luke straightened and surveyed the office. "Any video monitoring here?"

"No one is supposed to know, but due to the nature of Hank's business . . . yeah, there are a few hidden ones."

Thank you, Lord. Finally, a break.

"Where's the footage?"

Tanya moved to Hank's computer, typed in a series of passwords, and opened the main page full of dates. He squeezed her shoulder. "Thank you," he said as Declan entered.

"You guys okay?" Declan asked.

Kate nodded. "This is Tanya."

"She's bringing up footage showing who picked up Hank's trucks last week," Luke said.

Declan moved to stand behind Tanya's chair, Luke and Kate on either side of him, as agents—both FBI and CIA—flooded the warehouse. Soon the jurisdictional jabbing would begin, though the CIA had no sound footing. They were on U.S. soil, and the FBI, thanks to Declan, had arrived first.

"There," Luke said, pointing to the screen, his focus on finding out exactly who picked up the trucks. Hopefully, once they had a positive ID, they could link them back to Ebeid.

Tanya paused the footage.

"Go back two minutes," Luke asked. "There."

She paused it.

"Who is that?" Declan asked, squinting at the screen over Luke's shoulder.

"Can you zoom in on the man's face?" Luke asked.

"That's Cyrus," Declan said. "He was Ebeid's new right-hand man."

"Great. Now we just bring Cyrus in, get him to confess his tie to Ebeid, and—"

"Not going to happen," Declan said, cutting him off.

Luke frowned. "Why?"

"Cyrus's body was just pulled from the dumpster behind Kate's office."

Kate's jaw tensed. "What?"

"Trash crew called it in. Tim Barrows at the Bureau just identified the body."

"Why kill Cyrus?" Kate asked.

"Because he failed to kill us at CCI, and he was probably the bomber at the boat," Luke guessed. "Time of death?"

"Parker's on site now that Avery's recovering, and he said he'd guess over twenty-four hours."

"So if Cyrus was already dead, then who did this?" Luke asked.

21

Declan scrolled through the footage to the time Tanya said the shooting began. The men who entered the warehouse with semi-automatics were dressed head to toe in black.

"Well, that doesn't help us any," Declan said.

"What about the vehicle they arrived in?" Luke asked.

"Good thinking," Declan said.

Tanya switched cameras to the parking lot and *bingo*. "I recognize this. It's one of the trucks we lent out to the guy you called Cyrus," she said.

"I'll have traffic cameras start searching for the truck," Declan said.

"That's it." Tanya snapped.

Luke arched a brow. "What's it?"

"The *trucks*." Tanya switched to a different screen on the computer and again entered a series of passwords. "The video cameras weren't the only hidden thing Hank had going." She typed in several more number combinations. "Only Hank and I knew, but he installed GPS trackers on all his trucks."

"Seriously?" Luke said.

She nodded.

Thank you, Lord.

"Hank worked with some—well, let's just call

it like it is—monsters," she said, glancing at Hank's body being wheeled out the door by the ME. She swallowed hard, tears streaking down her cheeks. "It was his way of protecting his assets," she said, choking on a sob.

Kate handed her a tissue.

"Thanks." She sniffed.

"And the people taking the trucks didn't know?" Luke asked. It was a critical factor.

"No." Tanya shook her head as she blew her nose.

"Are you positive?" Declan asked.

She nodded. "Positive. A buddy of Hank's who is a total whiz kid when it comes to techie gear decked out all the trucks for him. Said it'd be nearly impossible to find them."

Nearly wasn't good enough, but there was hope, a chance.

Tanya found the screen she'd been searching for and grabbed a pad of paper. She started jotting down the truck numbers and their current locations. When she was done, she handed the page with trembling fingers to Luke, who handed it to Declan. It was her ticket into witness protection.

"There are four trucks here." Declan frowned. "I thought you said five went out?"

"Five did . . ." Tanya typed in some numbers, then frowned. "One isn't registering."

"Which one?" Luke asked, his gut sinking.

Tanya exhaled. "The one they drove here this morning."

"Any chance they figured out there was a tracker on board?" Luke asked. Their first break would collapse if Ebeid was aware of the trucks' GPS tracking devices.

Tanya shook her head. "Not from what Hank said."

"Could anything short them out?" Declan asked.

"Water," Luke said. "It wouldn't surprise me if they ditched the truck, submerging it somewhere in water, where it'd be unlikely to be found."

"Hopefully, we'll catch a hit on it from traffic cams," Declan said. "See if we can't deduce the direction it was headed and where it might have been dumped."

"And the other four?" Luke asked.

Declan clutched the paper Tanya had written the locations on. "All at the same address in Sparrow's Point."

"Let's pray that's where they have Bedan and the weapons holed up," Luke said, calling Mack to quickly pinpoint the location, while Declan did the same with the Bureau task force.

"Well?" Ebeid asked as Brandt entered.

Brandt cleared his throat. "I took care of all of them, but I was unable to locate Tanya."

He waited for Ebeid's response as the man

185

simply drummed his fingers on the desk before him. Ebeid was known as a man who did not accept failure, as evidenced by his predecessor's death, and he had flat-out failed his mission. He'd considered disappearing, but he wasn't a coward. He'd track down and kill that woman if it was the last thing he did, but he had to own up to Ebeid first.

Ebeid's fingers stilled and came together as he held his hand up and shooed away the man who'd been serving him tea.

"And how do you presume to excuse your failure?" he asked once the servant was gone.

"I do not excuse it, sir. I only ask for the opportunity to finish my mission."

"Finish your mission?" Ebeid arched a stark brow as he lifted his gold teacup just below his lips. "And how do you propose to do that?"

He clutched his black ski mask in his right hand, adrenaline pumping through him at a dizzying rate. "I will hunt Tanya down and finish the job."

Ebeid took a thoughtful sip of his tea, then set his cup down. "But you felt it better to come here and tell me you failed, rather than doing that first?"

He cleared his throat. "I'd thought . . ."

"Thought?"

"You'd want to know the status."

"I see. Well, I presume now that you have alerted me, you will complete your mission."

"Yes, sir." His stance reverted to the military one he'd known so well before becoming a mercenary.

"You have one chance." Ebeid lifted his teacup again. "Finish the job."

Khaled forced his hand to remain still, his fingers clasped around the cup, the unnerving sensation of unsteadiness shifting through him at the sight of the former young Marine now turned mercenary.

Perhaps it was his former service branch or his features so similar to Matthew's that had kept Khaled from killing the mercenary, but Brandt would finish the job—Ebeid read it in his predatory gaze. Before the day was out Tanya would be dead.

Matthew's young face on his Marine service portrait flashed through his mind.

Khaled's son was betrayed by America, just as his father had been. But very soon the country that took his son and his father from him would crumble. He almost wished he'd let "Caroline" live to see the day, but the whore deserved to die at his hands. It was the last time he'd gotten his own hands dirty until he'd killed Cyrus, and he'd forgotten how magnificent it felt to pull the trigger. He envied Brandt's next act, squelching the life out of Tanya as he had Caroline. Killing another person deserving of death was so liberating. He lifted Kate Maxwell's recon photograph, delight surging through him, knowing she too would soon be dead.

22

Luke studied the Sparrow's Point warehouse through his long-range binoculars as he very impatiently waited for Declan's task force to arrive. Hank's warehouse had been less than a five-minute drive away, while the team Declan requested had a healthy half-hour drive in front of them.

"We just got some news," Declan said, indicating the communications piece in his ear. "It doesn't bode well."

Luke was afraid to ask. "What?"

"The truck used for the attacks this morning was tracked by traffic cams and found parked behind a Best Buy."

"Not submerged in water?" Kate asked.

"Afraid not. The GPS tracker was stomped to pieces on the ground beside it."

Which meant the chances they hadn't bothered to check the other vehicles was zilch. He'd wager the trucks were gone and only the tracking devices remained in the warehouse. Luke swallowed hard. They'd lost their opportunity.

Declan exhaled. "Looks like the warehouse is empty. Thermal imaging indicates no warm bodies inside."

"The warehouse may be empty, but that doesn't

mean they didn't leave any surprises behind for us." Luke indicated the direction he wanted Declan and Kate to look with a lift of his chin. "Two and seven o'clock."

Declan lifted the binoculars, shifting to the warehouse across from the one they were raiding, and then handed them to Kate.

Two snipers. One on the southwest corner. The other on the northwest.

"Great," Kate sighed.

"Better warn your team," Luke said to Declan. "They will be sitting ducks if they arrive front and center." It's exactly why Luke always preferred finding a back way in and always observed first. Thankfully, he'd chosen a good spot, one the snipers couldn't see.

Declan asked the team's ETA over the comm. "Roger that." He looked at Luke. "Twenty minutes out."

"I'd instruct them to come in the same way we did. No sirens. No lights. Quiet as possible."

At least the day wasn't a total loss. They could capture the snipers, and get whatever information they possessed out of them. And there was no time like the present. He shifted, moving low and slow as to not draw any attention.

"Where are you going?" Kate whispered.

"To get the snipers."

"Are you crazy?" Declan's brows shot up. "Wait until our team is in place and you have coverage."

189

"And risk any other lives or the possibility of losing the snipers when the cavalry arrives?" Luke shook his head. "I've got this."

"It goes without saying, you're good," Kate said in a forceful but hushed tone, "but even with your training, taking on two snipers who maintain the tactical advantage is crazy."

"Aren't you the one who always told me that everyone needs a little crazy in their lives—it keeps 'em sane?" he asked.

"Yes, but . . ." she sputtered.

"No time to think." With a wink, he pressed a kiss to her lips and smiled at her bewildered expression. He'd most likely have to answer for the kiss later, but—one—he would deal with it *if* he survived and there was a later, and—two—it was better to ask forgiveness than permission.

If there was a chance he wouldn't survive—and in all probability, there was a high one—he most certainly wasn't leaving this world without one last kiss from the woman he loved.

Rapidly assessing the layout, a quick plan of attack formed in his mind. He moved up the right rear scaffolding as silently as possible and as he cleared the roof's edge and climbed on top, the first sniper's back remained fixed to him, his focus on the ground. His presence was sheltered from the second sniper by the HVAC unit, hopefully giving him enough time to move from one to the other without being seen.

Stalking as quickly and as stealthily as possible, he reached the first sniper and zapped his back with a shock stick, knocking him out cold. Then he moved toward the second target.

Moving quietly didn't work this time. The sniper rolled over as Luke approached, gun aimed at him—and fired.

Luke bobbed and managed to kick the weapon out of his hand. He lunged for the young Southeast Asian as the man pulled a knife from his leg sheath.

Luke dodged, but the knife slashed his right forearm, stinging hard. He bit back the pain as the man wrestled from his grasp and stood, holding the knife poised for a fight, his gun nearly a dozen feet to Luke's left.

Boot steps fell heavily across the rock-covered roof, and Luke glimpsed Declan moving for the unconscious sniper.

"Drop it," Kate said, racing forward, gun aimed at the second sniper's chest.

His eyes darted to his unconscious mate, and the realization that he was outnumbered flashed across his face.

"Don't do it," Luke said, rushing forward, but he was too late.

The young man darted toward the ledge and hurled himself over. A distant thud echoed up to the silent rooftop.

Death before dishonor.

"Medics' ETA?" Luke hollered, but he knew it was already too late.

"Five," Declan said, handcuffing the other sniper and holding him at gunpoint.

"At least we got one." But the likelihood of his talking after the desperate measures his fellow sniper just took was minimal.

SWAT teams, black Bureau cars, and an ambulance arrived within minutes.

Kate insisted Luke get his slashed arm attended to, so he relented and sat on the back edge of the ambulance, the bay doors open. His wound was soon to be one of many scars littering his body. He ignored the stinging as antiseptic seeped into the raw wound. He'd endured far worse.

Though, since being reunited with Katie, he was a new believer in mental anguish being equal to, if not harsher than, physical pain. Physical pain healed. If his relationship with Katie did not—and it was a long shot, at best—he doubted that the raw, pulsating inner agony would ever abate.

Declan's team infiltrated the warehouse, and as soon as Luke was cleared to proceed, they walked inside together.

"Anything?" he asked as Declan met him at the door.

"How's your arm?"

Seriously. It's just a flesh wound, people. "Fine. And the warehouse?"

192

"It's been cleared, but it's going to take a while to comb through."

Luke exhaled. "We were too late."

Declan's head dipped in affirmation.

Frustration flared inside of Luke. Ebeid had once again slipped through his grasp.

As Luke followed Declan through the warehouse, he was impressed. It had been transformed into three sections. There was storage—at least that was what the shelves and few remaining boxes attested to—living quarters, no doubt Bedan's, and most terrifying, Bedan's laboratory.

Declan insisted they await the hazmat team's clearance before entering the glass-walled storage container functioning as Bedan's lab.

Luke moved through the living quarters while he awaited the hazmat team's go-ahead, praying that, in the rush to flee, something, *anything* had been left behind to give them a fresh lead.

Ebeid had set up a comfortable environment for Bedan, probably knowing the more comfortable the scientist was, the better his work would be.

There was a galley-style kitchen, which still held a good amount of food. Closing the fridge door, he surveyed the cabinets and then continued moving through the space into the living room. There was a sofa, reclining chair, a couple accessory tables, and a TV mounted on the wall. Though, based on the impressive amount of reading material stacked on the side table, Bedan was not a TV enthusiast.

Luke scanned the book titles, careful not to touch anything until it was all properly processed, despite the gloves he had on. He knew Parker would step in for the still-recuperating Avery and photograph everything as it was found before *anything* was moved. Then the agents would spend hours, possibly days, cataloging and bagging every item.

With a sigh, Luke straightened and shook his head at the titles he'd just read. They were chasing a man with frightening knowledge and ability.

"Find something of interest?" Declan asked, entering the space.

Luke indicated the stack of books.

"Let me guess. Terrifying topics?"

Luke raked a gloved hand through his hair. "Extremely."

"So is this," Declan said, holding up a bagged sheet of paper with mathematical and scientific notations on it.

Luke's curiosity sped.

"The hazmat team found it behind one of the counters in the lab. Must have slipped behind during the rush to move out. From the state we found things in, along with the number of items they had time to move, I'd wager they discovered the GPS trackers in the truck early this morning, soon after they took Hank out."

"Which gave them several hours' head start on us."

Declan rubbed the back of his neck with a sigh. "I'm afraid so. On the plus side, they probably don't know how closely we were behind them, and they made a few significant mistakes, like leaving this"—he jiggled the paper again—"behind."

"And what is it, exactly?"

"I know it deals with chemical agents that bond with anthrax and sarin gas, but that's the extent of my mathematical and scientific expertise." He handed it to Luke.

Luke studied the page through the plastic evidence bag. "It looks like the notes around the edges are in some sort of mathematical shorthand."

"That would explain why I had no clue what it meant," Declan said.

"I think"—Luke's mind tracked back—"I've seen this before. . . ."

"You have?" Declan's brows furrowed.

"Unfortunately," Luke said, the memory fixing in place. "It's a form of shorthand used by Bedan's grandfather during his time with Operation Paperclip. There are samples in the classified records from that project."

"I'm assuming Bedan's grandfather left some of the paperwork behind, that he only stole certain files from the project?" Declan asked.

Luke nodded. "Correct."

Declan slid his hands into his trouser pockets. "Can you decode it?"

"I'm afraid not. I just know that's what it is."

"What was on the other pages you saw with this shorthand?"

"Formulas for biological weapons, if I remember correctly."

"Whatever happened to Bedan's grandfather?"

"It took them a few days to find him after the theft, but before they could bring him in for questioning, he committed suicide."

Just like their sniper on the roof.

"Since he committed suicide before he confessed, the Agency doesn't positively know Abel Bedan was responsible for stealing those documents." Declan shrugged. "So how do they know Bedan is currently working off them?"

"Because after Bedan's biological attack in Munich, he was forced to flee and leave most everything behind. When we combed through his office and lab, we found a few of the missing Operation Paperclip files."

"Just a few?"

"Afraid so. He's still got some of them."

"Any idea what's on them?"

"Not specifically, but we know the scope of the project centered around the use of anthrax as a biological weapon. In addition, some of Bedan's current work was left behind, and it was directly built upon the work done during Operation Paperclip."

"I can't believe he'd leave it behind. He had to know there was a strong chance he'd have to run following the Munich attack. He must have made preparations."

"That makes what he left behind even more terrifying."

"Why?"

"Because what we found was awful. If he felt secure leaving that level of work behind, I hate to even fathom what level of destruction he's working on now."

"Agent Grey," someone behind them said.

"Yes?"

A young agent motioned toward a window overlooking the lab. Inside, a hazmat team member held up an evidence bag with several aerosol cans in it. "Apparently, Bedan's big on his hair care."

"Those were in the lab, not the bathroom?" Luke asked.

"Yes, sir," the young man said.

"Not good," Luke said, striding over to the window.

"What is it?" Declan asked.

"Bedan's hair on a good day looks like Einstein's on his worst. No way Bedan spends time on his hair, and he definitely doesn't use product."

"So why the hairspray cans?"

The realization of what he was looking at struck like a thunderclap to his soul. "I'll need to wait until the notes are decoded and I take this apart, but I think I was wrong about Bedan's choice of dispersal method."

"Not food?"

Luke shook his head.

"Why? Because of some shorthand notes and a couple cans of hairspray?"

"These aren't cans of hairspray. I think they are prototypes."

Declan's eyes narrowed. "Of what?"

"Bedan's chosen dispersal method."

Realization dawned on Kate's face. "Aerosol dispersal? Is that even possible?"

"Not easily, but a man with Bedan's skills and heritage . . ."

"But how could he regulate it?" Declan asked. "Isn't anthrax sensitive to temperature fluctuations?"

"Yes. You'd need specific conditions, but if those were met, and the anthrax stabilized in the deployment device—essentially an oversized spray can—and with the proper prevailing winds . . ." Luke's eyes widened. "I've got to contact an old friend."

"An old friend?"

"If what my gut is saying is about to happen is truly the threat against us, he may be able to provide some insight."

"Okay." Declan nodded.

"Just so we're on the same page," Luke said, "as far as I'm concerned the threat level just went DEFCON 2."

"DEFCON 1 is *war*," Kate whispered.

"A terrorist attack on U.S. soil *is* war, and if I'm right about this, we're teetering on the brink of it."

23

Luke followed Declan into his FBI office to find Kate and Tanner waiting for them with lunch. Luke had contacted his friend David the day before yesterday, after the warehouse raid, and he'd be arriving through BWI shortly. They'd agreed to meet up at CCI, as David wanted to keep his visit as unofficial as possible. With the shattered windows replaced and the space patched up reasonably well after the sniper attack, CCI would make an excellent meet-up location off the books.

Luke had approximately half an hour before he needed to head over to CCI, wanting to be there in plenty of time to greet his guest. It was odd thinking of David as a guest, though he'd been one himself a time or two when their roles were reversed and David had required his intel.

Parker was in his lab at CCI, processing the evidence retrieved from the warehouse raid. Luke was anxious to discover what he had learned, praying they'd garner more of value from the raid. Thankfully, Avery was recuperating well, so according to Parker, she was resting at home and really antsy to get back to her job. And meanwhile, Griffin and Finley were on their way to North Carolina, still tracing the killer's steps as they made their way home.

Kate stood, assessing the bandage wrapped around Luke's arm. It'd been two days, but the wound was best protected with a bandage for another day or two. "Any luck with the sniper you brought in?" she asked.

"Still in a cell. Refuses to talk, so we'll keep him until he decides to cooperate," Declan said.

"Has he called a lawyer?" she asked.

"Nope. Hasn't even asked for one. Hasn't spoken a word, period."

"Good luck cracking that one," Kate said.

"Thanks," Declan said, before shifting his attention to Tanner. "I was hoping you'd accompany me for the next round of questioning."

She smiled. "You got it. Want to go now?"

"Sure, if you don't mind waiting to eat." He gestured to the carry-out they'd brought in.

"Nah, I'm good," she said.

The two disappeared before Luke could blink.

"Being a crisis counselor makes her a fabulous interrogator," Kate said, opening the bag of food, the smell of freshly baked bread swirling through the office.

"I imagine that skill set would be a strong asset." Though the Bureau's idea of interrogation and *his* experience with interrogation in the field were probably quite different.

With Tanner, he imagined the questions and approach were coming from a place of help and befriendment, whereas he went straight for the jugular. Then again, the men he was dealing with and the chaos of the crisis he was typically involved in during an interrogation didn't allow time to establish actions of perceived befriendment.

However, he was on U.S. soil now, working as a liaison with the Bureau, so he'd abide by their rules, and truth be told, he might prefer their rules now. Interrogation had never been his thing. He much preferred intervention over interrogation.

Kate pulled out a thick sandwich wrapped in white paper and handed it to him. "From Pitango's," she said.

"Thanks. I didn't realize Pitango's has sandwiches now." It'd always been a gelato specialty shop where he and Kate would get affogatos, chocolate gelato with espresso poured over it, for late-night study sessions. They'd get their fuel, sit on one of the benches lining the brick sidewalk in Fells Point, and study under the streetlamps. Then they'd walk along the water before making the drive back to campus. It had been a nice break from the monotony of studying.

Having grown up along the water, he wanted to be near it, on it, in it as much as possible and had returned to his Chesapeake Harbor home with Kate every weekend they could throughout college. His mom had insisted he not only sleep in a separate room from Kate, which he'd absolutely have done on his own, but she'd gone

one step further, making him sleep on an entirely separate floor—most often on the couch in his dad's den.

He had been glad to learn via Mack that when his parents retired to Florida—he'd never thought he'd see that day—his brother and wife had moved into the family home.

He wondered what it looked like now, how it'd changed over the years or, even more so, how it had remained the same. Did the floorboards still creak and the upper-right windowpane slide sideways for a bigger view of the harbor outside what had once been his bedroom?

"You still with me?" Kate asked at his prolonged silence.

He blinked out of memory lane. "Yeah. Sorry. Just thinking."

"About?"

Our life together that I was foolish enough to destroy. "Everything."

She let out a throaty laugh. "No wonder it looks like smoke's about to come shooting out of your ears."

"Ha! I haven't heard that one in a while."

Kate shrugged. "My mom's still got a thing for those old-fashioned sayings—itchy nose means someone is thinking about you, burning ears if someone's talking about you, though 'a penny for your thoughts' is still her favorite."

He set down his roast beef, gouda, and

horseradish sandwich and moved to her side—captivated by her presence and thrilled they had some time to themselves. "I remember," he said, his voice low.

Her expression shifted, the playfulness changing to a look of wariness.

He took hold of her hand, holding her palm against his cheek, her touch surging a pulsating current through him. "I remember it all. The way your silky hair falls through my fingers." He ran his free hand through her golden hair. It was the first time she'd worn it down in days, and while he liked her trademark ponytail, he loved her hair falling free across her shoulders.

He inched closer still, his voice deepening. "The scent of your shea butter lotion and the way it makes your skin so supple." He trailed his fingers along the underside of her left arm. He exhaled, trying to steady himself and his racing heart. "The way your lips feel against mine," he whispered hoarsely and, braving another slap, he cupped her face and lowered his lips to hers.

Tentative at first, she finally melted into the kiss, sliding her hands up the back of his neck and into his hair. Releasing a guttural moan of pleasure, he moved his arms around her waist and pulled her tighter against him, their kiss growing heady, powerful, reconnecting them body and soul.

"Oh!" A female squeak came from the doorway.

"I'm so sorry." One of Declan's fellow agents quickly retreated and closed the door behind her.

Kate instantly broke the kiss and stepped back, raking a hand through her tousled hair.

Her lips were full and rosy, the mark of his kiss evident upon them. He moved to pull her back into his embrace.

She held up her hand. "This is a bad idea."

He heard her words, but her eyes said something far different. "What happened to the audacious, dive-in-headfirst girl I knew?" he said teasingly.

"You crushed her heart."

His heart hammered in his throat, all playfulness vanquished. "I know." He swallowed. "Don't let my idiotic choice change you from the free spirit I knew into someone who is guarded. Even if you never forgive me—which I understand is a strong possibility—please don't lose that part of you." It was heartbreaking to see that shift in her and to know he was the cause of it.

She linked her arms across her chest. "Your leaving taught me how to protect myself."

"Protection is good, but not when it shuts you down." He knew that only too well.

She shook her head, a sarcastic huff expelling from her freshly kissed lips. "So I'm just supposed to put my heart right back out there for you to crush all over again?"

"No." He stepped toward her and tipped her

chin up, forcing her to look him in the eye. "I will *never* hurt you again."

"How can I ever trust you?"

"Only time will prove you can."

"What if I'm not willing to put my life on hold for you again? For however many years you will disappear next time?"

"As soon as this case is over and Ebeid is stopped, I'm out."

Her eyes widened. "Seriously?"

"*Seriously*. I'm leaving the Agency."

"Why?"

He linked his fingers with hers, intertwining them. "Do you really have to ask?"

"Don't do it for me."

"I want *everything* I do from now on to be for you."

She shook her head, backing away, shutting down. "You said that before."

"I know, and in my own messed-up, complicated way, I convinced myself my leaving *was* for you—to protect you—but I see now it was my selfish, immature way to have an adventure."

"There's that word again."

He frowned. "What word?"

She glared at him. "Adventure."

Why on earth did the word *adventure* bother her so much?

Suddenly, the office door swung open. "We've got a problem," Declan said.

"What is it?" Kate asked.

Declan rested his weight against the doorframe. "Guards went to move our detainee from his holding cell to the interrogation room and discovered he'd hung himself in his cell."

Luke's jaw tensed. "How?"

"Best we can tell, he waited until the guard standing watch got called away for a moment. He apparently had a length of paracord sewn into his waistband. Pulled it out and hung himself."

"Ebeid has them trained disturbingly well," Luke said. "They are so terrified he'll kill them if they talk—or do far worse *before* he kills them— that they'd rather take their own lives than face him."

"Or they truly believe they are serving a greater purpose and cause by taking their own lives rather than risking compromising the mission," Tanner said, entering behind Declan.

Kate shook her head. "I can't get over how ruthless Ebeid is. It's like he's got mind control over these men."

24

Griffin studied his beautiful wife, deep in slumber. She'd fallen asleep before they'd even reached cruising altitude. Though he wasn't surprised after the night they'd had, followed by another intensive and draining day.

Once drink service began, he took the cup of coffee from the flight attendant and settled in to work during their flight to Wilmington, North Carolina.

They'd spent the remainder of their time in Houston speaking with the final two detectives, who were both friendly, though not overly helpful in offering new leads. The most Griffin and Finley had gained from them was confirmation that the victims in both of their cases had endured at least three out of the seven words from Burke's list. The words neither case was tied to in a clear way were *leader, agent,* and *barn.*

Thankfully, they hadn't had another encounter with either of their intruders, but unease still raked through Griffin. Shifting, he scanned the passengers around them, wondering if the killer was aboard the flight, if he was following their steps.

He had a nagging feeling that wouldn't release its hold, suffocating the peace out of him. The killer was near. He could feel it. Perhaps not on their flight, but definitely on their trail.

He continued surveying the passengers, his gaze not locking on anyone in particular, so he settled back in his seat—though he wouldn't be truly settled until this case was over and the killer behind bars.

They'd also spoken with the victims' families before leaving, which had torn him apart, bringing back memories of the detectives who'd come to his home after Jenna's disappearance, and again after her body was discovered. He didn't know that they'd learned anything pertinent to finding the young women's killer from the families, but they now had a much better feel for the victims, and that was always helpful in an investigation.

According to their families, all the victims had been beautiful, vibrant, loving women. All in relationships—most with young men the parents didn't know about until after their disappearance. In addition, four out of the five Houston victims had recently moved from an old boyfriend to a new one in the months prior to their murders. It was an interesting, if not unique, thread. Jenna had secretly been involved with Parker, and the relationship was relatively new. New, but deeply intense, as the two were planning marriage.

He exhaled and reached for his coffee cup, the Styrofoam warm in his palm. Was there something in the victims' relationship statuses that the killer didn't like? It seemed too frequent an occurrence to be a coincidence. Perhaps, in the killer's warped eyes, he viewed the young women as betraying their families with the secret relationships, or perhaps betraying their former boyfriends.

If that was the case, it meant the killer had studied the victims or, at the very least, searched out young women involved in that type of relationship.

If he'd stalked them, as Griffin believed, there was a higher likelihood of catching the killer, because it tied him to the victim for a longer period, rather than if he had just randomly snatched them. No. Griffin bet he'd studied and stalked, and if that were the case, there had to be evidence of that somewhere—a trail to follow. They just had to find the beginning.

Thankfully, the victims' families had all provided some contact information—phone numbers and known or last-known locations of the victims' boyfriends at the time of the murders. All of them had been suspects, but eventually all had been cleared when no physical evidence tied them to the crime. That fact only strengthened Griffin's belief they were dealing with one killer.

It was a strong new thread to study and follow. Now, if he could just lose the sensation of the killer's presence hovering nearby.

• • •

Initially, Griffin had hoped to talk with the detective on Megan Atha's case after arriving in Wilmington, but when he called the station soon after landing he found out the detective had retired and moved to Amelia Island about three months back. He was gracious enough to speak with them by phone, though, and an officer at the precinct let them look through Megan's official case file. It was helpful but didn't offer anything new in the way of leads. As they entered the station in Topsail, Griffin prayed Julie Goss's case would be different.

Topsail was a small beach town about an hour northeast of Wilmington and about seven hours south of Baltimore. Griffin's family had spent a week every summer on its fine shores growing up. It saddened him to think one of the Shore Killer's victims had been found on those same shores.

The intake officer directed them to the desk of the detective who handled Julie's case. "Detective Cullen?"

"That'd be me," Cullen said with a smile.

The detective stood. He was a little over six feet tall, had a swimmer's build, short blond hair, deep blue eyes, and a tan.

"Hi, I'm Detective McCray and this is my wife"—he rested his hand on the small of Finley's back—"Dr. Scott-McCray."

"Right. Thanks for flying all the way out here to talk about Julie's case. Being in a smaller precinct, our cases don't typically garner much outside attention, but it sounds like Julie wasn't the only victim of the killer, according to your call?"

"We don't believe so."

"Why don't we head outside? It's a bit quieter than in here and it's a gorgeous day out."

"Fresh air sounds amazing." They'd been stuck in planes, rental cars, and police stations. And it really *was* a beautiful day.

Detective Cullen led them outside into the salty sea air that smelled wonderful, a moderate breeze blowing off the ocean, sand dunes rising in the distance.

"Julie Goss's body was found about three blocks from here, on the sound side." Detective Cullen pointed west. "I can show you, if you'd like."

"That'd be helpful." The more familiar they could become with the crime scenes, the better. So far they'd only found the dumping sites, though, never the location where the murder itself took place. It was possible the victims had been killed near the water before being dumped, but Griffin had a strong sense that the killer murdered the women in barns—since *barn* had been among Burke's key words—and then moved their bodies to the water. He wondered if the killer studied the currents to ensure the bodies washed up on shore. Did the killer want his work to be discovered? Did he want the world to see what he'd done? Was it some perverse need to show off his work? Or had he been unlucky, wanting the bodies to remain submerged, but they rarely did?

Detective Cullen led them across the two-lane road, the traffic light this time of year due to the lack of mainlanders, according to the detective. They proceeded down a side road and through the tall grass surrounding the marshy area leading up to the sound.

"Watch your step, Dr. Scott-McCray," Cullen said.

"Finley, please, and thanks." She held Griffin's hand, her bright pink ballet flats tiptoeing around the wet sand blanketing the shore.

"You're welcome, and call me Dirk," he said.

Like Griffin's favorite fictional character from Clive Cussler's novels, Dirk Pitt.

"Dirk it is." Finley smiled, glancing back at Griffin. She'd no doubt caught the connection.

About ten feet in, Dirk stopped at the dark bluish-green water's edge. The smell of brackish marsh—fish, algae, and brine—imbued the air. The lap of water lulled as it swayed the tall grasses surrounding the long and narrow estuary. "Julie was found right about here," Dirk said, pointing to a small sandy patch along the water's edge.

Griffin looked around at the tall grasses, sand dunes, and narrow path. "Hard to imagine anyone being found back in here."

"Thankfully, Julie was. Gave her poor parents some solace to at least bury their daughter."

"The way you talk about Julie, her family . . ." Griffin asked, sensing a tie there.

"My kid sister went through school with Julie. I know her family. You grow up in a small town . . ." He shrugged.

"I'm sorry," Griffin said.

"And I'm sorry," Dirk said. "I assume from the list of victim names you read over the phone that with Jenna's last name being McCray, there's a relation?"

Griffin rubbed the back of his neck. "She was my sister."

"Ah, man. I'm sorry. That sucks."

"Yeah, it does, which is why I want to get this guy so bad. I'm hoping you can help us."

Finley squeezed his hand, caressing his palm with her thumb in soft, soothing strokes.

"So tell me about Julie's case," Griffin said. "How was she found? By whom?"

"Some fishermen. Their names are in the file. We can check when we return to the station. They weren't local."

"Any chance the finders were involved?"

"No. We questioned them and they both had alibis for the time of death."

214

"Who's we?" Griffin asked.

"Me and Joel, my partner at the time."

"Joel?"

"Yeah," Dirk said. "He was new on the force, but raring to learn, so he shadowed me everywhere I went, asking questions, studying crime scenes, recording everything on that stupid tape recorder of his."

Finley swallowed. "Tape recorder?" Griffin knew what she was thinking. Perhaps Burke's key word *leader* really did mean a short strip of material at each end of a reel of recording tape for connection to the spool.

"He said it helped him study. He planned to take the detective's examination, but with this being such a small town, the chance of an opening here was slim. He heard Houston was hiring"—Griffin saw Finley's eyes widen just as the certainty hit him—"so he transferred out there. Did his time as a patrol officer, took the test, and made detective not long after. . . ." His eyes narrowed. "Why do you both look as pale as that albino alligator they got down at Fort Fisher Aquarium?"

Griffin found his voice. "Are you talking about Joel Hood?"

"Yeah. You know him?"

"He was the detective on one of the murders linked to the same killer."

Dirk's easygoing, low-key persona tensed.

215

"I'd like to say it's a small world, but even to a country boy like me, I'm afraid the likelihood of that being a coincidence is rare." He shook his head. "Joel?"

"What can you tell us about him?" Griffin asked.

"Why don't we head back to the station? I'll pull his employment file."

"That'd be great," Griffin said, still trying to wrap his head around what he'd just heard. Of all the detectives and the one agent they'd spoken with, he'd never have pegged the affable Joel Hood as the killer. Was it possible?

"Then we can head to the barn where Julie was killed, if it would be helpful," Dirk said.

Griffin stopped stone-still. "You found the barn where she was killed?"

"We did."

He was torn between which lead he wanted to start with.

"If you'd like, we can grab Joel's records and go over them while we drive out to the edge of Holly Ridge where the barn is."

"That would be great. Thanks."

Joel Hood? He could still barely wrap his mind around the possibility. Had he shaken the hand of Jenna's killer?

Fury flared like hot iron through his veins.

25

Dirk grabbed Joel's employment record and handed it to Griffin as they climbed into Dirk's patrol car, headed for Holly Ridge—about a twenty-minute drive from the station, according to Dirk.

Griffin scanned the document. "Joel transferred here from a Wilmington precinct?" That's where Megan Atha had been killed.

"Yes. Like I said, he was eager to learn, and no one there was willing to take the time and let him shadow them, so he moved here. But he's originally from Maryland, I believe."

Griffin's jaw slackened. "Maryland?"

"Yeah. Was a travel agent or something up there while he got his degree in criminal justice. Moved down here not long after he graduated, applied to the police academy in Wilmington, and then graduated from there."

"How long after he joined the Wilmington force was Megan Atha killed?" Griffin asked Finley.

She calculated it. "Roughly three months."

He turned to Dirk. "And how long had he been working with you when Julie Goss was murdered?"

Dirk swallowed, tapping the steering wheel. "About the same amount of time."

Finley leaned forward from the back seat and placed her hand on Griffin's shoulder as rage flared inside of him. He had shaken the hand of the man who'd tortured and killed his baby sister. It took all his restraint *not* to leap from the car and jump on a plane back to Houston, but that was not how they'd nail the scum. "Do you know anything about his life or his family back in Maryland?"

"Nah. He didn't talk about it much."

"I'll call my partner, Jason, ask him to do some digging," Griffin said as they pulled up to an old, rickety barn. "How'd you track the killer here?"

"It was a combination of factors, actually." Dirk stepped from the car and shut the door.

Birds scattered from the sycamore trees overhead.

"First, Julie had splinters embedded in her skin. Since she was only in the water a few hours, we were able to remove and analyze them."

"Only a few hours?" That was a far shorter timeline than with the other victims. Perhaps he was too early in his killing spree to really understand the currents and how they affected a dead body.

"The splinters came from aged wood over a hundred years old. There's only so many buildings that old in the area. Two homes and this barn," he said as they walked toward the entrance. "I figured an old barn near the game land made a lot more sense than one of the homes in town."

"Game land?" Finley asked.

"It's about seventy-five thousand acres of land used for hunting half the year, hiking the other half."

"So if she was killed during hunting season, the sound of a gunshot wouldn't be out of place?"

Dirk tapped his nose. "You got it."

They stepped inside the barn, an oppressive sense of darkness swooping over them.

Finley shuddered as if she'd just gotten a chill.

"You okay?" He rested his hand on the small of her back.

She nodded, but he could tell she was feeling the same thing he was. Something awful had occurred here.

"Did you find any evidence of Julie's murder?" he asked.

"The killer attempted to clean up, but from what you've told me, he was early in his craft." Dirk looked at Finley. "Forgive the base word, but that's how I'm sure he views it."

Finley crossed her arms over her chest, rubbing her arms with her hands. "I'm sure he does."

It was disgusting.

"Wilmington sent a CSI crew up here, and they went through the barn and the site where Julie was found. Like I said, the killer tried to clean the place, but the team still found evidence of blood—a fair amount of it. They were able to match the splinters in her skin to the floorboards, and we found a busted-up chair they determined she'd been tied or cuffed to, based on the markings on her wrists and the indentations in the chair's arms."

Griffin clutched Finley's hand, knowing this would shake her, as it was shaking him. He couldn't help but wonder if the same thing had happened to Jenna.

After gathering all the information they could from Detective Cullen, Griffin and Finley thanked him and made the drive back to Wilmington. Any evidence to this point was circumstantial, so they decided not to do anything that might tip off Joel Hood to their suspicions. They'd be catching an eight thirty flight back to Maryland—apparently Joel Hood's home at one point, as well.

Luke glanced at his watch. His colleague would be arriving any moment. *Colleague* perhaps wasn't the right word, since they were agents for different countries, but he viewed David as a colleague just the same. They had partnered together many times for common purposes, and worked together in conjunction with Interpol—both part of the race to catch Ebeid before he wreaked more destruction.

"Luke," David said, entering the office as if on cue.

"David." Luke moved to shake his hand. "Thank you for coming."

"To stop our common enemy? Anytime."

"Come on in and meet everyone." Luke ushered him inside. "This is Kate." The bell over the door rang, signaling Declan and Tanner's arrival.

He turned to greet them. "Hey, guys. Allow me to introduce you to—"

Tanner's eyes grew remarkably wide. "Dad?"

"Tania?" David said, his eyes equally wide. Eyes the same color as Tanner's.

"This is your dad?" Declan asked Tanner.

She nodded, clearly confused by his appearance. "What are you doing here?"

"Luke called in a favor."

Tanner's eyes narrowed on him. "Luke?"

"David and I work in conjunction from time to time," Luke explained, just as befuddled as she was.

"The CIA and Mossad?" she asked.

"We share a common enemy, Tania," David said.

"Tania?" Declan arched a brow.

"It's her given name, before she Americanized it," her dad snapped.

"I prefer Tanner."

"She prefers anything that is opposite of her heritage."

"Really, Dad? This isn't the time or place."

"No. You are right. We have far more important matters to attend to."

221

"Any luck with the shredded paper the team pulled out of the trash?" Luke asked, trying to defuse a clearly awkward family reunion as Parker entered the main room.

"Yes," Parker said, handing Luke a piece of paper. "I was able to re-create one section of what the shards they pulled from the trash once made up. I'm still working on the remaining sections, but at least it's a start."

Luke studied the paper, his gaze narrowing. "Is this a wind chart?"

David inhaled sharply.

Luke arched a brow. "What?"

"You mentioned you found the warehouse where Bedan was working?"

"Yes."

"And you said you found aerosol cans?"

"Yes."

"Can I see one?"

"Sure. I'll grab one from the lab," Parker said, heading down the hall.

"What are you thinking?" Luke and David shared an ominous look. Luke knew it was most likely the exact thought he'd had when he first saw the cans.

Ebeid intended to spread the anthrax spores via aerosol dispersal.

26

Tanner's father leaned toward her as they waited for Parker to return.

"I don't understand," David said in a low whisper. "What are you doing here with Luke? You work for the Global Justice Mission."

How did he . . . ? "Have you been checking up on me?" Had he actually shown an interest in her life since she left Israel?

"Your aunt . . ." He shrugged. "She talks to your mother."

Uh-huh. His body language was clear. He had been checking up on her, which was flat-out shocking, considering they hadn't spoken since she'd left Israel more than a decade ago.

"I'm with the Bureau now," she said, "and this"—she indicated the group—"is the team heading up the task force set up to stop Ebeid and his impending attack."

Her dad's dark, inquisitive eyes narrowed. "You leave your homeland only to fight the *same* war for another country?"

She cleared her throat. He was so stubborn . . . overbearing. It was flooding back—his heavy-handedness, his controlling manner. "Dad, this isn't the time or place."

"It never is," he said, disappointment welling in his eyes.

"I'm Special Agent Declan Grey," Declan said, clearly attempting to break the tension in the room. "It's a pleasure to meet Tanner's father."

"I'm sorry for not introducing you," Tanner said, looking softly at Declan and then to her father. "Dad, this is my boyfriend, Declan."

Her dad's brows shot high. "Boyfriend? A federal agent?"

"Yes."

He shook Declan's hand while scrutinizing him. "I look forward to getting to know you better." Which meant raking him over the coals, but she wasn't worried in the least. Declan could more than hold his own.

"As do I," Declan said.

"Thank you again for coming, David," Luke said, clearly trying to steer the conversation back to the case.

David nodded. "Anything to stop our common enemy."

"I'm sure you have already figured it out," Luke said to the group, clearly unsure of who knew what, "but David is Mossad. We've worked together frequently in pursuit of Ebeid."

David nodded. "We are both trying to combat the growth and spread of sleeper cells being staffed with young men out of Southeast Asia."

Tanner and her family had spent a short part

of her youth living in Southeast Asia. All the threads of her life seemed to be coming together in this very moment in time. As if God had been preparing her.

Her dad shifted his hands to his pockets, jingling the change in his right one, just like he had when she was a little girl—though she doubted he'd pull the magic trick of the disappearing coin at her age, or given their surroundings. They no longer had that kind of relationship. They'd had no semblance of a relationship *period* since she'd accepted Christ as her Savior.

Awkward silence filled the room, only the occasional jingle of his coins breaking it.

She still couldn't believe Luke and her dad had worked together, though it made sense given Luke's focus on Muslim extremists in Southeast Asia as well as her dad's—at least during their time there. It'd been through that period of her youth that she'd felt the call to go back as an adult and serve. People there—woman and children, especially—needed help. It was why she'd requested to be assigned to Cambodia when she went to work for Global Justice Mission.

She wondered how long Luke and her dad had known each other, where all they'd worked together. There was a mentor-mentee, father-son vibe going on. Her dad clearly liked and respected Luke, and Luke clearly looked up to her dad. It was surreal.

"When was the last time you saw Bedan?" Luke asked.

"In Paris after he fled the Munich attack." Her dad's presence was as commanding as ever. He was still strong and refined, but he had wrinkles creeping in at the corners of his dark brown eyes, and whispers of gray edged his temples.

"Is that where you've been working?" she asked, unable to curb her curiosity. "In Paris?" He'd never been allowed to say where he was going when he traveled, other than when they were living on-location, of course. But she had occasionally guessed—or at least attempted to guess—where he'd been from the small gifts he brought her when he returned home. But now she was part of the task force, so maybe he'd actually share his full knowledge with her. She caught herself holding her breath as she awaited his answer.

"Tania, you know I cannot say."

"But you just told Luke you were in Paris. . . ."

"I did so to comment on Bedan's location. Not mine."

Same old silence.

"Of course," she quietly said, just as she'd always done.

But this time it felt even more wrong. She *was* part of the circle, not to be relegated out of the room as she'd been when she was young and visitors came to see her dad. Not that they came often. They didn't have friends over for dinner. Didn't do things her other friends did. Hers wasn't a typical family growing up, but as she got older and gained a better understanding of her dad's high position in the Mossad, she understood why.

No wonder her dad had always been so cautious of his speech around her.

She still remembered the terror in his eyes when he'd discovered her hiding in his office while he was on, what she could only assume looking back, a Mossad business call. She hadn't meant to be in there. She'd been playing hide-and-seek with her gray lop-eared stuffed bunny, pretending they were secret agents like her papa. She froze when she heard him enter the room, too frightened to move. She'd be in severe trouble for being in his office, period. It was off-limits, but she and Mr. Rabbit weren't civilians—not on that wonderful, carefree afternoon while her momma ran to the market and her nana was asleep in the living room recliner. She and Mr. Rabbit were secret agents, just like her papa.

At age seven, she'd been too young to understand anything that was discussed on that call other than a few words, which stuck in her mind—surveillance, payment, and dead.

It was then she'd discovered just how different her papa's job in the Mossad was from that of her friends' fathers and just how good he was at sensing another's presence in the room.

She remembered the soft sound of his footsteps, his shadow looming over the slit in the cabinet she and Mr. Rabbit were hiding in. The door swung open and she gaped up at the barrel of a gun. It wouldn't be the last time she'd had a gun pointed at her, not in her line of work, but it was a memorable *first* seared in her mind. Mr. Rabbit tumbled to her feet as she shook in fear.

Papa had been livid, chastising her for being where she didn't belong, and after that day, right up until she'd joined the Global Justice Mission, she'd never felt like she belonged.

Parker returned with the aerosol can and handed the black canister to David.

He studied it with a creased brow.

Declan rubbed Tanner's shoulders from behind. "You okay, love?" he whispered as everyone else's attention shifted to David's scrutiny of the device.

Tanner swallowed. "Just in shock."

"Luke had no idea. . . ." Declan began.

"Oh, I know. It's just . . . he's the last person I expected to see when I walked through that door."

"When was the last time you saw him?"

"When I left Israel over ten years ago."

David exhaled, slowly setting the canister on the tabletop. "It appears Bedan has succeeded in his design. Perhaps a finishing touch here or there, but he's got it."

Luke was the next to exhale deeply. "So Ebeid's going to be able to spread anthrax effectively via aerosol."

Her dad swiped a hand over his thinning crown of hair. "I'm afraid so."

"Which explains the wind charts," Luke said. "Bedan needs wind to carry the spores. With the right prevailing winds, the spores could carry, undetected. . . ." Luke cut off the thought. "We need to find the new location of that warehouse before Bedan puts those finishing touches on his weapon of mass destruction."

27

"I can't believe you worked with Tanner's dad," Kate said as Luke drove them to yet another hotel for the night.

Luke tapped the wheel. "Crazy, right? I had no idea."

"David seemed . . ."

"Solemn? Reserved?"

Kate shifted in her seat. "Yeah."

"He's so high up in the Mossad, I don't even know the level of his position."

"Seriously?"

"Seriously." He blinked in the glare of the oncoming headlights. The large SUV passed on his left, and he caught a glimpse of long blond hair in the reflection of his headlights.

He stiffened.

"What's wrong?" Kate asked as a *thwack* sounded, and their car swerved.

"It's Lauren."

Another *thwack*. Another tire blown out.

He hit the brakes, but the pedal just pumped without catching. *What on earth?*

Kate's eyes were wide in the dim shadow of the streetlights.

Lauren U-turned and sped up, moving directly for them as the steering went out next.

He clutched the wheel, glancing at the silver guardrail lining the narrow bridge, and then down to the dark, flowing water below, the moon illuminating its cascading rush.

Lauren had timed it perfectly.

He released the gas pedal, but the car continued its forward momentum, powering headlong against the bridge's guardrail.

Lauren slammed them from behind in her large, dark SUV.

Luke pumped the brakes again out of instinct, but Lauren had somehow rendered his controls useless.

"Luke?" Kate said, bracing herself for another impact.

This time Lauren rammed harder, shoving their car over the metal bridge railing.

"Hold on!" he shouted, struggling to power down their windows to prevent the force of the water from sealing them in, but all power in the vehicle was gone.

Nose-diving, they careened headfirst into the roaring river with bone-jarring impact.

"Luke!" Kate clutched his hand.

The murky water quickly swallowed the vehicle, entombing them. Bullets riddled down through the dark surface.

"Take a gulp of air." Lauren couldn't fire forever. It was late, but someone would surely have heard the car breaking through the metal barrier and hitting the water.

"What are we going to do?"

"We're going to have to swim for it." Pulling his weapon, he shot his window. The bullet's exit created a web of cracks, before the cold water surged in. Kicking out the glass shards to create safe passage, he took Kate's hand and swam out with her right behind him.

Sticking close to the side of the vehicle, he waited until Lauren needed to reload, and then they swam for it, bullets soon swirling through the dark water as red lights flashed overhead.

The firing ceased, and he breached the surface just in time to see Lauren peel away. One of the police vehicles quickly took off after her, but Lauren was too good to get caught. She'd outmaneuver the officer, just like she'd outmaneuvered them.

She hadn't followed them from CCI. He'd seen no tail. And she'd come from the opposite direction. So how did she know the path they'd be taking or the hotel they were headed to? Had she slipped a tracking device onto his rental car? He'd check, but with his car at the bottom of the river, they'd likely never know, and he couldn't take time to fixate on that. He needed to take Kate someplace safe and warm, but where?

"I've got it," Kate said after they'd been released by emergency personnel and Declan had reluctantly dropped them off at Kate's car. He'd argued for them to stay at his place, but neither of them wanted to risk bringing Lauren to his door.

Luke frowned at her. "Got what?" he asked.

"A safe place to stay." Chris's lighthouse. It was about as off grid as you could get. Only reachable by boat and providing the ability to see anyone approaching from miles away.

Why hadn't she thought of it sooner?

Maybe because she'd been so shaken up by her home being turned into a thousand little pieces of shrapnel that she plain hadn't been thinking since—rather, she'd spent the last four days simply reacting.

"Are you sure?" Luke asked.

Kate shifted gears, tearing down the road in her Mini Cooper. "Trust me."

Perhaps tonight Luke would finally manage to get a few hours of sleep, a few hours of peace in what had been close to eight years of war—maybe not on a battlefield, but a war just the same.

She drove them along winding back roads, watching his curiosity grow with each turn. To her surprise, he didn't ask any more questions, just remained silent—watching, waiting, *trusting* her.

Reaching the end of the dirt road, she cut the ignition.

Luke climbed out and surveyed the space. "Well, we certainly weren't followed." He turned to her and lifted his chin in question. "You wanna let me in on where we're headed?"

Pulling the Maglite from her glove box, she shone it on the rowboat tied at the isolated pier.

His brows hiked up. "Seriously?"

"Trust me," she said.

"Okay."

Warmth filled her despite the brisk breeze rolling across the bay.

She grabbed the duffel of clothes kindly provided to them by Tanner and Declan, and Luke took it from her with an outstretched hand, hiking it over his shoulder. Tomorrow, she'd grab the rest of her necessities from CCI, though the way things were going, she was due for a shopping spree.

The rowboat shifted beneath them as they climbed in. They sat facing each other in the center of the two wooden seats to steady its rocking.

Luke grabbed the oars. "Want to give me a heading?"

"Start rowing due east."

The water rhythmically lapped across the flat face of the oars each time they dipped in and out of the dark water.

Luke's breath shone in puffs in the halo of light cast from the Maglite settled between his feet.

Twenty minutes out, as Luke's breath clouded in vapor, she bent and lifted the Maglite to reveal a tiny bay island with a small, round lighthouse. "We're here."

Luke tied the boat to the pier and gazed up at the white-and-green lighthouse. "What is this place?"

"My friend Chris's second home."

"Your friend owns an island and a lighthouse?"

"Yep. It's been in her family for generations. The land was originally deeded to one of her ancestors in 1747 by Lord Baltimore. He deeded out several islands, as a matter of fact, two of which are still owned by the original families—Chris's and Talbot Island."

"Interesting."

"I know." She smiled. "The main house is on the barrier island about five nautical miles that way." She pointed southwest. "After having several shipwrecks on their barrier island, they built the lighthouse. They hired someone to run the lighthouse, and that"—she shone the light at the small, run-down cottage—"belonged to the lightkeeper and his family. Over time a bigger lighthouse was built about a half-dozen nautical miles farther out in the bay, and there was no longer any use for this. It fell out of memory and into disrepair until Chris's dad died and passed it on to her. She had fond memories of playing pirates here and decided to restore it with her husband. They finished the lighthouse first and are starting on the lightkeeper's cottage next."

She unlocked the lighthouse door and punched a code into the security panel.

"A security system for a lighthouse?" he asked, clearly impressed.

"We'll be safe here for the night."

She flipped on the light as they entered, and Luke stared at the full-blown security system, and video monitors showing the entire surrounding area.

"Chris is upper echelon at a security firm and a complete tech nerd, so let's just say she's a little over the top when it comes to security."

She led him up the winding wooden stairs, and they moved to the windows, staring in awe at the stars and the sea and God's magnificent creation.

The water set her soul at ease, and the line from Horatio Spafford's "It Is Well with My Soul" rang through her mind. *When sorrows like sea billows roll . . ."*

The ocean had been her gift of solace from God during Luke's absence. It was where she felt at home—in His arms and on the sea.

"So, will this do?" she asked Luke as she leaned against the pine railing, praying against all odds that the cop chasing down Lauren had caught her and she was securely behind bars. She doubted it though. They appeared doomed to be targets.

28

Luke studied Kate in front of the round window of the lighthouse. Moonlight streaked across her face.

He drew near. "It's perfect."

"So maybe you'll actually get a good night's rest?" she said.

"What do you mean?" Had she brought them to the secluded safe house so *he* could rest? And all this time he'd been so thankful she was finally appearing to be taking extra safety precautions for herself.

She leaned back against the window, the moon illuminating her silhouette, the flame from the lantern she'd lit dancing across her high cheekbones.

Cheeks he loved to caress, but lately, he'd only been wiping away her tears—tears he'd caused.

"You're tired," she said, her voice sounding sleepier than he felt.

Being with her in such a remote and stunning place renewed his energy and fueled his longing to be with her. *Only her. Always her.*

Katie was a starlit night filled with the bursts of fireflies. She was the pummel and froth of a waterfall booming in his ears, the surge of a plane jetting into the bright blue sky, pressing him back against the seat, his chest tightening with excitement. She was a tender movement of a slow dance on the front porch to the soft melody of crickets. She was every sensation, every good moment, every emotion rolled into one. One person. One love. It was *her*.

He'd known it all along, and yet he'd walked away. Talk about the definition of madness.

It was time to make things right.

To *be* right.

For that to happen, he needed to be at her side.

Without her, he didn't exist—not fully, not the way she awakened the light within him. Around her, his every sense was alive and on fire.

He existed to be at her side. To be one with her.

She was the piece his soul was missing.

She pushed off the panel and walked toward him. "Too tired to reply?" she asked softly at his silence.

"Too mesmerized by you." She'd always had that effect on him. Ever since he'd first laid eyes on her, he'd been hers.

She looked down, her hair slipping forward, hiding the blush he knew was creeping across her skin. He knew her, mind and soul. Now, in a moment of perfect clarity, he longed for nothing more than to marry her . . . and soon. Making her fully his, and him fully hers.

He swallowed and dropped to one knee.

Her eyes widened. "Wh-what are . . . you . . . doing?"

"Katie." He pulled the ring he'd worn for years on the chain around his neck, hidden by dog tags—dog tags of a true friend, one who'd died in front of him in Baghdad.

He slipped the ring off the chain and offered it to her with a trembling hand. "I bought this the day I left as a promise to myself I'd return and make you my wife. I've been married to you this whole time in my mind, but I know there's so much more to it than that." He bent his head, praying for the courage to be brutally honest with her. "I promise you, I *will* leave the Agency as soon as Ebeid is stopped and I know you are safe. Then I *am* going to marry you."

Her chin jutted up at his bold declaration. "Oh, you *are?*"

He stood. "Yes."

She shook her head and moved to turn.

He tugged her arm, wrapping her into his hold. He backed her up against the window, unwilling to let her pull away or shut down. "I know there's a part of you that hates me, and you have good reason."

She sighed and looked down.

He tipped her chin up, unwilling to let her hide any longer. It was time to have this out. He was a man of action, after all, and he desperately needed to get this off his chest.

"But," he said, softening his voice, "I also *know* you love me."

Her jaw shifted. "Someone thinks highly of himself."

"Tell me I'm wrong." Kate was never one to lie. Never had been. It was one of his favorite qualities about her.

She nibbled the corner of her lip. "You're awfully confident for a man I slapped not too long ago."

She held true. Not lying. Not denying. Only attempting to misdirect.

"Only a woman still in love would be that angry."

She laughed. "That's your reasoning?"

"Tell me I'm wrong."

"What does it matter? I won't marry you."

"But you love me."

"I loved you then, and look where it got me." Tears rolled down her cheeks.

"And it will take the rest of our lives for me to make things right, but *please,* Katie, give me the chance. I'm only asking for the chance."

"You're asking me to risk my heart getting pummeled again."

"Your heart is already pummeled because of me." He rested his hands over hers, intertwining their fingers. "Now let me do the right thing for once and start mending it."

She sniffed back tears. "And how do you plan to do that?"

"One kiss at a time." He nudged her nose with

his, brushed his mouth along her hair to hover over her ear, and whispered, "Let me love you, Gracie."

She swallowed. "You're not fighting fair."

"Darling, I will fight however hard, fierce, and long it takes to have you back in my arms forever. Marry me, Gracie."

She didn't move, not a single inch, just remained in his embrace, tears streaming down her cheeks, her heart thumping against his rib cage, her breath tickling his neck.

"I love you, Katie," he murmured, his forehead resting against hers.

"I love you too," she said between sobs.

He nearly collapsed to his knees in relief. *Thank you, Lord.*

He pulled her tighter to him, kissing her forehead, the tip of her nose . . . grazing her neck and earlobe before bringing his mouth to hers.

He stepped back, but only long enough to lift her hand, ready to slip the ring on, but she pulled back.

"Whoa!"

His stomach dropped. "I don't understand." She'd just said she loved him.

"Let's get through this alive first. You officially leave the Agency, we spend some quality time together, and *then* I'll marry you."

"Fair enough. But will you please let me place this ring on your finger as a sign of my promise?

I've been waiting more than seven years to do so."

"And I've been waiting more than seven years for you to do it." Shaking, she held out her hand, and he slid the solitaire diamond on her ring finger, inexpressible joy flooding him. He wanted nothing more at that moment than to take her and disappear, leave everything behind, but he knew Ebeid would never stop. It was up to him—he truly believed God had chosen him to bring Ebeid down. But afterward he would stand at the end of the aisle, awaiting his bride. Awaiting Katie.

He clasped her hand as he rested it against his chest, feeling the ring on her finger, *finally* where it belonged. He knew all the hurt he'd caused wouldn't magically be erased, knew it would be years for the wounds he'd inflicted to heal.

Still floored Katie had agreed to join him on that healing journey, he uttered another prayer of thanks.

It seemed too good to be true, and suddenly the immense fear of losing her knocked the breath from his lungs.

"What's wrong?" she asked as he tensed.

Just terrified of losing what I love most. "Just anxious to get Ebeid behind bars."

She nestled back against him. "We'll get him. All of us together. I trust God will equip us to prevail."

But how long would it take, and how many more lives would it cost?

She tensed.

"What's wrong?" he asked this time.

"Nothing. Just want to show you something . . ."

She reached for her shirt.

He arched his brows.

"My tattoo," she said, rolling her eyes.

"You're finally going to let me see it?"

"Since we're going to get married, it only seems appropriate." She smiled and tugged down the neck of her shirt, scooting back against him so he could look.

He smiled. It was a beautiful conch shell, but it was what nestled inside that brought joy to his soul—a starfish—just like the ring he'd given her back in college.

She turned back to face him. "I wanted something that tied me to you in a tangible way, because I knew whether you stayed or left after this mission that you'd always be a part of me." She cupped his cheek, her hand warm. "The best part of me."

"I don't know about that." He'd messed up so much.

She held his jaw firm, keeping his gaze locked on hers. "I do," she said, lowering her pink lips to his.

Hours later, torn between the bliss of Katie back in his arms and the reality they faced with Ebeid, Luke sat on the futon with Katie asleep beside him. The two had argued over who would take the bed, neither relenting, so they'd ended up sitting there, feet propped up on the coffee table, each trying to outlast the other.

Finally, his head bobbed, his eyes closed, and his mind drifted to the vivid image of bodies littering the ground. The image continued flashing as the nightmare shifted to fully engulf his mind.

He walked through a silent park, choking on the anthrax-filled air. He couldn't see the spores, but he knew Ebeid had won. He walked by his friends' bodies one by one, his soul crushing tighter and smaller with each body.

Declan. Parker. Griffin. Finley. Avery. Tanner.

And there at the end stood Kate, her back to him.

Relief washed over him. She was still standing.

He called her name, and she turned, her abdomen covered with blood. Ebeid stood behind her laughing, gun still in hand. "A loved one for a loved one," he said as Luke lunged forward, jolting awake.

"What's wrong?" Kate asked, tumbling to the floor.

"Sorry." He reached down and lifted her back up on the futon as the sunrise gleamed streaming shafts across the pine floor.

He swallowed, his skin clammy, his hair drenched in a cold sweat. "Nothing," he said, trying to shake out of it. "Just a bad dream."

And yet . . . it felt so real. Every detail nearly tactile—vivid and eerily present.

"A loved one for a loved one."

Was his dream a message from God? What had Ebeid been talking about? Had he lost someone he loved? Had their background report on him missed something . . . or *someone?*

Could that be fueling his actions and the impending attack?

He raked a hand through his hair as Kate did the same to hers, both disheveled. Despite Kate's wish for him to grab some sleep, he'd planned to stay awake and alert, but sleep had overcome him all the same. Unfortunately, rather than getting a good night's rest, he'd had a horrific nightmare, and Kate, by the way she was tenderly moving, had a serious kink in her neck.

"Kink?" he asked, walking over to her as she stood and stretched.

"Yeah." She nodded, then winced with the motion.

"Here." He put his hands on her shoulders. "Let me help." It didn't take long for his fingers to feel the knot at the base of her neck. Gently, he applied pressure.

"Thanks." She remained still, pliable to his touch, but fear tugged at him, pricking his subconscious. He had Katie back. What would he do if Ebeid took her away?

Please, Lord, don't let Ebeid take her away. Don't let me lose her. Not again.

Even if he'd chosen to leave the first time, he'd still lost the woman he loved for seven years—all because of his desire to serve his country and to see Ebeid brought down. But when was enough, enough?

Not yet, God whispered. *I have chosen you. You will overcome. Trust me.*

But what more might he lose in the process?

Katie shifted as he found another knot in her shoulder, and he lessened the pressure.

He'd promised to give all to God, to not hold *anything* back. If God was calling him to this battle, to face this Goliath, he had to do so, even if it meant death.

He thought of King David, so fearless for his age and stature, but he knew God had chosen him. He thought of the fear Joseph must have felt being dragged away from everything and everyone he loved to be sold into slavery, and yet God had raised him up and used him to save His people.

He was hardly comparing himself with David or Joseph, but God had entrusted this fight to him. He knew that as surely as he knew of God's love for him. Even now, even after all the compromises, God's love held strong. It was an anchor in the storm. His anchor. It'd taken reentering his old life for God to finally break through his thick skull, but He'd done so. He'd revealed how strong His love remained for Luke. How strong it had always been.

Thank you, Lord, for your patience with me, for never ceasing to love me. Please equip me to serve you wholly. I pray I make it through this mission, and that I get to spend my life by Kate's side. Amen.

Kate moved away from his massage and turned to him, studied him.

"Sorry, I was just . . ."

"I know you'll say 'distracted,' but I don't think that's it."

She knew him well.

"Oh?"

"No. You were thinking deeply."

"And praying."

She smiled.

"What?"

"I didn't know. . . . You've been gone so long, I didn't know—"

"If I still had a relationship with Christ?"

"I knew you did. To what extent is what I wondered."

He raked a hand through his hair on an exhale. "I'm not going to sugarcoat it. It's not where it should be on my end, but God has held on tight and never let go." He pulled her into his arms. "Just like I'm never letting you go." He kissed her forehead.

She closed her eyes and rested her head on his chest. "Never again?"

"Never. I promise."

"A loved one for a loved one" continued to run through Luke's mind.

"What's up?" Kate asked as she packed her things in their duffel.

"Just something tracking in the back of my mind."

"Care to share?"

He did. Leaving out all the gory and heart-wrenching details, he explained only Ebeid's words, and she quickly inferred their meaning.

"That's what has you so spooked. You're worried Ebeid's coming after me because I'm with you."

Especially now. Especially if he learned how deeply Luke loved her—that they were to be married. For her safety, he should have waited, but he could no longer deny the truth of what he felt for her. Couldn't have stood in her presence one nanosecond longer and not asked her to be his wife. He'd spent the last seven years hunting Ebeid. He might not have caught him yet, but he wasn't putting his life on hold any longer.

He shook out his hands, the image of her wounded and bloody replaying through his mind. "If he discovers how much you mean to me . . . ."

"No offense, but I'm pretty sure he's already

fully aware of how you feel about me. He blew up my home after all, and attempted to do so with us in it."

"True." She didn't pull punches—another thing he loved about her. He bent, kissing her ring, his fingers tracing over the small diamond. It'd been all he could afford back then. "You'll definitely need an upgrade," he said. "Now that I can afford one." He'd give her the wedding of her dreams.

"No," she said, holding it up so the sunlight bounced off its princess-cut surface. "It's perfect."

He smiled. She would think so.

"A loved one for a loved one."

"Hey." She cupped his face. "It's going to be hard—I know that—but I really believe God will help you—help us—triumph."

He did too, but at what cost?

29

Rowing back in the rising sunlight across the still morning bay, Luke longed for nothing more than to stay at the lighthouse forever with Kate. It could be their shelter from the world, their secret hideaway.

He might have to talk with Chris and see if she'd be willing to sell. He could easily handle living there, though he would require a quicker getaway vehicle than a rowboat, just in case . . .

Just in case . . .

He shook his head. It was ingrained into him. He was going to live the rest of his life this way—always watching his back, always alert for danger, even after Ebeid was stopped. But at least he'd be doing it at Katie's side.

"Hey," he said as they tied the boat back up to the pier. "I've got a brilliant idea."

She smirked. "Brilliant, huh?"

"After I leave the Agency, I still want to work in law enforcement of some kind, so I was thinking . . . what if I came and worked with you?" Anticipation and a tad of trepidation streaked through him as he awaited her response.

"I'd love that, but do you really think you'll feel fulfilled doing PI work after . . . ?" She gestured at him.

"I'd pretend to not know what that means, but I got ya." He was highly trained. "But being at your side and doing what God's called me to do—which is striving to see justice done, through whatever method or place that may be—is all the fulfillment I need."

She laughed as he tossed their duffel in the trunk. "Well, you would definitely bring a new skill set to the office."

Luke considered where they'd end up tonight—though, looking back at the water and the lighthouse it hid, he was seriously considering staying there again tonight. It was obviously off Ebeid's and, it appeared, Lauren's radar. And it was full of the best memories he'd made in years, thanks to Katie. He glanced at the ring, *his* ring on *her* finger, and smiled.

She caught his gaze and smiled back. "Where are we off to now?" she asked as they climbed into her car and he started the engine.

"Your office."

She frowned. "Not Declan's office?"

"I need to dig up some information on Ebeid, and that's going to require *your* particular set of skills."

"Hacking?"

"Exactly." He winked, anxious to see her in her element. She'd been good with the computer back in college, but from how all the guys talked, she had garnered mad skills during his years

251

away, and he couldn't wait to see her in action.

He also needed to set up a meeting with Malcolm, needed to let him know that Lauren had gone off reservation. Malcolm had brought her in, but no way he'd ordered her to kill them. Even he wouldn't go that far.

An hour later, Luke checked in with Declan to update him about what they were doing. Declan agreed that Katie's work was best accomplished from CCI.

Declan and the team were combing through all the evidence recovered from the warehouse, searching for a clue as to where Bedan may have relocated. If Ebeid hadn't had a backup location set up, they'd just gained a day or two while he configured and equipped one, but knowing the man he'd been tracking for nigh on a decade, he'd bet his life Ebeid had planned for all contingencies.

The clock was rapidly ticking down, and the threat was higher than ever.

"So what am I looking for?" Kate asked.

"Anyone close to Ebeid who was killed."

"By . . . ?"

"Anyone related to the U.S. via a raid, bombing, accident, hit . . ."

"Okay, and by anyone close you mean . . . ?"

"A lover."

"Isn't that against the rules for a Muslim?"

"Yes, but intel on Ebeid shows he didn't become

a practicing Muslim until he was in his early twenties. Prior to that, he lived unconventionally, for an Iraqi. I never thought to check who he may have had ties to before his conversion because it appears once he converted, he left everything and everyone he knew behind."

"So you think he may still have cared for someone he left behind?"

"It's possible. Just because you leave doesn't mean you stop loving." He knew that full well. Though it seemed almost impossible that a man as cruel as Ebeid could care for anyone or anything other than his cause.

"So I'm looking at his life in 1990, while he was in France?"

"Correct."

"And he's how old now?"

"Fifty."

He leaned over her.

She arched a brow. "Are you going to stand there the whole time?"

He tilted his head in the affirmative. "Was planning on it. Why?"

"You're a bit of a distraction." Her cheeks flushed.

He swiveled her chair around so she faced him and then leaned her back. "Is that right?"

She smirked. "Do you want me to figure this out?"

"In a minute." He took that minute to kiss her—long, slow, and tender.

"Well, that'll help me focus," she said after he pulled away and spun her back around to face the computer.

He glanced at his watch. "I'm going to call Malcolm."

"Sounds good."

Kate fanned herself after Luke excused himself to make the call. What was the man doing to her? She was strong, focused, determined. One kiss and she was swooning. It was ridiculous.

Tapping into the databases she needed to begin with, she started combing her way through, searching Ebeid's name and scrolling back through time.

30

Kate felt as if she were watching Ebeid's life play out like a movie in reverse. She observed a lot of content before something *finally* captured her attention—something key.

"Luke," she said, turning and jolting back when she saw he was standing less than two feet behind her, propped against the wooden post, his arms linked across his chest, and a charming smile on his lips.

"Sorry I spooked you," he said, pushing off the post. "You were so engrossed, I didn't want to disturb you."

"Okay." Her heart started to return to a somewhat normal beat. "But we're going to have to work on you either not being so stealthy or, if that's not possible, at least announcing your presence."

"Deal," he said, coming to sit beside her. "It was fun watching you doing your thing."

She shook her head with a smile. "You're weird."

"Never claimed otherwise." He shrugged with an impish grin and indicated her laptop with a tilt of his handsome head. "You're really good at what you do."

She tucked a loose strand of hair back into her

cobalt headband. "Thanks. How'd it go with Malcolm?"

"He swears vehemently he would never order a hit on us. He agrees Lauren's gone off reservation."

"Because you turned her down? That's just crazy."

"Malcolm fears she might have accepted a contract from Ebeid. There's been an occasional rumor of her taking a contract on the side, but no concrete proof ever came of the rumors."

"Are you kidding?"

"I wish I were."

"So, now what?"

"He's got a team searching for her. They'll bring her in."

"Yeah. If they can find her. You said yourself, she's one of the best."

He leaned over her shoulder and shifted the conversation. "Looks like you're on to something. . . ."

"I found a handful of pictures of Ebeid with this woman." Kate pointed to the woman in said pictures. She was tall, blond, and slender. "These photos were taken right around the target time period, and they look like surveillance photos to me."

Luke's brow furrowed. "You think the two were involved?"

"From this image . . ." She pointed to one of

them on a picnic, the woman's head in a young Ebeid's lap, Ebeid staring down at her with loved-filled eyes.

"We need to find out who that woman is," Luke said.

"No need."

Kate startled, and she turned to see David standing behind Luke. What was up with these stealthy spies?

"David." Luke moved to shake the man's hand. "You know this woman?"

"Yes. Her legend was Caroline Ladew."

Luke arched a brow. "Legend?"

David nodded. "She was working for your Agency."

"She was CIA?"

"She was a field agent, and an excellent one at that."

"Was?"

"Ebeid killed her, and then discovered the biggest surprise of his life."

31

Griffin and Finley entered the small but cozy reading room at the Brightview Senior Living Community in Ellicott City, Maryland. There were numerous Brightview facilities throughout the state, and as far as senior-living facilities went, Griffin had heard nothing but good things about them.

The facility was beautiful, clean, and well kept, and based on his interaction with the staff over the phone, and now in person, they appeared knowledgeable and compassionate.

Miss Sally, as the lady in her upper fifties and with a distinct southern drawl had introduced herself, led them to the room where Veronica Hood was reading.

"Roni," Miss Sally said, "you have some visitors."

The woman's sparkling green eyes lit. "Do I?"

Though her face was wrinkled, she was strikingly beautiful with gray hair styled in a fashionable twist knot. However, he'd bet money her hair had been brown in her youth.

Like all of Hood's victims, she was petite— maybe about five-foot-four, one-hundred and twenty pounds at most. Now to see if she was the overbearing sort.

He squeezed Finley's hand before letting go and stepping forward to greet Joel Hood's mother.

Veronica smiled as she slid her Kate Spade glasses on—the fashion knowledge courtesy of Finley. "My, aren't you a handsome visitor?" Veronica said. "And"—she looked past Griffin at his wife—"a beautiful young lady." She set her book aside. "Have we met before?"

"No, ma'am," Griffin said.

"And polite as well." She shook her head. "I always tried to raise my Joel with manners, but he required constant reminding. Such an inept boy. Just like his father."

Ouch. Most definitely an overbearing mother.

"Joel . . . your son?" Griffin said, sitting beside Finley on the floral love seat facing Veronica Hood.

"Do you know my Joel?" Veronica asked.

"We had the pleasure of meeting him in Texas," Finley said.

"He likes it down there. Only comes home to visit twice a year." She certainly didn't seem pleased with that.

"On special occasions?" Finley asked.

"Well, he claims his May trip is for my birthday, but I know it's really for *her*."

"Her?" Griffin asked, scooting forward on the loveseat.

"Stacey," Veronica said with a touch of disdain, her teeth—stained by time—clenched.

"And Stacey is . . . ?" Finley gently pressed.

"She was Joel's college sweetheart," Veronica said.

"And he still comes back to visit her?" Griffin asked, though he feared there was a far darker dynamic at play.

"Oh no," Veronica said, swishing her hand as if swatting away an unwanted insect. "Stacey went missing right before the end of Joel's junior year in college."

"In May?"

"Yes. Early May. The sixth. At least he's always here for the sixth. Sometimes he comes a few days before and stays through the sixth. And sometimes he comes on the sixth and remains a few days after to visit, but he's *always* here on the sixth."

"And your birthday is?" Griffin asked, wondering why she was so confident Joel's visits weren't for her birthday.

"Not until the end of the month," she said. "The twenty-eighth. Oh, he says work is always more hectic at the end of the month. That's his excuse for coming earlier, but I know it's a farce. He comes for the anniversary of when she went missing. It's for her. After they met, *everything* became about her."

He was coming back to celebrate the anniversary of murdering his girlfriend. Griffin stiffened. *What a sicko.* "And the other time of

260

year he visits?" he inquired before they got knee-deep in questions about Stacey and the thread got dropped. Always best to be thorough, and Veronica had said Joel came twice a year.

"Christmas," she said. "He comes the twenty-fourth and leaves the twenty-sixth. But I suppose at least he comes. Most folks here have no one at all at Christmastime. No one even brings them a gift." She shook her head. "Shame on their family members. It's not right. After all the work we do raising them, they just ignore us as we get older. At least Joel comes twice a year."

"Is Joel your only child?"

"Yes."

So that aspect of the profile had been correct.

"Is Joel married?" He'd hoped not, for a myriad of reasons.

"No. He never married. Poor thing. He was going to propose, and then Stacey went missing. He was heartbroken."

"He told you he was going to propose?"

"Yes. He begged me to give him my mother's ring, but he came back that night and was never quite the same. Stacey went missing a few days later." She clutched her bony fingers together, wringing her hands. "I tried talking to him, but when pressed, he just said she never showed up for their date the night he planned to propose." She sniffed and rolled her eyes in disdain. "Of course, I knew that was not the case. He was heartbroken over her disappearance. Most assumed something bad happened to her, but I think she ran off with the man she was seeing behind Joel's back."

"Stacey was cheating on him?"

"He didn't know, but I did."

Griffin was a bit afraid to ask how, but it was crucial information. "How did you know?"

"We come from money." Veronica smiled. "Lots of it. When I realized Joel was getting serious about Stacey, I had someone keep tabs on her."

"Someone?"

"Yes, Albert. He is our estate manager and serves a variety of essential duties."

"And he saw Stacey with another man?" Finley asked.

"Oh, yes. Intimately with another man."

"Did you tell Joel?" Griffin asked.

Veronica's hand shifted to her purple blouse as she clutched the linen fabric. "Oh no. I would never harm him like that."

"But weren't you concerned about him marrying her?" Finley asked, his wife's thoughts no doubt mirroring his own. Was it possible the mother had Stacey removed from their lives?

"Albert reported that Stacey actually had shown up the night Joel planned to propose. She turned him down, of course, so I decided not to hurt him further by telling him about the other man. But, honestly, I couldn't blame her."

Griffin tried not to gape. She didn't blame

Stacey for cheating on her son? "Why's that?"

"Because she and I were very much alike. Joel didn't deserve her."

This woman was beautiful on the outside, but absolutely cruel on the inside.

"Did he date again?" Finley asked. "I mean, did he recover?"

"Oh yes. He dated here and there, but to this day, I don't think he's had another serious girlfriend. Then again, his work consumes him."

And his murders.

"It seems we've gotten off track," Veronica said, patting her styled gray hair. "As I was saying, at least Joel visits and brings gifts for my birthday and at Christmas. They are never worthwhile, but he rarely does much that is."

Definitely overbearing.

"That must have been hard as a mother," Finley said, "having a son who didn't excel."

"Goodness knows I tried. Hired him the best tutors. Sent him to the best schools, but he was just like his father—mediocre."

"How terrible for you," Finley said, knowing how to play the interrogation game, how to get to the heart of people, even if it was an ugly heart down deep. She had a way of encouraging them to share what mattered most.

Veronica sighed. "It certainly wasn't easy being surrounded by those who couldn't rise up to the privilege afforded me."

263

Finley tilted her head. "The privilege?"

Veronica reached across the space separating them and placed her age-spotted hand on Finley's for a moment. "The money, dear. I came from it. Not my husband. I came from a family with a grand heritage of accomplishment."

"How nice for you."

"It was a marvelous upbringing. We had the best of everything. We *were* the best. But Howard, Joel's father . . ." She rolled her eyes, not even bothering to refer to him as her husband. "Fool that I was, I married him for love—or what a silly seventeen-year-old girl thought was love—but he turned out to be nothing but a disappointment."

"And Joel?" Finley asked.

"Ha!" Veronica released an amused exhale. "He was even worse. Oh, he put in the work. Got decent grades. Worked while he was in college—as a travel agent, of all things. He dreamed of traveling. That was his problem. He was a daydreamer rather than a doer. Then he met Stacey Marsden and everything shifted. He became distracted and obsessed."

Griffin arched a brow. "Obsessed?"

"He needed to be with her every moment. Followed her around like a dog. It was ridiculous. Be a man, I say."

"And Stacey? I take it she didn't like all the attention?" Finley said.

"How could she? She was a lovely girl. Smart.

Talented. I would have loved having her as a daughter-in-law, but even her influence on Joel wasn't enough to bring him up to our level."

"Our?"

"Stacey's and mine." Veronica shifted, lifting her teacup she'd ignored until then. "As I said, we were very much alike."

And one day Joel snapped and decided he didn't want to be looked down upon or bossed around by an overbearing mother, let alone a girlfriend—one who Griffin bet he'd discovered was cheating on him. Question was, where did he kill her and what had he done with her body?

"Mrs. Hood," he said, scooching forward.

"Veronica, please."

He nodded with a smile. "Veronica. Do you know if there was someplace special he liked to take Stacey? A barn, perhaps?"

"The barn?" she laughed. "Why would he ever take her to that old place?"

Griffin looked at Finley, then back to Veronica. "What old place?"

"Our family grounds are extensive, and far out on the property there's an old barn where we used to keep horses while my husband was alive. I had no desire to keep those animals after Howard passed, so I sold them, much to Joel's anger, but that boy didn't know what he really wanted or needed. That stupid barn has stood empty ever since."

"How long ago did you sell the horses?"

"Close to twenty years. Howard had a heart attack in his early forties. I wasn't surprised, considering the way he ate and how he never exercised."

"And the barn is still on your property?"

"Yes. Just because my son put me in here doesn't mean I sold the estate. You're welcome to go see it, if you're in the area. Albert is still managing it all for me, and I've left everything to him in my will. At least I can trust he'll take good care of it, unlike Joel. . . ."

She appeared to consider something for a moment. "No, I doubt Stacey ever stepped foot in that rickety old barn. They spent most of their time down at the boathouse and out on the water on one of our boats. They typically chose the rowboat. Though why, when we have so many other options, I don't know. I think, in his feeble mind, Joel thought it romantic. Who knows? Perhaps he thought that stupid barn was romantic too."

A flirtatious smile widened on her wrinkled face. "It did hold nice, soft hay. I imagine to two young people in love . . . or at least Joel was in love. Stacey was too smart for that. She quickly saw Joel wasn't the man she needed. Wasn't really a man at all. More a boy trapped in a man's body."

Ouch. Mom of the Year. But thanks to her,

they'd just discovered Joel's connection to a barn and to water. Now they just needed to politely excuse themselves and head for the Hood estate. And thanks to Veronica Hood, they'd just been given permission to explore.

32

"Go on," Luke said, anxious to hear the rest of David's intel. How had he been assigned to Ebeid all these years and never known the entirety of Ebeid's past when David did? Why hadn't Malcolm read him in to the intel? Or had Malcolm himself not been read in?

"I'm piecing together years of recon and bits of information that I was able to obtain," David said. "I'd wager there's a top-secret file somewhere in the vaults at Langley on all this, but this much I know . . ."

David proceeded to fill them in on Ebeid's past, his relationship with Caroline Ladew, and the discovery of her role as a CIA agent.

"He tracked Caroline down to where she was living under a new alias in South America. He killed her, but he learned after the fact that they had a son who she gave up for adoption. He started searching, but quietly through a third party, and after years of searching, finally discovered that his son—Matthew—had enlisted in the Marines at a young age and was killed overseas by friendly fire within months of graduating from basic training.

"Ebeid's rage toward America grew, and it's rumored he believed the Americans killed

268

Matthew outright and covered it up as 'friendly fire.' I have no idea if he was correct, but I've heard whispers he vowed revenge for Matthew's death. So he moved forward with his plan to punish 'the country of liars and pigs' via terrorist attack—and he plans to do it on the anniversary of his son's death."

"Which is?"

"Two days from now."

Luke sat back, stunned, trying to process it all and wondering why he was never informed of such pivotal information—and why, if David had known all along, he was just now deciding to share.

David looked at Luke. "I'm sorry, friend. I was ordered to remain silent until we had proof Bedan possessed a working dispersal method. Told it wasn't pivotal to your mission."

They seriously felt two days was enough time to combat this level of threat? "How could you not tell me?" Luke asked.

David hung his head. "Orders, my friend. Orders and timing are essential to what we do. You know that."

Luke exhaled, remembering all the information he'd been asked to withhold or to falsely plant over the years. It was part of the life of an agent. A part he could no longer play.

But first he'd make sure Ebeid was stopped.

33

Griffin and Finley drove to the Hood estate located outside of Annapolis proper. Veronica hadn't been exaggerating when she used the term *expansive*. Looking at the map, Griffin estimated the estate covered over one hundred acres. In that area of Maryland, they were talking major money. The wrought-iron entrance gate was locked, and apparently Albert wasn't home, because no one answered when they pressed the call button.

Finley gestured to the ten-foot-high brick wall running along either side of the gate and as far along the property line as they could see. "I doubt a property so vast is completely surrounded by a brick wall."

"Excellent point," Griffin said, and sure enough they found where the brick wall ended and a simple three-rail horse fence began.

Griff glanced down at Finley's red heels. "Might want to grab your tennis shoes out of the trunk before we go trudging about."

"Good idea."

She changed her shoes, and Griffin held out his hand and helped his wife, who wore a coastal blue and crisp white striped dress and purple Treks tennis shoes, climb over the wood fence. She hopped down on the grass, the lawn still surprisingly green and plush considering the time of year and the cool nights they'd been having.

Griffin hated to imagine the cost of maintaining such expansive grounds.

Finley pulled her cobalt blue cardigan tightly about her and buttoned it up as a brisk wind fluttered through the autumn leaves overhead.

"You want my jacket?" he asked, pulling his fleece over his head without waiting for an answer.

"It's not necessary."

"Please humor me," he said, handing it to her. She needed it far more than he did. There was a crisp bite in the air.

"Thanks." She slipped the charcoal gray North Face fleece over her head, the sleeves hanging at least four inches beyond her fingertips.

He smiled as the wind rustled her red hair, so striking in the golden shafts of sunlight streaking through the light cloud coverage. "You look adorable."

She smiled back. "This smells like you," she said, zipping it up and burrowing further in.

"Shall we?" He smiled, loving that he could provide her with comfort.

She nodded, and they headed toward the bay. Having no clue where the barn sat on the property—they'd been hoping to ask Albert— at least they could locate the boathouse by following the shoreline.

Within a half hour, they found it. A beautiful white and Nantucket-blue boathouse, the structure larger than Griffin's oversized three-car garage, where he worked on his refinishing projects.

The motorboat was up on a dry ramp and seal-wrapped for the end of the season, but the rowboat simply sat against the far wall, where one could easily flip it onto the launch ramp and into the greenish-blue bay.

"I can see why this would be a romantic spot," Finley said, looking out across the Chesapeake, small whitecaps occasionally fluttering along the otherwise smooth and still surface.

Griffin opened his mouth to speak as something smacked the back of his head with a pain-searing *thwack.* Then everything went black.

Tanner walked beside Declan as her dad examined the warehouse with Luke.

David strolled methodically, observing, touching with gloved hands. According to Luke, Bedan was nothing if not meticulous. In addition, nearly all the evidence had been cataloged and moved to FBI headquarters, but her dad took time to sit on the high stool where Bedan had no doubt sat while working. David inhaled, exhaled, and tapped the white lacquer countertop. "Still no idea where they moved Bedan to?" he asked Luke.

Luke shook his head. "No. I spoke with

Malcolm before we headed over to see if the Agency has learned anything new, but unfortunately when it comes to Bedan, they still know very little."

"Malcolm." David chuckled. "I haven't heard that name in a long time. How is he?"

"Hard to say," Luke said.

Tanner shifted. At times, most times, Luke spoke just as vaguely as her dad. Perhaps a tool of the trade.

Her father studied Luke for a moment and then asked, "I don't believe you had a chance to respond to my earlier question. *Do* you believe Ebeid had an alternate location ready, or do you think you gained some time while they're trying to regroup?"

Luke shrugged, his hands in his tan pants pockets. "Considering both Bedan and Ebeid's thoroughness and meticulous attention to detail—" Luke sighed, raking a hand through his brown hair—"I fear they had a backup location. And in all honesty, we have to face the possibility that we might not find it in time. We need to focus on determining the deployment locations and intervening before they release the anthrax into the air."

David rubbed his chin. "I agree. You have to plan for that contingency, but let's pray we find the new location so it doesn't come down to the wire."

"We?" Tanner said. Had her father just said *we?* As in, he was planning to join their efforts? She had expected him to declare he was off on another case—posthaste.

Her father's brown eyes fixed on her. "Yes, Tania. I plan to stay and see this through. To be of any help I can."

"So, you're staying?" she asked.

"As long as I'm able, but that depends on my boss."

Before she could react—or most likely overreact—Tanner politely excused herself and moved into the main warehouse storage area, her ballet flats nearly silent as she walked along the concrete floor.

Her chest constricted. Her dad in her life, daily, after all this time.

Declan's footfalls echoed behind her, the soles of his loafers tamping along the floor. He wrapped his arms around her from behind, engulfing her in the big bear hug she loved so much, and rested his head on her right shoulder, nuzzling his cheek against hers. "You okay with this? With your dad staying on with the team?"

"I don't have a choice." It was nice in some ways to see her dad, but in others, it only brought hard memories of her childhood flooding back.

"I know." Declan sighed. "And I'm sorry, but on the plus side, it appears he has a lot of intel to offer."

"Yeah." She swiped the moisture from her eyes.

"Hey." He squeezed her tighter. "I'll walk right beside you through whatever his being here brings."

She leaned her head against his strong chest, his muscular arms and six-foot-three solid frame making her feel safe, protected, and most importantly, loved. A line from her favorite psalm floated through her mind.

"He will cover you with his feathers, and under his wings you will find refuge."

Declan had her, but even more importantly, *God* had her, and her Savior would never let go.

Calm settled in her soul as she reflected on God's presence and protection in her life. She wished her parents knew Jesus. After she became a Christian, she'd tried sharing the abundant, overflowing joy she was experiencing as a new creation in Christ, but her parents had only attempted to shame her for leaving her Jewish faith behind. By believing in Jesus and His truth, she'd severed the threadbare string that had connected her to her parents. And they'd effectively disowned her.

It'd been a decade since she'd seen them, and now her father—her stern, secretive father—was here in her space, in her life. And his stoic demeanor indicated his hard heart hadn't softened much in their years apart.

Deliberate footsteps sounded behind them, and

then her dad stood before them. After pressing a kiss to her temple, Declan straightened and moved to clasp her hand, interlocking their fingers.

"May I have a word with my daughter?" her dad asked.

At least he still acknowledged she was his daughter, though he hardly treated her as such.

Declan looked to her and lifted his brows.

She nodded in affirmation, unable to stem the curiosity of what her dad wanted—would it be another chastisement or lecture this time?

Either way, she'd stop it in its tracks.

"Thank you," her dad said as Declan excused himself, giving Tanner's hand a reassuring squeeze before leaving.

"I'll just be in the kitchen," he said, assuring her he'd be within earshot if she needed him.

Her dad slid his hands into his trouser pockets, watching as Declan walked away. "He's quite protective of you."

"Yes, he is." But in a respectful, loving, supportive way—so unlike her dad's authoritative and controlling protection.

"You two are serious?" her dad asked, gesturing back toward Declan's retreating form.

She couldn't believe her father was taking an interest in her life. Or perhaps he was just assessing the situation as he always did—trying to determine the dynamics of the relationships of those around him, and summing people up.

"Yes," she said.

"I see." He rocked back on his heels.

She waited for him to condemn her. Declan was far from Jewish.

"He appears to be a good man."

She gaped at him. Had he just given a sign of approval for a choice in her life?

"Does he take care of you, treat you well?" he asked, shuffling his feet.

She narrowed her eyes. Was her dad *nervous?*

"Yes, he does, but I also know—"

"How to take care of yourself," he finished for her.

And for that, she had to give him credit. Being the only child of a Mossad agent, she'd been taught self-defense and combat skills from a young age. She'd always assumed it was because he wanted a son . . . but perhaps, *just perhaps,* he'd worked her so hard because he loved her?

He'd never showed signs of affection, but maybe he felt them all the same, or maybe she was reading far more into his questions than existed.

"Yes. You taught me well," she finally said.

"You were a spirited learner, a fierce fighter for such a little thing."

"I didn't have a choice." He had trained her every day he was home, save the Sabbath—and instructed her to practice two hours a day every day, save the Sabbath.

"I wanted to make you strong."

And I wanted to be loved.

"You always had such a soft heart," he continued.

"That's not a weakness."

He frowned. "You believe I viewed it as one?"

"You said I was little, gentle—that I needed to learn to be strong."

"Yes. You were already gentle. I wanted you to be strong too. To be both strong and gentle."

"What?" Shock radiated through her. Was he actually saying he approved of her gentle side?

"I knew the tender heart you possessed, and if not paired with the skills I taught you, I knew if my enemies ever got a hold of you . . ." His jaw tensed.

"But I thought . . ."

"Thought what, Tania?"

That you didn't love me. "That I was weak."

"No, weak and gentle are two very different things. Gentle has its own strength, but gentle, unfortunately, does not protect you from enemies." He shook his head and his features softened. "You were so tiny when you were born. I held you in the palm of my hand, your legs resting along my forearm. I knew when I looked in your beautiful brown eyes you were spirited, and I knew it would serve you well."

Tanner stood rooted in place, speechless. Her father viewed her so differently than she'd believed all these years, but why had he waited so long to say so?

"Everything okay?" Declan called, popping his head around the kitchen doorframe.

She smiled. "Just fine."

Declan nodded and ducked back into the galley-style kitchen.

Her dad chuckled. "I see he takes very good care of you, and I'm sure you do the same for him." He put a hand on her shoulder and squeezed gently. "Go to him, my Tania. We will have more time to talk."

Tanner just stared as the dad she was beginning to realize she had never really known smiled warmly at her and walked away.

"How'd it go?" Declan asked as she moved into the kitchen.

"Very different than I anticipated."

"Oh?" Declan's brows arched as a smile curled on his lips. "He finally saw the beautiful, strong, passionate woman I get the honor of seeing every day?"

She loved this man with her whole heart.

"Sorry to interrupt"—Luke stood in the doorway—"but Malcolm's here with some news."

34

Luke watched Malcolm join the group, and particularly observed how Malcolm greeted David with reserved appraisal.

David's cell rang. "Excuse me," he said. "I need to take this."

Luke nodded as David left the room.

Malcolm cleared his throat, directing his full attention at Luke. "Can we speak privately?"

Luke nodded. "Of course."

The two moved into what had been Bedan's living room.

"I understand David told you about Jennifer McLean."

"Who? Oh, you mean Caroline Ladew? You knew?"

"Not until very recently."

"And you didn't feel I needed to be read into the situation?"

"The cause for Ebeid's hatred of America isn't pertinent to stopping him."

"No, but the date of the attack sure is."

"I don't get to choose what I get read into or when."

"What if David hadn't come?"

"Then I assume we would have been notified before the time came, but the focus needs to remain on finding them *before* the attack date. You're obviously close. You found this warehouse. You're right on Ebeid's heels, and Langley knows that. You've never failed to come through, and the higher-ups know that as w—" Malcolm stopped short, his penetrating gaze shifting just beyond Luke's right shoulder.

Chanel No. 5.

Without hesitation, Luke spun around, low to the ground, kicking Lauren's feet out from under her.

She fired but missed. Not like her, unless . . .

"Malcolm?"

No response, but he couldn't take his eyes off Lauren until she was unarmed and subdued.

Heavy footfalls rushed toward them.

"Stay back!" Luke hollered as he wrestled with Lauren, both fighting for control of her gun.

Declan entered, gun drawn, followed closely by Kate.

Lauren kneed Luke below the belt and rolled over, firing an instant after Declan leapt behind a metal column.

The bullet pierced the aluminum, and Luke feared his friend had been shot through the slender column, but he took the small tactile advantage he had with Lauren on her stomach, momentarily faced away from him, and flung himself on her back, gun drawn, muzzle flush with the back of her head.

"Drop your weapon," he ordered.

"Never!" Her fingers slid for the trigger, and a nanosecond into her squeeze, he did what he had to do and pulled his trigger.

Tanner, running in, gasped.

Luke moved off Lauren's limp body, moving the gun now loose in her hand.

Concern flared through him. *Malcolm.*

He spun around to find him laid out on the floor, a bullet wound to his chest.

"He's not breathing," Tanner said, rushing forward and commencing CPR.

Luke called in the crisis code, and while Tanner worked from the right, he knelt by Malcolm's left side, willing him to breathe.

The *whoosh* of a helicopter's blades whirred overhead, growing louder as it came closer.

A specialized team moved in and, within a matter of minutes, Malcolm was onboard the helicopter en route to shock trauma.

Both FBI and CIA agents flooded the building in streams.

One of the medics checked Lauren's vitals, but Luke had called it. The check was in vain. Lauren Graham was dead.

Griffin woke to a thunderclap of headache. He lifted his aching head but discovered his hands were cuffed behind his back, his legs duct-taped around the wooden rail-back chair he was restrained in.

He blinked, the space dim except for shafts of light flooding through the second-story window.

Panic ricocheted through him. *Finley.*

He scanned the space and attempted to shout her name, but duct tape covered his mouth too.

"Look who's finally coming to." Joel Hood moved in front of him and revealed Finley secured in a similar fashion to a chair thirty feet away at his ten.

Tears streamed down her face, and a thin bloody streak ran the length of the left side of her neck.

Griffin yanked against his restraints, trying to break free, but Joel only laughed.

"Don't worry. I waited to start the real fun until you were awake to watch."

He strode to a table with a black leather roll case laid out, displaying the knives, razors, and other tools of destruction it held. He fingered the instruments, his demented mind apparently carefully considering which to use.

"Outside your hotel room in Houston . . . that was me. The rose was placed by a man I utilize occasionally when I want to send a message, but I digress. When I stood watching you that night, contemplating what to do, I considered killing you quickly and then having my way with your wife. But I think it's far more profound and painful this way, don't you think?" He slid a serrated blade from the leather case.

Griffin would get out of this. He had to. He just needed to come up with a plan.

Joel stalked toward Finley, and horror riddled through Griffin's veins.

"Now, it's no fun if you can't hear the punishing you're inflicting." He ripped the duct tape from Finley's mouth, her lips and skin red and raw. "And trust me," he said, moving for Griffin, "out here, it's actually true—no one can hear you scream." He chuckled.

Joel Hood was truly demented.

Following suit, he ripped Griffin's duct tape from his mouth. It burned, but at least now he could wage a battle.

"Not even Albert, who should be back on the property soon?"

"Albert," Joel said, twisting the blade back and forth, watching the light streaming through the upper loft windows and reflecting off the steel with a glint. "This barn is too far from the house for anyone to hear." He smiled wickedly. "Trust me, both Stacey and your sister discovered that in the most exquisitely painful way."

Griffin lunged forward so fast and hard he split the duct tape around his torso.

"Whoa!" Joel laughed, jumping back with a mocking grin. "Aren't we the fierce one? No matter. You'll never break those cuffs."

Perhaps not, but he knew how to get out of them—a trick Parker had taught them all back in college while they were criminal justice majors. He just had to dislocate his thumb and his hand would slide right out. It took a bit of maneuvering and a fair amount of pain, but he'd done it before.

Joel circled Finley like a lion circling its prey and then leaned over her shoulder, holding the knife blade to the right side of her neck. "So you paid Mother a visit today. I should thank you. It turned out to be a highly valuable interaction. One in which I learned several things—such as the need to dispose of Albert. I took care of that, but with you two on the way, I was forced to rush my work, which I loathe doing. I mean, where's the fun and craftsmanship in that? But no matter, I'll make up for that now."

How did Joel know the details of their conversation with his mother? Did he have her place bugged? Had he been hidden somewhere in the room or nearby? It wasn't worth asking, because after Griffin got loose, it wouldn't matter. Joel Hood would finally be behind bars, where the monster belonged.

Joel rhythmically slid the flat face of the blade along Finley's ivory neck.

Griffin's fists tightened. He was going to kill him. He swallowed and refocused. He needed to mess with Joel's head until he managed to dislocate his thumb or, better yet, thumbs. "Why'd you start killing? All because some girl cheated on you?" he asked, working to pop his thumb out of joint.

Joel's face reddened as he moved toward Griffin. But Griffin's moment was coming, and with one more pop of his thumb, he'd be ready.

Joel bent, his face so close to Griffin's he could smell garlic and onion on the man's vile breath. "Trust me, I shifted the power over that witch into *my* hands, where it still resides and forever will."

Griffin shifted. "What do you mean *still?*" He wasn't seriously suggesting Stacey was still alive?

"I mean she's locked in a watery grave that I control. She'll never be free—not even in death."

The boathouse. He'd buried Stacey under the water and somehow restrained her there.

Joel stepped away before Griffin could lunge. "I'd put your wife there when I'm finished with her, but that spot is reserved for Stacey. The rest are simply trash to be dumped."

"In water?"

Joel nodded. "Sometimes they wash up on shore like the refuse they are, and other times they remain below."

"How many, Joel?"

He pointed the tip of the blade in Finley's direction. "Your wife will be an even dozen. But don't worry—she won't be the last. There are so many women out there deserving punishment, and I track them down, making them pay for their actions."

"Punishment for cheating on their boyfriends, or sneaking out to meet them, like Stacey did?" Griffin got his other thumb popped out of joint and silently slid out both hands, one after the other, then fisted the cuffs in his left hand, leaving them behind his back until the right moment. "Let me guess, you caught her sneaking out one night to rendezvous with her lover?"

Joel rushed at him, blade lifted. "Don't ever call him that."

"It's true, isn't it?"

Joel paced back and forth with marked agitation. "Stacey was a betrayer. They're all betrayers."

"Not Finley. She's never betrayed anyone. She doesn't deserve to be punished." He watched his wife lean closer to the table of weapons—she was going to try to grab one, try to work her cuffs free.

"She's just going to have to be for fun, for pleasure, plain and simple," Joel said. "It's not like I can let either of you go."

"People know. My partner knows. My boss knows," Griffin said.

"That was a mistake," Joel said. "Perhaps you deserve to be punished too." He stalked toward Griffin and bent over him, and Griffin took that opportune moment to swing a right hook with full force into Joel's face, so hard he knocked Joel back onto the ground, dazed but not unconscious.

He unwound the duct tape around his legs and stood, slamming Joel with the chair as he attempted to scramble to his feet. The chair shattered, wood splintering around them. Joel still struggled, swiping at Griffin frantically with the blade.

Griffin punched him in his neck—not hard enough to break his windpipe and kill him, but enough that he was gasping for air.

Grabbing the knife from Joel's shaking hand, Griffin moved to free Finley, who kept her gaze fixed on Joel to make sure he stayed down while Griffin freed her.

"He put our phones and your gun in the trough over there." She indicated the wooden feedbox with a tilt of her head.

Anger surged as blood dripped on his hand from his wife's neck. The desire to choke Joel was fierce, but vengeance was God's.

"I'll hold him with a knife," he instructed Finley once she was free of her restraints, "while you get my gun."

She nodded and retrieved his weapon, which he then held at the edge of Joel's perspiring forehead while Finley dialed 9-1-1 and cuffed him.

Griffin read Joel his rights, and within fifteen minutes police swarmed the barn, hauling Joel to his feet.

Griffin wrapped his arms around his wife, kissing her quickly before the paramedics set to work.

He sat beside her on the back of the ambulance as a dive team arrived to search under the boathouse for Stacey's remains. Not only did they find her remains fettered to the underwater portion of one of the pilings, but they found a rope leading to a metal, waterproof box that, when they lifted it from the water and busted it open, revealed eleven victims' mementos.

Griffin swallowed, slid a pair of gloves on, and lifted Jenna's heart-shaped locket, clutching it tightly in his hand.

We got him, honey. We finally got him.

35

The gang finally headed back to CCI in Declan's Suburban—Lauren's body having been removed from the scene by the ME while Malcolm was transported to shock trauma, and David surprisingly on his way back to Israel sooner than anticipated.

His boss called him home after a discussion with "a contact" in the Agency "looking to protect their asset from a possible terrorist attack on U.S. soil." It had clearly been Malcolm's, or possibly even Lauren's, way of removing David from the picture before either arrived at the warehouse today. Whoever had made the call, it had worked, and David was on his way home.

A crew was still in place processing the warehouse, but their group needed to keep their focus on stopping Bedan and Ebeid. The weight of all that had occurred hung heavy and thick in the enclosed space of the car.

Luke glanced out the window, the sky overhead dim and gray. They passed warehouse grouping after grouping. He shifted in his seat. Could it be that simple? *One way to find out*. "There are a ton of warehouses in this area, and Ebeid and his crew had an awful lot to move before you raided the other warehouse. Something tells me they didn't move far."

"You really think Ebeid's backup warehouse would be close?" Declan asked, clutching the wheel.

"It's the last place we'd think to look."

"True," Declan said. "And they most certainly need to be using another warehouse just based on the space and storage they require. Most of the warehouses in this area are empty."

"So let's check the ones that aren't," Luke said, clasping the back of Declan's seat. "Have a satellite pass over the area and note the warehouses in use."

"Smart, Luke," Declan said. "There can only be a handful."

Declan called in the request, and well before they could make it back to CCI, they were rerouting back to three occupied warehouses in the same general vicinity as the first, just on the other side of the water.

Luke unfolded a copy of the page filled with scientific notations and Bedan's shorthand they'd found at the first warehouse, smoothing it out to study it. Might as well do something useful while riding back to the warehouse district.

"Bedan was definitely working out the needed equations to stabilize anthrax into an aerosolized form," Luke said. But the side notations—in a form of shorthand he'd matched to lecture notes of Bedan's that were still available online via Hanover Medical School—frighteningly enough indicated that Bedan was dabbling with also mixing a few grams of plutonium dust in with the anthrax.

But to what purpose?

"Radiation," he said suddenly.

"What?" Declan frowned in the rearview mirror.

Luke took a moment to explain his findings and went on to lay it out as he saw it happening. "Plutonium dust is heavier and wouldn't travel as far as the anthrax spores, but think of the logistical nightmare it would cause when emergency response teams try to go in to treat the people exposed to anthrax. They would need proper radiation gear and it would delay response time and allow the anthrax to spread farther." Luke went still. "We've got to find that warehouse."

"Pulling up to the first one now," Declan said.

"But wait," Kate said. "How would emergency personnel know radiation was part of the equation? Radiation sickness takes time for its effects to become identifiablc."

A frightening thought crossed Luke's mind. "Maybe this paper was left behind on purpose."

Declan turned to look at him like he was crazy. "What?"

"If we figure out Bedan is mixing the anthrax with plutonium dust, then we'll clearly warn emergency personnel."

"So Bedan is using us to delay a response time and give his anthrax longer to spread and infect," Declan said with shock resonating in his tone.

Luke exhaled. "I certainly fear that could be the case."

The sun was midway down in the sky as they approached the third and final warehouse in the district. The first warehouse had been a drug bust, and DEA was now in charge of that raid. The second warehouse was home to a group of hackers. Not the good kind, like Kate, but rather the very dangerous kind—criminals extorting money from people, hacking bank accounts, stealing funds, and inputting viruses into mega corporations for a high fee from their competitors. Kate was currently working in conjunction with the cybersecurity unit of the FBI on that raid.

Vehicles were parked out front at the last possible warehouse, and the last SAT photo they received over Declan's phone showed three white trucks like the ones Hank had lent out parked by the loading docks.

Hope filled Luke. This might finally be it and, if so, he was uber thankful Kate was surrounded by a unit of federal agents and happily occupied with busting the hackers, because he had zero doubt that if they were in fact at Bedan and

Ebeid's warehouse, the raid would not be without casualties.

Federal Agent Tim Barrows and Declan lay on either side of Luke on the rooftop of the warehouse next to the one in question.

"Well?" Declan said.

"Thermal imaging shows at least a couple dozen warm bodies inside—all near the trucks on the back end of the warehouse."

Luke stood and moved for the fire escape, which was the fastest route to the ground.

"Hang on," Declan said. "With anthrax and possible plutonium in there, we can't enter without hazmat gear. The full team and SWAT are on the way. We just have to wait. They have the gear we need."

"No time," Luke said, proceeding to the fire escape.

"What are you doing?"

"Going in."

Declan shook his head. "It's not safe."

Ignoring his friend's warnings, Luke moved with gun in hand toward the northwest door, where no heat signatures had been detected. It appeared to be the safest way in, though, knowing Ebeid and Bedan, the warehouse was likely rigged with booby traps. Inhaling a strong, steadying breath and puffing it out, he picked the lock and opened the door as a shrill alarm sounded.

They knew he was here.

The alarm screamed overhead. Someone was inside the warehouse with them, and Khaled was certain it was Garrett Beck.

He reached over, grabbed his laptop, and pulled up the security camera feed, only to confirm his suspicions.

It had been almost seven years since he first saw that face—so like his son's. Young, idyllic, believing in the country he was serving. How futile and pathetic. If Garrett Beck only knew the truth, if only Allah opened his eyes to true understanding and he could see how his country was using him, just like it had used his son, Matthew.

Matthew Ladew was adopted days after his birth and his name changed to Matthew Sullivan. Caroline hadn't even given Khaled the courtesy of gifting their son with *his* last name, though considering she'd never bothered to inform him that they'd had a son that wasn't surprising.

Matthew had grown up to serve as a U.S. Marine and had died shortly after graduating boot camp and being deployed to Afghanistan. Authorities had called it "friendly fire," but Khaled doubted there was anything friendly about it. In his mind, someone must have discovered Khaled was his biological father and ordered someone to take out his son.

Anger flared through his limbs, searing up through his lungs. He would not allow Garrett

Beck or the country that had misused him and his son to stop his retribution. Matthew deserved better. It was why Khaled was in the United States, why he'd chosen Baltimore as his home base. After Caroline had given Matthew up for adoption, he'd been raised in Baltimore before joining the Marines.

Bedan raced around the corner of Khaled's office, sweat beading his brow. "Someone is here."

"It's Garrett Beck."

Bedan swallowed. "But the shipments. Only one has left. The rest aren't fully loaded yet."

"We'll get them off. Don't worry."

Khaled silenced and rearmed the alarm so it would sound again if anyone else entered the building.

"How do we get out of here?" Bedan asked.

"Go gather your things and meet me back here. Don't worry. You'll be well taken care of." Just as his predecessor, Dr. Kemel, had been.

No loose ends.

Khaled loaded his gun, clicking the magazine into place. "I'll take care of Beck myself."

Bedan nodded and rushed off.

He actually believed him. *Such a fool*. A brilliant fool, though. He'd created his masterpiece. It was finally complete and working. Bedan's role had been served. There was no further use for him.

Khaled exhaled his wrath for Garrett Beck and

stood, knowing the safeguards he'd put in place would buy him the time he needed to escape and for the other three trucks to set off for their destinations before Beck could stop them. He'd be too late, and it would cost him—and those he loved—their lives.

Striding to the rear office door, he punched in the code, opened the door, switched on the tunnel lights, and closed the door behind him. Moving quickly through the drafty underground tunnel, he hurried his way to safety and his waiting vehicle.

Luke carefully avoided the trip wire an inch inside the warehouse door. It was impressive that Ebeid had planned for unwanted visitors even at the secondary warehouse. Impressive, but sick.

Luke shook his head. *A trip wire?* That was so cliché. He'd have thought men of Ebeid's and Bedan's brilliance—disturbingly applied as that intelligence may be—could have come up with something more innovative.

He took another step in, realizing it had been rash and even a bit reckless for him not to wait to get properly suited up in hazmat gear, but as long as he didn't enter the lab, he should be okay.

"We're in gear and moving in," Declan said over Luke's comm.

Before Luke could respond, the alarm rang around him. It was odd working with a team.

He'd always worked solo, or occasionally with a small tactical unit like the one Lauren had run. But certainly not on a full federal team like this.

"Watch out for booby traps," Luke said. "This place is seriously—"

An explosion—small and contained, but unfortunately lethal for the agent who hadn't heeded his instruction—sounded throughout the warehouse.

". . . rigged," Luke finished his sentence.

36

He should have known there was a reason the heat signatures were all in one quadrant. He knew Ebeid too well to fall for the man's trap, but he'd been acting on instinct and adrenaline. If he'd stopped to think it through . . .

But it was too late now. At least they were in, and while losing an agent was awful, so far it had just been one casualty. Who knew how many would have been killed if they'd attempted to waltz in the warehouse front door. Knowing Ebeid, there was probably a rocket launcher aimed and ready for anyone foolish enough to try that approach. Ebeid was not a man to trifle with.

Declan approached Luke from his six, and he turned to greet Declan, Tanner, and Tim Barrows, who were following close behind.

"Ebeid knows we're here. Let's move."

According to Declan, SWAT now had the place surrounded. No more trucks could leave, but one had already gotten away. Now they needed to ensure that Ebeid and Bedan did not.

Rushing across the next open expanse, a flare of warning shot through Luke, and he jarred Declan back, but Tim didn't heed his halting signal, barreling forward as swiftly as he could until something clicked beneath his boot.

"Duck!" Luke hollered, lunging with Declan and Tanner behind an old conveyer belt base as the modified claymore mine shot projectiles with voracious power in all directions. All around them, agents dropped to the ground.

Something pierced Luke's leg with splintering force, and once the arsenal of screws, ball bearings, and who knew what else finally ceased, they had a handful of agents down and in need of serious medical attention, but it was too late for Tim. He'd taken too many hits in too many vital places and was already gone.

Tanner swallowed back tears, her face reddening, clearly trying to contain the over-whelming sadness battling to break loose. She shifted her weight and coughed back what Luke could only assume was a sob.

Declan wrapped her in his arms, sheltering her for a moment as he called it in that they had agents down. He looked over Tanner's bent head at Luke's bleeding thigh. "You've got a screw sticking out of your leg."

"I'm aware. It's okay. Missed the femoral artery." *Thankfully.* He ripped a length off the bottom of his shirt and, bracing his weight against the wall, with a grunt and extreme shot of blistering pain yanked the screw out and quickly wrapped the length of cloth tightly around the wound. It hadn't hit the artery, but he was still bleeding at a decent clip.

"You okay, man?" Declan asked, his expression mirroring Luke's pulsating pain.

He nodded. *Man alive, that one hurt.* "I'll be fine. We need to keep moving."

"We're with you," Declan said, and the uninjured members of the team moved forward, entering a maze of nearly ceiling-high wooden shelves filled with decrepit grain sacks and wooden crates. The old factory's storage room.

Stacked crates littered the floor between rows, the entire room a well-crafted maze, no doubt Ebeid's doing.

Where was the door to the interior portion of the warehouse?

Cautiously, Luke scanned the perimeter surrounding them with each step. He led the team slowly through the maze, his chest tight, blood seeping warm down his left leg.

A rifle leaning against the metal shelves looked out of place. An agent moved to lift it just as Luke waved him off, but not fast enough. Another click. Another explosion. This one knocked the wind from Luke's lungs as he slammed against the concrete floor, flames searing the heels of his boots.

"Everyone okay?" Declan asked over the comms. "Check in."

Names filed through, some missing based on Declan's further call-outs.

Tactical medics moved in as the uninjured

301

agents managed to push forward, finally reaching the other side.

Bruised, bloodied, and in a lot of pain, the team made it to the main working area of the warehouse, where they were instantly met with gunfire.

Returning fire, they pushed their line slowly forward until they'd taken down the dozen or so men in the room, knowing another dozen probably lurked somewhere.

Declan signaled a group to move for the loading docks.

Luke indicated he was headed for the location that appeared to be Bedan's lab and living space. He wanted Ebeid and Bedan.

Declan nodded and alerted his men over the comms that he and Tanner were accompanying Luke, but that they were to take full control of the warehouse. Confirmation came back, and Declan and Tanner followed Luke through the makeshift living space that had been erected for Bedan.

Luke indicated for Declan and Tanner to move for the lab and Bedan. He was going after Ebeid, who no doubt had an office in the building. This project was the man's baby. He would be remaining close, especially after the first warehouse raid. Unless he'd already found his way out.

Luke prayed he wasn't too late.

The feds were coming, and Ebeid was nowhere to be found. Although, after how Ebeid had taken care of his predecessor, Isaiah Bedan wasn't surprised this would be his fate. However, unlike Kemel, he'd prepared for this possibility.

Ebeid's office door kicked in, and CIA field agent Garrett Beck stood before him—bleeding, his left thigh wrapped, blood staining his pants. Scorch marks marred his shirt, his face bruised. His gaze darted around the office. "Where is Ebcid?"

"Gone," Isaiah said on an exhale, knowing the fate that awaited him, but it was a fate *he* was in control of. He would have his say, make sure they understood the magnificence of his genius and creation.

Luke moved around the room, looking for something, no doubt trying to discern how Ebeid had managed to escape.

Isaiah had been wondering the very same thing ever since he returned to find Ebeid's office empty.

Luke moved to the security panel on the wall, then slid his hands across it. He grunted and called for someone to come blow a door.

A door? Ebeid had a secret door out? Of course he did.

Within minutes, Bedan was handcuffed, hauled to his feet, and the security panel was being overridden instead of the door blown. It worked, and a door hidden along the wall slid open, revealing a tunnel—a tunnel Ebeid could have easily taken him down too. All loyalty to Ebeid died as Isaiah stared down the lit path the traitorous man had taken without him.

Fury and frustration whirred inside Luke. Ebeid had eluded him *again*.

"Figure out where this tunnel comes out," he instructed two of the team members. "But watch out for more booby traps."

They nodded and set off down the tunnel.

"I'm sorry," Declan said, entering with Tanner. "You'll get him."

Anger heated Luke's body at the realization he'd once again lost Ebeid.

He turned his wrath toward Bedan.

"We're going to have a talk."

Bedan's Adam's apple bobbed in his throat.

37

Luke and Declan entered the interrogation room that held Bedan. Luke had been informed the warehouse's tunnel came out nearly a mile away. Ebeid no doubt had a car waiting and was now in the wind. Teams were combing Ebeid's home and office at the Islamic Cultural Institute of the Mid-Atlantic, but there was no sign of him.

Luke's injured leg throbbed, every nerve ending on fire, his whole being screaming to find Ebeid. They also needed to discover where the one missing truck was headed.

The three trucks that had been onsite when they'd arrived had been stopped before they could pull away, the drivers and guards now in custody and being questioned by Tanner. They'd then be questioned by Luke and Declan until put behind bars.

They needed to crack someone because they needed to know where the fourth truck was headed. Declan had put out an APB and set up blockades on all roads out of Baltimore, but depending on when the truck had left, it could already be out of the area.

Luke exhaled and kicked back in his chair, trying to give Bedan the impression they had the situation under control. They weren't even close, but Bedan certainly didn't need to know that.

"Where is Ebeid?"

"Fleeing the country, I suppose."

"To where?"

"He didn't say, but he told me *we'd* be long gone before my creation was unleashed."

Luke interlocked his fingers. "Guess he left you behind."

Bedan simply nodded, scribbling on the steno pad they'd provided in case he agreed to write out a confession.

"I suppose it's a better fate than Kemel's."

"Indeed," Bedan said casually.

Too casually.

He'd been searched, patted down, and wanded—and the only things that set off the alarm were his belt buckle and the metal rims of his glasses. He was clean, according to security.

Luke sat forward, resting his arms on the table. "Since he dismissed you so carelessly and left you for us, why protect his destination?"

"I told you. Ebeid did not reveal the details of our getaway."

Luke narrowed his eyes. Bedan was hiding something. "You know more than you are saying."

"Very well, I'll tell you where Ebeid is headed—I have no more loyalty to him—*but* only after I share what I need to."

"Which is?"

"The beauty, intricacy, and genius of the zenith of my career."

"Your anthrax aerosol deployment devices?" Bedan may be brilliant, but he was a nutter.

"Yes," Bedan said, leaning forward, his voice dancing with excitement. "But it is so much more."

Luke bit back what he wanted to say and worked to get the answers he needed. "Please, go on. . . ."

He needed to find Ebeid before the man disappeared for good. They didn't have much time, but it was clear Bedan wasn't going to reveal what he knew before he was ready. Luke could read it in his eyes.

"Do you realize the significance of what I've created?" Bedan asked.

"A deployment device of biological warfare that falls into the *weapons of mass destruction* category?" The man was mad. Didn't he realize the devastation his creation would wreak? The lives that would be lost? And here he was talking as if it were a piece of art.

"Don't you understand? My creation is a thing of beauty."

"Beauty?" Declan laughed. "Are you serious?" He looked to Luke. "Is he serious?"

Luke swallowed. "I'm afraid he is." At least that's how Bedan saw it.

"You're clearly missing the intricacy of what

307

I created, of what no one before was able to accomplish in a working manner."

"Anthrax," Declan said. "And . . . ?"

They wanted Bedan to confirm what they discovered in his notes, to be certain it was in fact plutonium that he'd mixed in.

Bedan's lips twitched, trying to smother a smile. "Why do you think there's anything else?"

"Because we found a page of your notes you left behind at the first warehouse."

"And you understood them? Interesting." Bedan pushed his glasses up the bridge of his nose.

"Those notes indicate you mixed something radioactive with the anthrax," Luke said.

Declan looked over at him, eyes wide.

"You are a smart one, Agent Beck. I like you."

He most definitely wasn't taking that as a compliment. Interesting that the man didn't know his real name. Luke wasn't about to fill him in on the truth. He hoped Ebeid was under that same impression.

"What is it?" Luke pressed, wanting Bedan to clearly state that he'd used plutonium. They needed to be one hundred percent sure what specific threat they were facing, so they could properly combat it.

"Oh, you know a scientist can never give up the details of his masterpiece—not until it's been patented."

Patented? He wanted to patent a biological

weapon of mass destruction? Bedan was beyond mad. Though considering his lineage . . .

"The more you give us, the more we can help you," Declan said.

"Help?" Bedan laughed. "Is that what you call it? Well, thank you . . . Agent Grey, is it? But I don't need your help." He lifted a hand to adjust his glasses. "I've got this covered."

A shot of warning ricocheted through Luke as Bedan's eyes shifted to a look of glorious resignation. He grabbed Declan and yanked him toward the door. "Get out now!"

The guard waiting outside rushed in as Luke and Declan ran out.

"No!" Luke yelled as the door swung shut behind him.

"What on earth?" Declan asked, spinning around to grasp the doorknob.

Luke stilled his hand as they looked through the vertical glass pane in the door to see Bedan and the guard convulsing on the floor, both foaming at their mouths.

"We've got to help him," Declan said, his gaze fixed on the dying guard.

"We're too late, and you need to call hazmat."

Declan did so, then turned to Luke. "How'd you know Bedan was about to do that?"

"I just had a very bad feeling."

Declan rubbed his head. "I can't believe we lost another man and our biggest lead."

And Ebeid's whereabouts. Or so he thought. After hazmat entered the room and determined Bedan had released sarin gas via an ingenious, albeit disturbing, deployment device on his glasses, they quarantined the room. But when they replayed the video footage, Luke saw Bedan scrawl something on the steno pad they'd given him at the start.

He leaned in, narrowing his eyes on the image. "Stop," he told the tech. "Zoom in on that pad."

"It looks like he wrote . . . *Niue*."

He couldn't believe he was thinking this, but . . . *Thank you, Bedan.* He'd given them Ebeid's intended destination.

He looked to Declan.

"I know," Declan said. "Go. I'll find the truck."

Luke nodded and clasped Declan's shoulder before racing down the hall, ignoring the searing pain in his leg.

"Head to BWI. I'll have a jet waiting," Declan hollered to him.

"If you talk to Kate before I can call her, tell her I'll be back—and that I love her," he hollered as he headed for BWI—and Niue of all places.

38

Declan met Tanner as she exited interrogation room three. "Any luck?"

"Not with that one." She looked past him. "Where's Luke?"

"He went after Ebeid."

She frowned. "But one of the trucks got away. We have to assume . . ."

He squeezed her hand. "He knows we can handle it."

"Does Kate know he left?"

"Not yet." That was one conversation he wasn't looking forward to. "Shall we head into interrogation room four?" That room held the guard of the third truck. So far, all the men, according to Tanner, were holding out, believing they were serving a higher purpose, and they were willing to face the death penalty for terrorist actions against the United States, but maybe, just maybe, Declan prayed, they'd get some answers out of the last man.

Lord, we're walking in here as a last hope. We need to know where that truck is headed, and we need to stop it fast. Please help us. We're desperate for your help.

They entered the room and introduced themselves.

"And you are?" Declan asked.

They were still running facial recognition and fingerprints through the system, as none of the men had any identification on them.

The man simply stared back at them.

Tanner asked him again in Malay, and his eyes fluttered.

"You speak Malay?" the man asked.

"Yes, and you speak English."

He nodded.

"I'm Tanner."

"Abdul."

"Abdul," she began, "can you—"

A knock sounded on the door.

"Excuse me." Declan stood, answered, and took the file from the clerk.

"Abdul Megat," Declan said, reading the report they now had on the young man seated across from them. Twenty years old, according to his driver's license. Why had it taken the system so long to find him? He scanned the list of aliases. That's why.

"You're from New Jersey?"

"I'm from Malaysia, but I've lived in New Jersey—"

"Since you were four," Declan said in shock.

Abdul nodded.

"So you've lived pretty much your whole life in our country. A country of which you are an official citizen, and you still plan to aid in the launch of potentially the worst terrorist attack we've incurred?"

Abdul shifted.

Declan narrowed his gaze, *really* studying the man, his body language, his movements. He was different from the rest.

Clearing his throat, he leaned forward. "Abdul, I'm going to go out on a limb here and say you joined up because"—Declan read the list of the other men's names in the file before him—"your older brother, Amin, talked you into it."

He straightened. "Amin doesn't talk me into anything. I am my own man."

"Then *be* your own man. Don't go to death row because you refuse to do what you know in your conscience is right to do."

"My loyalty is to my homeland."

"*This* is your homeland." Declan pounded the table with his fist, shaking the surface, the coffee in his cup sloshing. *Sorry,* he mouthed to Tanner as her coffee sloshed on her white blouse.

She winked back.

Man, he loved her.

He shifted his focus back to Abdul. "I can see you're torn. Do as you said. Be your own man and tell us where that truck is headed, and I'll see you are spared the death penalty."

Abdul swallowed.

"Let us help you," Tanner said.

Abdul shifted, his knees bouncing against

the underside of the table. "If I tell you, you guarantee I won't face the death penalty?"

"You have my word," Declan said.

"Can you put it in writing?" Abdul asked, sweat beading on his brow.

"Absolutely."

Declan rushed through the process as quickly as time would allow before Abdul lost his nerve, but Tanner remained with him the entire time, talking with him, soothing him as Declan watched on the video feed.

He returned and handed Abdul the signed paperwork.

Abdul's dark eyes scanned it, his knees still bouncing, his brow dotted with sweat. He swallowed.

"I held up my end of the deal. You hold up yours." Declan's chest tightened. "Where is that truck headed?"

"Atlanta."

Declan swallowed hard. "Atlanta?"

Abdul nodded. "We were to meet up with fellow brothers-in-arms. Bedan has a friend there. Someone who works somewhere high up. He was going to help us."

Bedan's "in" at the CDC.

"When was deployment set for?"

Abdul's gaze darted about the room as he inhaled, shook out his hands, and then said, "On the anniversary of Ebeid's son's death."

As they suspected. "Matthew?"

Abdul nodded.

"Two days from now?"

Abdul nodded again.

"So all of this is an act of revenge?"

"Yes," Abdul said.

"If you'll excuse me again, I'll be back."

Tanner nodded as Declan exited the room.

Once the door was solidly shut behind him, he bolted down the hall. They needed to intercept that truck before it reached Atlanta.

Or should they find it, follow it, and wait to see who rendezvoused with it? If Bedan had a "friend" at the CDC, they needed to know who it was. Plans shifted in his mind as he rushed for his boss's office.

39

Luke hurried across the tarmac on the far side of BWI to the jet that Declan had waiting. Once inside, he called Kate.

"How's it going? Did you get anything out of Bedan?" she asked. He'd called her on the way into the FBI office to update her.

"Yes. Ebeid's destination."

"Destination? You mean there's only one deployment spot?"

"No." Luke covered his ear to better hear her as the plane engine roared to life.

"What is that?" she asked.

"You still working on the hacker case at the warehouse?"

"Yes. What's the noise on your end?"

The plane began taxiing down the runway. "I don't have much time to talk. I'm on a plane, headed to intercept Ebeid."

"What?"

"He's on the run. I have to find him before he disappears for good."

"What about the attack?"

"Declan's on it."

"You're leaving again?"

Again. That hurt. "Yes, but just until I catch Ebeid."

"The last time you left to catch him, you were gone for more than seven years."

"That's not going to happen again. Trust me."

The plane started its ascent.

"I'm going to lose you in a minute." He prayed it was only over the phone and not permanently, not when he'd just gotten her back. But this was something he had to do. He couldn't let Ebeid get away. "I love you. I'll be back. . . ."

Silence.

"Kate . . . Katie?" The call was gone, but he prayed she wasn't.

Kate excused herself from the warehouse for a moment. Stepping outside, she rounded the corner of the metal frame building, making sure no one was watching before bursting into tears. She understood Luke's need to stop Ebeid. Really, she did.

But last time he'd left, he'd been gone a lifetime.

Sobs wracked her body.

What if he didn't come back?

Declan and Tanner hurried down the ramp to B terminal at BWI, heading for their flight to Atlanta.

The boarding call for their flight was announced over the speakers.

Declan's phone rang. "It's Kate. You go ahead. I'll be right there."

"All right." She pressed a kiss to his cheek.

"Hey, Kate," he answered. "Tell me you've got some good news."

"I've got great news. I found the truck en route to Atlanta. Are you sure you don't want to intercept now?"

"I'm positive. Have them monitored without letting them know they are being followed. I've already talked with the Atlanta Bureau chief. He's got a team ready for us. We'll wait until the truck arrives at its rendezvous spot and nab Bedan's CDC mole."

"It makes me nervous."

"I know, but we can't risk losing the mole. Can you imagine the havoc he could wreak from inside the CDC? As long as we don't lose the truck, we're good."

"I'll see to it."

"Last boarding call for Flight 28 to Atlanta," the attendant announced over the intercom.

"Gotta go."

"Be safe."

"We're going after a truck full of weaponized anthrax and plutonium dust. What could go wrong?"

"Not the time for humor."

"It sounded like you could use a little."

"I'm fine."

"He'll come back, Kate."

"You don't know that."

"I do."

"I wish I had half your confidence. Now go catch your flight."

Luke knew what frustration felt like. It was geography competing with time in a chase where he was behind.

He was headed toward New Zealand, then over to the non-extradition island of Niue, if necessary. With the Bureau's help, Luke had tracked Ebeid's chartered jet to JFK, where Ebeid had boarded Flight 1124 to Guangzhou, China. China wasn't cooperating with flight information, but the airline flying the route from Guangzhou International into Auckland, New Zealand, had one of Ebeid's aliases listed on a first-class ticket. So Ebeid was staying with that planned final destination of Niue. Getting ahead of him was the problem.

Luke pulled strings to get on a flight to Auckland, to see if he could cut him off there. If not, he was heading to Niue, where he'd have to figure something out.

What he wasn't going to do was let Ebeid get away again.

40

Ebeid stepped off the private plane that had just landed in Niue, looking tired, disheveled, and like a man who had been flying halfway around the world. He had changed his appearance at JFK enough that if Luke hadn't seen the security video footage, he might not have recognized him.

The man took a moment to stretch and look around. It was dark outside. Silent. Trees swaying in the warm breeze. There were just their two private planes currently on the tarmac. Ebeid squinted at the sight of Luke's plane, but Luke remained hidden.

Ebeid straightened his shirt collar, rolled his sleeves up to his elbows, and flung his white jacket over his shoulder before striding confidently forward. He believed he'd gotten cleanly away. And he nearly would have if it weren't for Luke's amazing pilot, who'd flown him from Auckland to Niue in record time to get him there moments before Ebeid landed.

With a steadying inhale and a prayer, Luke took *immense* pleasure in stepping out of the shadows and into Ebeid's path, gun aimed at the man's heart.

Ebeid's face paled in the tarmac lights, even paler than the makeup had made him. "You have no jurisdiction here. It's a non-extradition country," he said smugly.

"You're right, but I'm going to get you on that plane back to Auckland," Luke said, pointing at the small plane that had made the three-and-a-half-hour trip in just over three hours thanks to the wickedly skilled pilot, Hauger.

"You'll have to kill me first," Ebeid spat.

"Not a problem." Luke kept his gun aimed at Ebeid's heart "Your choice. Get on my plane or die now."

Ebeid looked back at his pilot, who upon seeing Luke armed, quickly retreated onto his plane and closed the entry door. Ebeid looked to Luke's pilot, but he only waved. Luke was tipping Hauger big time. Luke had spent the three hours, or a good portion of it, explaining Ebeid's depravity and intent for evil. But thanks to a quick call to Declan while switching planes in Auckland, he'd learned Declan, Tanner, and their Atlanta team had stopped the threat. Not only did they have the driver in custody and the anthrax seized, but they were interrogating Bedan's accomplice from the CDC, a scientist by the name of Barak Notauli. An interrogation that Luke bet would last a long while.

"I'm losing my patience," Luke said, having given Ebeid more than a second's reflection. "What's it going to be?"

Defiance washed over Ebeid's face. In a flash, a gun appeared in his hand.

Luke fired, shooting Ebeid in the heart.

Ebeid stumbled back, firing, the bullet hitting Luke in his collarbone.

Staggering backward in blistering pain, Luke fired again, shooting Ebeid in the head.

Ebeid dropped to the ground, his body going limp, the gun slipping to the dirt runway.

It was over. Ebeid was gone.

Relief washed over Luke in a way that he hadn't experienced in over seven years, not since the day he'd let Malcolm recruit him into the Agency.

It was *finally* over.

His head swam and his vision blurred as Hauger rushed toward him.

"You okay, ma—"

41

Parker knelt along the shoreline where Jenna had been found. *Sweet Jenna.* Moonlight illuminated the waves crashing offshore, the sand cool beneath his knees.

He laid down the bouquet of yellow hibiscus, Jenna's favorite, that he'd managed to get imported from the Big Island of Hawaii. It'd been their dream to visit Hawaii. They'd even considered honeymooning there.

He sniffed back the sobs threatening to wrack his body. So many dreams, so much future ahead of them—all gone in the blink of an eye.

When Avery had been shot in front of him at CCI, the intense horror of losing another woman he desperately loved had nearly destroyed him. But it was in that instant that he knew he loved Avery differently than he'd loved Jenna. Not less, or more, but different. What he and Avery shared was deeper—partially because of all they'd been through and partially because they were older. Jenna was and always would be his first love. She would always hold a special place in his heart, and Avery—wonderful woman that she was—respected and honored that. She loved him for it rather than in spite of it.

"You would have liked her, Jen," he said, his

voice cracking. "I'm so glad you can finally rest in peace. We got him. Griffin got the monster who took you away."

Warm tears slipped down his cold cheeks, the late fall air dipping to near freezing.

"I know you're in a better place. I know you're whole and happy and at peace, but I still miss you, *Mo grá*." He hadn't said the Irish phrase for *my love* out loud since Jenna's death, but in his final good-bye, he thought it only fitting. Her killer was behind bars, and it was time to move forward fully with Avery, though doing so would never minimize what he and his *grá* had shared. Jenna had been his love and his treasure. And now she could rest in peace.

Parker stood and turned, shocked to find Griff leaning against his car alongside the road.

"Didn't want to disturb you," Griffin said, pushing off the car and striding toward him with his own bouquet of flowers. So he was saying good-bye too.

Parker stopped a few feet from him, unsure what to say. It seemed wrong to belittle the moment with speech.

"Thank you for loving my sister so much," Griffin said.

Parker swallowed, hard, then nodded, praying more tears didn't fall—not in front of Griff. "I'll leave you to your good-bye."

"It's only good-bye for now."

Parker nodded. "Until heaven."

Griffin smiled softly—the love only a sibling could have welling in his eyes. "Until heaven." He stepped past Parker, then paused and turned. "See you and Avery at CCI?"

"We'll be there."

"About time you put a ring on her finger, isn't it?"

Parker inhaled. Griffin understood his love for Jenna was his past, but Avery was his future. "I couldn't agree more."

"See you in a few."

Parker nodded.

The gang sat down with their Chinese takeout boxes around the coffee table in Kate's office. It'd been an incredibly busy week, but it still hadn't been distraction enough to keep Kate's thoughts off Luke.

Where was he?

Had he left her again?

Would it be another seven years?

Fear trickled inside.

She tried to shake it off by distracting her thoughts, thinking back over all that had happened in the last week. Declan and Tanner's work in Atlanta. Griffin and Finley finding Jenna's killer. Finding and recovering Stacey Marsden's body, the first victim, so she could finally be laid to rest by her family.

Hood would be going away for the rest of his

life. According to Griffin, in an attempt to avoid the death penalty, he'd already admitted to all eleven murders.

Griffin was thrilled about being able to give a sliver of peace to their families—the knowledge that their daughter's killer was finally behind bars. It'd been a long time coming, but he had a new measure of peace, and so did Parker. She could read it on them both.

"Katie, eat something," Parker said.

She grabbed an egg roll and took a bite, then, unable to help herself, looked to the doorway again, only to find it dark and empty. She sighed.

"It'll take time," Declan said, either sensing her angst or catching her hundredth glance at the door. "Luke had to travel far to catch Ebeid."

"Have you heard from him?"

"Not since he landed in Auckland."

"Which means Ebeid could have killed him."

"Or he's got Ebeid in custody and is bringing him home."

"Then why not call?"

"Perhaps he doesn't want to risk calling you with Ebeid in earshot."

"He'll come back," Tanner said. "I'm sure of it."

"I'm glad you are." Because she sure wasn't.

"Sure about what?" Luke asked from the doorway.

Of course, the minute she'd looked away from the door, he appeared. She jumped to her feet and rushed to him, wrapping him in her arms.

He winced.

She pulled back. "What's wrong?"

"Got shot." He pulled his V-neck sweater away from his body, showing her the bandage across his collarbone.

"You're okay?"

"Yep. Nothing a little surgery on a third-world island couldn't fix."

"Ebeid?"

He nodded.

"And he is . . . ?"

"Dead."

Thank you, Lord.

"And you didn't call because?" She'd been waiting a week, beginning to believe the worst.

"I was chasing Ebeid, then out of it from the surgery. . . ."

"And then?" she pressed.

He shrugged, pulling a bouquet of flowers from behind his back. "I thought I'd surprise you."

"*Seriously?* You *really* thought that these were good circumstances to surprise me in?"

He offered a cheesy I-know-I'm-in-deep-trouble smile. "Surprise."

Kate exhaled. "You're lucky I don't shoot you myself."

"You know, I think we ought to be going, Av,"

Parker said to Avery, who had healed remarkably well. She was a fighter too.

"Yeah . . ." Everyone else stood as Avery did, excusing themselves one by one.

"Night," Tanner said before being the last one out the door, leaving Kate and Luke alone.

Tears sprang to her eyes. "I was so worried about you."

Luke pulled her gently into his arms. His chest had to be sore as all get-out. "I'm sorry. I should have called. I was so focused and excited to get back to you, I just kept moving in that direction."

She rested her head on his shoulder. "Is this okay?"

"Better than okay."

She looked up at him. "I'm not hurting you? Or your wound?"

"You could never hurt me, baby. And I promise I will never hurt you again."

"And the Agency?"

"Already put in my resignation."

"Seriously? You have time to call Malcolm, but not to call me?"

"Clearly I messed up. I'm sorry. It's going to take me a while to get the knack for these types of things again."

"I'll be patient," she said, attempting a stern face, "but only for so long."

"I was just trying to get everything in order, so I could walk through that door and tell you it's all over." That he was here and ready to begin a new life with her.

"It's really over?"

He nodded. "As of today, I'm *all* yours."

"Ooh." She smirked. "Now, what am I going to do with you?"

"Anything you want." He smiled, bringing his lips to hers. He was going to *love* civilian life.

EPILOGUE

Luke remained with Kate in her car, trepidation filling him.

"They are going to be ecstatic to have you home," she said.

He'd waited until his parents returned from their European cruise and had traveled back from their retirement home in Florida to Chesapeake Harbor for Thanksgiving before making this final move back into his normal life—returning to his family. How on earth would they react? How would he explain? He swallowed, rubbing his hands up and down his thighs, the friction off his jeans warming his hands. It was a cold November day, the first snow having already fallen. Now he was just stalling. He summoned the courage to ask Kate the question burning in his soul. "What if . . . ?"

"What if what?" Kate tilted her head. "Luke, they are your family. They love you."

"Sometimes I think being a CIA agent was less intimidating."

"Please." Kate rolled her eyes. "You'll do just fine. You got past me, and I'm the hard one."

He chuckled. "That is true."

She clasped his hand. "I'll be right at your side."

He lifted her hand to his mouth, placing a kiss on her engagement ring. "Forever."

She smiled. "Forever."

He exhaled.

Jesus would carry them through this *together*. He needed her, just as she needed him. God had created them for each other. They were designed to be one. And with her at his side, there wasn't anything he couldn't do.

Stepping from the car, he took her hand and moved for the house, catching sight of the rest of the gang playing flag football out back. Swallowing, he walked around the corner and stopped at the sight of his brother.

Gabe's gaze met his, and he dropped the ball. "Luke?"

Luke nodded apprehensively.

"Luke?" Gabe's eyes widened and he rushed forward. "Mom, Dad, it's Luke! He's back!" he hollered as he engulfed his brother in a hug.

He was home.

LETTER TO THE READERS

Dear Readers,

There are so many books out there. Thanks for picking up *Dead Drift*! I'm honored and humbled.

Thank you so much for sharing Luke and Kate's adventure with me. I hope you've had a chance to read all the books in the CHESAPEAKE VALOR series, and I truly hope you enjoyed the conclusion. I loved spending time with this gang of characters and will miss them. But I look forward to my upcoming COASTAL GUARDIANS series and meeting a lot of new friends. I hope you will too.

For lots of extras and behind-the-scenes information, be sure to check out my website (www.danipettrey.com) where you'll find recipes, *Dead Drift*'s story playlist, Pinterest board, Book Club Kit, and much more!

Blessings, Dani

ACKNOWLEDGMENTS

To Jesus—for being my anchor. For blessing me with a love of words and the beautiful joy of getting to share that love with others.

To Mike, Kay, Ty, Calvin, and Brenn—I love you all silly and beyond measure. You fill my days with joy, laughter, adventure, and beautiful chaos—and I wouldn't want it any other way. I thank God every time I think of you. Thank you for making my life so rich and full, and for all your support, especially during deadline craze.

To Lisa—for always being there and for being the best, best friend a girl could ask for. Love you!

To Karen—for your meticulous eye, helpful feedback, prayers, and friendship.

To Jen—for your amazing work!

To everyone at BHP—I'm so honored, humbled, and blessed to be part of the BHP family.

To Janet—thank you for your support, encouragement, wisdom, wit, and friendship. I'm blessed by you! And you're never allowed to retire!

To Dee—for your continued support, encouragement, inspiration, and friendship. Thanks for sharing this journey with me.

333

To Katie Cushman—for being my friend and partner-in-crime. Can't wait to see what our next adventure holds!

To Donna—for keeping me sane.

To Ali—you are absolutely amazing and I adore working with you.

To Dad—for all your help on this one! Loved the chats.

To Barry—for taking the time to read my stories, provide feedback, and champion me on. I appreciate you.

I have so many people who bring joy and richness to my life. Thank you for the amazing support to Debb, Annie S., Carrie S., Rissi, Lisa Kelly, Rick Estep, Heidi Robbins, Eli, Amanda Dykes, and all my awesome Suspense Squad Street Team members. You guys rock!

ABOUT THE AUTHOR

Praised by *New York Times* best-selling author Dee Henderson as "a name to look for in romantic suspense," **Dani Pettrey** has sold more than 400,000 copies of her novels to readers eagerly awaiting the next release. Dani combines the page-turning adrenaline of a thriller with the chemistry and happy-ever-after of a romance. Her novels stand out for their "wicked pace, snappy dialogue, and likable characters" (*Publishers Weekly*), "gripping storyline[s]," (*RT Book Reviews*), and "sizzling undercurrent of romance" (*USA Today*). Her ALASKAN COURAGE series and CHESAPEAKE VALOR series have received praise from readers and critics alike and spent multiple months topping the CBA bestseller lists.

From her early years eagerly reading Nancy Drew mysteries, Dani has always enjoyed mystery and suspense. She considers herself blessed to be able to write the kind of stories she loves—full of plot twists and peril, love, and longing for hope and redemption. Her greatest joy as an author is sharing the stories God lays on her heart. She researches murder and mayhem from her home in Maryland, where she lives with her husband. Their two daughters, a son-in-law, and two adorable grandsons also reside in Maryland. For more information about her novels, visit danipettrey.com.

Center Point Large Print
600 Brooks Road / PO Box 1
Thorndike, ME 04986-0001 USA

(207) 568-3717

US & Canada:
1 800 929-9108
www.centerpointlargeprint.com